THE COMPLETE CASES
OF THE MARQUIS OF BROADWAY,
VOLUME 2

John Lawrence

THE COMPLETE CASES OF THE MARQUIS OF BROADWAY

VOLUME 2

JOHN LAWRENCE

ILLUSTRATIONS BY
JOHN FLEMING GOULD

ALTUS
PRESS

BOSTON • 2016

EDITED AND DESIGNED BY
Matthew Moring

PUBLISHING HISTORY

"The Stars Said Murder" originally appeared in the March, 1939 issue of *Dime Detective* magazine. Copyright 1939 by Popular Publications, Inc. Copyright renewed 1967 and assigned to Steeger Properties, LLC. All rights reserved.

"Old Wives Tale" originally appeared in the April, 1939 issue of *Dime Detective* magazine. Copyright 1939 by Popular Publications, Inc. Copyright renewed 1967 and assigned to Steeger Properties, LLC. All rights reserved.

"Death for Twelve Months" originally appeared in the June, 1939 issue of *Dime Detective* magazine. Copyright 1939 by Popular Publications, Inc. Copyright renewed 1967 and assigned to Steeger Properties, LLC. All rights reserved.

"Man Hunt" originally appeared in the October, 1939 issue of *Dime Detective* magazine. Copyright 1939 by Popular Publications, Inc. Copyright renewed 1967 and assigned to Steeger Properties, LLC. All rights reserved.

"Albino Alibi" originally appeared in the December, 1939 issue of *Dime Detective* magazine. Copyright 1939 by Popular Publications, Inc. Copyright renewed 1967 and assigned to Steeger Properties, LLC. All rights reserved.

THANKS TO
Chad Calkins and Joseph Laturnau

TABLE OF CONTENTS

THE STARS SAID MURDER 1

OLD WIVES TALE 79

DEATH FOR TWELVE MONTHS 119

MAN HUNT 159

ALBINO ALIBI 219

THE STARS SAID MURDER

LIEUTENANT MARTY MARQUIS, THE TOUGH LITTLE CZAR OF MANHATTAN'S MAIN STEM, NEVER THOUGHT HE'D FALL FOR ASTROLOGY, BUT WHEN HE DID HE BIT HOOK, LINE AND BULLET-LEAD SINKER. THAT WAS THE NIGHT THE STARS BLOTTED OUT THE WHITE LIGHTS OF THE TENDERLOIN AND THE CONSTELLATIONS SPELLED M-U-R-D-E-R. FOR THE MARQUIS' BIG SIDEKICK AND RIGHT BOWER, JOHNNY BERTHOLD, HAD TAKEN SEVENTEEN DRINKS TOO MANY AND RUN AMOK IN A 45TH STREET BAR.

CHAPTER ONE
BIG JOHNNY RUNS AMOK

IT WAS exactly eight minutes after eleven when big Johnny Berthold stumbled into Lippertz' shoddy little bar-and-grill. He had some difficulty in getting his big, broken hands on the bar, and croaked his order to the bartender in a hoarse whisper. His usually bright blue eyes were shot with red, his big, battered face pasty and strained, and the too-small hat that usually rode on the back of his shaggy blond mane was missing. This was his eighth port-of-call and, when an audit was made, it was unbelievable that he could still stand upright. In two hours of progress across Forty-fifth, starting at First Avenue, he had gulped down upwards of twenty drinks of rye whiskey.

So small a thing as a simple tooth had touched him off. Ironically, the big Broadway detective was one of those who cannot face the dentist. Neglect had caught up with him earlier in the evening. An ulcerated molar had started to work, turned to white, tormenting fire in his head, driven him irrational and sent him raging for relief to the nearest bar—and to subsequent bars.

He was not a drinker at all. Since one memorable occasion, eleven years earlier, when, deep in his cups, he had practically demolished a popular Broadway restaurant single-handed, seriously injuring two people, he had rigorously avoided the bottle. This was on orders. The Marquis,

barely saving him from dismissal not only from the Broadway Squad but from the Force, had set a limit on the big
man's consumption—a limit of three drinks. And strangely, some faint distortion of this order remained in Johnny's
brain. In no one place did he order more than three ryes.
Working unswervingly across Forty-fifth, he had stumbled
into one spot after another, stood with his fingers white
on the mahogany while his drinks were being served,
gulped them down, then weaved on to the next place.

Nowhere did he speak to anyone. The terrible intensity
of his single-minded efforts to drown out the torture of
his tooth-ache made him oblivious to everyone. No one
knew about the molar, of course, and by the time he had

The big giant drove his right straight
into Curran's face and smashed the
greasy little shyster's nose to a jelly.

reached Lexington Avenue, word was running ahead that
the big Broadway strong-arm detective was running amok.
A dozen phone calls had gone in to the Times Square
Ticket Agency that was the unofficial headquarters of

Lieutenant Marquis and the Broadway Squad, but by ill luck, the Marquis was out, and out of touch.

No one of the jittery owners of the places lying in big Johnny's path dared to call any police help, other than the Marquis. Any headquarters squad would have cracked down with savage relish. To make a spectacle of one of the Marquis' cordially hated squad would be a crack at his precious prestige that would warm the heart of his worst departmental enemy. The harried bar-owners knew all about that. They also knew that the Marquis would devote special attention to anyone who put him in such a hole. So nothing was done—up till the time he reached Lippertz', at eight minutes past eleven.

THE WEASEL-FACED Lippertz, after a moment of agonizing debate, finally decided to brave the Marquis' wrath, rather than risk the ruin that an explosion on Johnny's part would positively mean. He noted the time while he sweated in the phone booth, calling the Riot Squad.

The greasy little lawyer, Curran, and the big pink-eyed politician, Helwig, came into the picture then.

Helwig was in the latticed-off dim-lit rear half of the establishment, alone at a table. Curran—stubby, bald-headed, black-eyed—pushed through the front door, waddled swiftly down the bar, making for Helwig's table.

In his right mind, big Johnny would never have spoken to, or even taken notice of the odorous little shyster. Temporarily, Curran was under the wing of Max Helwig. Helwig had some unofficial, more or less mysterious connection with the reform administration in City Hall. No one knew exactly what it was, any more than any one could fathom why the big man had taken a fancy to the greasy

Curran, but the connection was valid and the big, pink-eyed man swung too much influence downtown for the Broadway Squad to antagonize him needlessly. Without Helwig's protection, the scheming, crooked little lawyer would have succumbed long ago to one of the host of dangerous enemies he had made for himself.

For the past two or three years, the politician had literally held the lawyer's bald head above water—procured him a connection with Dopey Daniels' policy empire, entrusted him with his own personal legal affairs, and let it be known definitely that, grudges or no grudges, Curran was not to be harmed—by anybody. It was even a reasonable guess that Helwig had managed to keep him out of a cell following the recent crash of the policy organization.

There was no sense to it. It was purely a personal fancy on the big man's part. Certainly Curran, now without a connection or friend on Broadway, reputedly so dead broke as to be unable even to get out of town, was no asset. Yet the politician still chose to cover him—meeting him in Lippertz' place alone served notice on that. Like most of Broadway, big Johnny vaguely looked forward without pain to the moment when the inevitable gun or knife would overtake the greasy little schemer, but his feelings would not, ordinarily, run to personal molestation.

He was on his third drink, catching his breath before downing it, when the bandylegged lawyer walked in. Lippertz, wiping sweat from his weasel face, was standing first on one foot, then the other, far back by the phone booths, now overwhelmed by belated panic for having called headquarters—panic at how the Marquis might receive the news. The dozen-odd customers in the latticed-in rear of the establishment were seemingly oblivious. The waiters were a watchful little knot around the kitchen door. The bartender had found an excuse to go down-cellar. The bar was gloomily empty save for Johnny. The big giant, subconsciously uncomfortable at the large space accorded him, had edged down almost to the end of the mahogany nearest the lattice.

Curran's doughy face was drawn and preoccupied. He flicked nervous, pinpoint black eyes over the detective's crouched, sodden figure as he came abreast. Recognition came belatedly and he fastened a hasty, sick smile on his mouth, circled a little warily, mumbled some appropriate pleasantry, tried to hurry past—and the explosion came.

Big Johnny literally spat a glass of whiskey out of his mouth, whirled himself away from the bar in a flashing, stumbling motion, big hands clawing for the lawyer.

He yelled, "What? Why you —— ——— little ————!" and one big hand clutched the front of Curran's green suede topcoat. The other drove smackingly, with all the force of the big giant's dive, straight into Curran's face, forced the lawyer's terrified squeal back down his throat, flattened his face into a bloody jelly, and slammed him wildly into the edge of the arch of the lattice.

BLOOD STREAMING from nose and mouth, Curran hit with a jar that ripped the lattice from its moorings, sent him careening from a table corner and threw him heavily, screaming to the floor.

Big Johnny almost fell, staggered into the opposite—the uninjured—side of the arch, caught himself, swaying. Above the now-explosive uproar in the place, no one could hear, what he was saying, but his lips moved. His eyes were like sunken red coals. As the sobbing lawyer scrambled frantically to get to his feet, big Johnny dived again, teeth bared.

Big Johnny's ham-like fist crashed squarely behind his ear, lifted him fairly from the ground and pitched him headfirst—straight into the pink-eyed politician, Helwig, who was struggling to get out from behind his table, roaring.

The two men and the table went over with a deafening crash. A dozen people saw the gun flash in Helwig's hand as he yanked it from his hip. He flailed the sobbing little Curran off his chest, tried to fling himself up from the ground. Big Johnny stumbled forward, stood over him, eyes trying to focus, legs spread, grinning fatuously.

Curran suddenly yelled, "No! No! Max—no…." and somehow writhed up with the big politician, grabbing wildly at Helwig's gun wrist. Then big Johnny evidently saw the gun for the first time and the grin was wiped from his face. He growled low in his throat, lurched forward, snatching at it. A woman patron screamed. Tables were flung over as the customers dived for safety. They saw big Johnny's fist whip over at the struggling, purple-faced politician's jaw. They did not see the blow land. The distracted Lippertz had finally reached the switch box, plunged the melee into darkness.

Then came the shot—the shot that did not hit anybody, did no damage, but gave the newspapers the lead around which most of the headline stories were built.

It was a sudden, racking, blue-orange spurt in the darkness. There was the sound of big Johnny's hoarse grunt, the vicious, driving smack of blows, roaring, cursing—and then it all blended in one mad uproar in the blackness.

For the space of ten seconds the deafening uproar was continuous. Then it was ended by the ear-splitting screaming of a siren as the first police car squealed in to the curb in front. The Riot Squad, with years of experience at arriving too late, had timed their descent in answer to Lippertz' earlier phone call, to the exact moment.

A searchlight bloomed through the window and the uproar died. Men and women froze in the blue glare. Patrolmen ran through the door, snapping on more flashlights—and Lippertz threw the switch closed again, letting lights blaze up.

THE PATRONS—THOSE who had not managed to get out through the kitchen or otherwise—were a wide, frightened-eyed circle around the walls of the little table space. Linen, dishes and silver were strewn on the floor, tables overturned, the left half of the lattice was leaning drunkenly.

Big Johnny stood in the middle of the floor, still spread-legged, shaking his head as though to clear it. Two men lay at his feet. The blond politician, Helwig, was on his back, his eyes closed, and the bloody-faced Curran lay aslant him, on top of him. Both were unconscious, breathing heavily. The shiny revolver lay a few inches from Helwig's outstretched pink hand, on the floor.

Evidently the gleam of the metal caught big Johnny's eye. He cursed growlingly, lurched down toward it. A youngish, olive-faced officer in plainclothes at the head of the still in-streaming bluecoats, ripped a hasty order from the side of his mouth. Six coppers, nightsticks swinging, hit big Johnny at once. There was the cruel sound of locust whacking bone and the big man went down, stayed down.

Two white-coated internes, running in after the bluecoats, were already diving in to kneel beside the fallen men. They bawled at the bluecoats, who drew back from the smashed, bloody, unconscious big Johnny. One interne made a hasty examination of him while the other was going over the already-moaning, greasy-faced little lawyer, Curran.

The one who was examining big Johnny grunted: "Ambulance. Just a few lumps, maybe concussion."

The other said, after wiping the blood from Curran's pasty, beaten face. "About the same here. Some teeth out. Maybe a busted nose."

They piled the little lawyer off the big, blond politician and both knelt beside Helwig. Sudden urgency came into their movements. For seconds they worked with swift fingers. The blond interne's hand finally went under the politician's big neck, came away with a streak of blood. He sat back slowly on his hunkers, looked up curiously, exchanged a quick, questioning glance with his companion, then told the tight-lipped young detective above him: "Not so good. This one got a crack at the base of the skull. His neck's broken. He's dead."

In the instant hush, the olive-skinned, almost-womanish, small-featured face of the officer went suddenly tight and hard. He drew in breath almost audibly, said through stiff lips, "Nobody move," and swung for a phone booth.

A siren snarled at the curb outside as a prowl car squealed to a vicious stop. Its door banged open and the Marquis walked into the shambles.

CHAPTER TWO
IT WAS JOE DUVAL

NO ONE spoke in the ninety seconds after he reached the edge of the ring of bluecoats and stood looking down. No one had to. Without the details, the Marquis' heart was down in his boots, his scalp crawling. He could read enough in what was under his eyes to recognize disaster.

He stood with his round, pink-cheeked, weathered face blank, his deep-set China-blue eyes almost gentle on the laboring stretcher bearers as they loaded their burdens. He still had a piece of billiard chalk in one small, black-gloved hand, carried from the spot where the urgent summons had reached him, but he was dapper and immaculate, his tight black silk scarf neat, his expensive hard hat jaunty on his coal-black, crisp hair, his carefully tailored Chesterfield coat wrinkle-less. Inside, he was stormy, devastated. In his mind's eye, he could see this news racing over the wires at this very moment, could see the gloating of his host of departmental and political enemies, and—most crushing of all—the staggering, almost fatal blow that it would be to the painfully nursed prestige of his little Broadway Squad.

He was too numbed at the blow to even rail at the fate that had set big Johnny's eruption in the presence of the two shadowy border-line characters—Curran and Helwig—in the first place. He was too numb even to stir his agile mind to look for something constructive. At the moment, he scarcely had more than a mild curiosity even as to what charge they would nail on big Johnny. It looked like clear-cut manslaughter, and there would be no departmental protection. The Force considered the Marquis' little band of twenty-two irregulars outlaws. It was a certainty that big Johnny would get no mercy, much pitiless publicity—and the Broadway Squad would be pilloried. It did not seem that anything could make it worse.

That was while the officer with the almost girlish olive face and long-lashed black eyes was still in the phone booth.

A taxi squealed to a stop outside and there was a sudden ripple through the center of the swarming restaurant. Asa McGuire, chubby, redheaded, burst through the circle, came to a dead stop, panting, at the Marquis' side.

"Marty—for God's sake—what...." His cheerful eyes were stunned, aghast, as the stretcher bearers brushed past him.

"Go and phone Izzy," the Marquis said dully. "Tell him to meet Johnny at the hospital."

"Izzy? The lawyer?"

The Marquis nodded absently—and then the full flavor of the cruel little masterpiece of disastrous circumstance was made clear. The young officer finished his telephoning and came from the booths, was suddenly standing across from the Marquis, hands in the slash pockets of his trench coat, his dark face stony and shining under his dark-gray snap-brim. The Marquis' eyes jumped in recognition, just as a silvery headed sergeant in uniform pushed through beside him and said hurriedly: "Sergeant Immerman— Tom—listen—the reporters are out there."

The olive-skinned Immerman never took his jet eyes from the Marquis' shaded blue ones as he said: "Keep them out. Mac—you're in charge of the raiding squad. I've just received a temporary appointment to Homicide—the Inspector is willing that I go along with this case, since I found it. Get it, Marquis? I'm in charge of the job."

The Marquis got it.

There had once been a Zeke Immerman, an explosive, uncontrolled, mercenary schemer commanding one of the borough raiding squads. On the eve of his dismissal from the Force for extortion, the Marquis had taken him on the Broadway Squad, had him little more than a year, wakened one morning to find himself framed for murder by the overly ambitious ex-raiding-squad commander. Zeke Immerman had been shot while resisting arrest, shot by big Johnny Berthold, under orders from the Marquis. The imagination of the Marquis' worst enemy could not conceive any more disastrous twist than that Zeke Immerman's brother, Tom, should control this already desperate situation.

The Marquis' blue eyes were cool and steady across the sprawled body of the dead blond politician. He asked quietly: "What are you going to make of it, Immerman?"

The other aped the Marquis' soft tones, but his paper-thin lips scarcely moved. "Murder in the first degree, Marquis. Your overgrown, vicious thug came in here dead drunk. He tried to commit mayhem on an innocent party. He practically succeeded. That makes it a felony. In committing the felony, he killed a third party. That makes it murder in the first."

The Marquis' forehead showed faint flush—the only sign of his consternation.

"You're overdoing it." His voice was still quiet. "You can't make that stick."

"I can try."

A MEDICAL examiner with a shining bald head, carrying a little black bag, elbowed past the Marquis and said: "Well, well. Here we are, a little late, but I venture our friend here doesn't mind waiting, eh? Ha-ha!" He knelt beside the dead Helwig and said, *"Hmmm,"* pinching his lips. An assistant meandered behind him.

"Turn him over," the bald-headed man directed and the gloomy assistant complied, exposing the small pool of blood that had collected under the dead politician's neck, and the break in the skin at Helwig's hair-line. There was not much blood, not much of a cut, but the loose lolling of the carelessly handled big blond head was gruesome.

Asa McGuire suddenly dived to the Marquis' side, jerked at his arm. "Marty—come here. Maybe—"

The Marquis looked down at him blankly, allowed himself to be led back and around the still thick circle of officials and police, till they were standing beside the row of three phone booths.

"Did you get Izzy?" the Marquis asked.

"Yes—he's on his way to the hospital by now. But look at this." He unfolded a handkerchief in his hand and displayed a small clipping from a newspaper.

It was the "Daily Horoscope" as forecast by "Neptune" of the *Daily Sentinel* and read: *Today is a day of achievement—a day to go forward boldly—to bring current plans to a culmination. Fortune will favor the fearless.*

"Well?" the Marquis asked.

McGuire turned it over. Mixed with dirt, there was a strawberry-shaped stain of fresh, bright crimson blood on the back of it.

"Look—" McGuire pointed down at the floor beside the rear phone booth. "I saw it there when I came to phone Izzy." His forehead was wrinkled in intense concentration. "I think there's something here, chief, though I don't quite get it. Wait a minute!"

For a second he was silent, absorbed. Then he said gropingly: "Look—say this is blood from the dead man—which it obviously is. Somebody must have dropped this horoscope near him. Somebody must have stepped in the blood, stepped on the horoscope, walked out here, and—" He made a vague gesture with his hand toward the kitchens. Then his chubby face became suddenly startled. "Marty—listen! Anybody that was close enough to Helwig to step in his blood—hell, it must have been while the lights were out—nobody has come near him since—and if the person that trod in that blood— Hell and damnation, Marty—maybe Johnny didn't kill Helwig!"

For an instant, the Marquis' blue eyes were suddenly questioning, then he shook his head. "It won't stand up. There's no sense kidding ourselves, much as I'd like to. It's simply beyond coincidence that anybody but Johnny did it. That slip of paper could have been tracked here by anybody. No, there's no sense cooking up pipe dreams, Ace. All we can hope to do is find something that Izzy can use—something to ease the rap this maniac Immerman is trying to build."

Both their heads turned, as the group around the body suddenly became a moving, chattering little swarm, heading toward a table at the far corner of the room. The moving group came to a halt, and the Marquis stepped backward, and up into a phone booth. The extra three or four inches of height this gave him let him see over the shoulders of the group.

Immerman's brittle voice was telling the bald-headed medical examiner: "Here's where the shot went. It ripped up this tablecloth, ricocheted there into the wall. Helwig drew the gun, tried to fire up, but the shot obviously just went wild."

Through the swarm of men, the Marquis saw a white tablecloth covering the table. A few ashes were on the cloth and a tall glass, full to the brim with amber fluid. Beside the glass there was a rip in the tablecloth and fresh, splintered wood showed beneath.

The Marquis stood transfixed. Asa's, "Hey! What...?" went unanswered.

The knot of men around the group talked confusedly for a few minutes, then moved back to the body, leaving the table utterly deserted.

The Marquis' barely audible voice said quickly in the redhead's ear: "Get the waiter that served that table. No, wait a minute. Come on."

HE STEPPED down, strolled casually over to the shot-splintered table. No one was paying any attention to them. Small hands still in his coat pockets, he bent over the scar on the table-top. He looked into the tall glass, bent closer to the table-top, let his cheek touch the glass, then smelled it. To the eye, he was solely interested in the bullet-mark.

He stepped back, strolled casually back to the phone booth. McGuire's puzzled blue eyes were bursting with question.

"It's warm," the Marquis told him.

"What's warm?"

"That rye-and-ginger-ale."

"What the hell of it?"

"Go to the bar and order one."

His eyes anxious and bewildered, McGuire hastened to the bar. He came back with a glass identical to that on the table, crammed with ice and darker amber.

"What in hell...?"

"The glass on that table hadn't been touched, stupid," the Marquis' soft voice said. There was no blankness in his eyes now. "Somebody sat a long time in front of that glass without touching it. Long enough for all the ice to melt. If it was the same as this one, it would take well over an hour."

"So?"

"I'm getting as high as you. Now I'm wondering if Johnny did do this. If by some crazy miracle—go and get that waiter, on the quiet."

"What are we going to do?"

"Do? We're going to take a long, deep look into the affairs of Helwig and Curran."

"You know, by God, it's not impossible!" Asa's undertone started rising in excitement. "If someone *was* after Helwig, and following him, then this opportunity would be made to order! Say he—"

"Get that waiter," the Marquis clipped. "He may be a gold mine. And keep it quiet."

FROM THE phone booth, the Marquis presently looked down at a dumb-looking waiter with bucket ears and frightened gray eyes.

"You know who I am?" the Marquis asked quietly.

The waiter gulped and nodded.

"Would you like me to have my men take you out to the country and beat the living hell out of you?"

The waiter's face was like starch. "No," he gulped.

"That is exactly what will happen if you repeat what I'm going to ask you. You served the drink on that table? Keep your voice down."

"Ye-yes."

"It was full of ice—like this one?"

"Ye-yeah. See, the guy ordered it a long time back and the ice melted and—"

"You probably had your eye on him a lot, waiting for him to order another, eh? What was he doing?"

"He—he wasn't doing nothing. Smoking cigarettes."

"What did he look like?"

"He—" the frightened waiter stared at the floor, groping for words desperately. "He had a long face, with great big teeth, kind—kind of sallow-like and little gray eyes, kind of—well, they always reminded me of a toad, like—"

"Always! You'd seen him before?"

"Well, sure," the waiter seemed anxiously surprised. It was Joe DuVal—" He came out with this startling information as though it were elementary.

McGuire nearly choked. "DuVal, the private gumshoe?"

"Yeah. Sure."

"I know that rat!" McGuire's excited undertone became hoarse. "He's got an office in the Horatio Building—way downtown on William Street. By God!"

For just a second the Marquis' dark eyes were shifting round the room. Then he said, "We'll run it out, anyway," and turned toward the street door.

On the threshold, they ran into the long, drooping, washed-out looking Harry Derosier. The skinny Broadway sergeant's pale blue eyes were aghast, his English face full of concerned question as he pulled at his bleached mustache. "Marty—"

"Out," the Marquis said.

On the sidewalk, he choked off the Englishman's flood of questions with: "Joe DuVal, the private detective. Find out where he lives."

"The Rathbone Hotel," Derosier said.

"Then go and hunt him up. Don't brace him—just get behind him, and call in at the ticket agency so I can catch up to you. Make it fast—there's no time to fool with explanations now. Ace and I are going to glance over his office."

CHAPTER THREE
THE GIRL AT
THE CELLAR DOOR

THE REDHEAD'S excitement soared as they were in the cab speeding downtown. "We're just like real detectives," he exulted. "We spot clues—and bang we have the right answers!"

"Have we?"

"What! My God—we know that this killing grew out of some trouble between Helwig, Curran, and Joe DuVal. That DuVal was following them—or Helwig anyway. That he was close to the fight in the dark, tracked away that horoscope clipping, ducked out the back door. In fact, by God, that DuVal, tailing Helwig, wanted to kill him and when Johnny blew in like an act of providence, damn well did."

"Why?"

"I've even got an answer for that! By accident!"

"Accident!"

"That's what I said. I can't see Joe DuVal trailing around after Helwig, lying in wait for a chance to kill him. Helwig was too big. But I can see DuVal—or any one of a thousand other Broadway tough guys—going after the shyster Curran that way. Think it over. Say Curran has crossed DuVal—like he's crossed any number of others. DuVal is raging. He's looking for Curran, knows the shyster will meet Helwig sooner or later so he's tailing Helwig. They're sitting in Lippertz'. Curran comes in. The fight starts. It's a natural—big Johnny for the fall guy. But it takes DuVal a minute to see the chance. Meanwhile the lights go out.

He jumps in, just a second late and, in the dark, gives it to the wrong man."

"Having been impelled to action by reading the daily horoscope," the Marquis said disgustedly, "which tells him, in effect, to do it now. Or maybe Joe DuVal hated Curran enough so that he kills Helwig first, not daring to harm the lawyer while Helwig is alive. Killing Helwig leaves him a clear field for finishing off Curran later on. Or maybe Helwig hit himself in the back of the neck and died of old age."

The redhead flung himself sullenly in a corner of the cab. "All right. I'll shut up."

"Don't shut up," the Marquis said. "But don't mix fancy with fact. The only facts up till now are that big Johnny went haywire, that he blew up in the presence of three damned suspicious people—Helwig, Curran and DuVal—and, since DuVal did an awfully fast sneak, it's a fair guess that the three of them are mixed in some picture together.

"What we've got to prove is that that picture sprouted Helwig's death. That big Johnny's advent was just an opportunity for someone else to murder. If we can get a square enough look at the picture, maybe the whole business will be clear. That's what we're looking for—that picture. It would be nice to find it in DuVal's office."

THEY HAD no such luck, but the fourth personality came into the picture here, giving it the first tinge of money.

The building was dingy, ancient, three stories high. The Scandinavian night-watchman was evidently tongue-tied. He looked at their badges, listened to their explanations without a word, gave them a glare of suspicion and led them up two flights of rickety wooden stairs, turned and went back down, leaving them there.

Most of the gold paint was peeled off the door that had once said—*Joseph DuVal & Co—Confidential Investigations*.

The office—when the Swede's pass-key had let them in and the Marquis had switched on weary lights in the ceiling—was one littered, dust-covered, messy room. Papers were strewn on filing cabinet, scarred flat-topped oak desk and flat table, and spilled out of the full waste-basket. There were 'Wanted' circulars on the walls and dust over everything.

Five minutes expert, swift combing through the papers got them only the impression that DuVal was practically without legitimate business, and kept no records that they could find of his illegitimate doings. But the search brought up the black-lettered red card.

It was in the top drawer of the desk, buried among papers. It bore DuVal's name, office address, and a code number assigned him by the Telephone Secretary Service, to which he was obviously a subscriber.

"What's that?" Ace asked curiously, as the Marquis sat down and reached for the phone.

"A service that answers your phone when you're out and takes messages. Let's see."

He called the Secretary Service, and repeated the code number. "This is Mr. DuVal. Were there any calls for me while I was out?"

After a minute's wait a feminine voice informed him: "I have a message for you to call Rhinelander 1—8994. Evidently the party called twice. Once at ten five. Once at nine minutes to eleven. No other calls."

The Marquis hung up, immediately released the hook and made another call—police headquarters. When he had the proper bureau, he said, "Give me the name and address of the folks who have this phone number," and repeated the Rhinelander sequence.

A minute later he slowly hung up the phone and said in a choked voice: "Judge Brockway Hoffman."

"What! The millionaire—the reform administration's campaign angel? He was calling Joe DuVal?"

"Twice."

The Marquis' eyes were thoughtful, intent. "He lives in the Sixties, off Park."

"My Lord—are you going there at this hour?"

"Why not? Unless Harry Derosier has located DuVal in the meantime...." He picked up the phone once more and called the ticket agency, but the lean, English-looking sergeant had not been heard from.

"But Hoffman's a big shot," McGuire protested when they were once more in the speeding taxi. "You can't barge in on him—especially after midnight."

"We'll see when we get there. If this thing wants to break fast, I'm not the one to stop it. Our luck seems to be in. At least if Hoffman is part of this picture, we're damned lucky to have discovered it."

THEY LEFT the taxi on Park Avenue, walked silently round the corner—and were opposite the house. It was old, small, exclusive. It nestled just behind the skyscraper apartment that fronted on Park. Its small lawn was enclosed with iron-picket fencing. It was dark from cellar to garret with the exception of one bay window on the ground floor—the window nearest the apartment house.

"What's the scenario?" McGuire whispered. "Are we—"

"Let's take a look. The service alley of that apartment house runs right beside that window."

They went noiselessly down the alley. Only the iron fence separated them from the house. When they came into the square of light thrown from the bay window, by standing on tiptoe they could see in.

They saw a comfortable, office-like library, done in black oak and red leather. A phone began to ring inside.

A little pouter-pigeon of a man came in sight. He had strange, excited brown eyes in a small, barbered-pink face. He stood not more than five feet five and had lifts in his heels. His hair was cut to produce what were suspiciously like sideburns and was dyed black. The shoulders and chest of his black-and-gray broadcloth suit were padded and his paunch was suspiciously absent. He picked up the phone in fat little brown fingers, and, while they could see his lips move, no sound reached them.

"Is that Judge Hoffman?" McGuire whispered incredulously.

"Yeah."

They watched him, while he finished his phone conversation.

When he had walked again out of their sight, McGuire asked: "Well—what?"

The Marquis moved slowly, thoughtfully, back down the alley. When they were just opposite the pitch-black strip of lawn on the other side of the fence, he started, "I'll go in alone—" and got no farther.

A sudden spurt of light seemed to come from the bowels of the earth, just in front of the house next door, and both men stopped dead in their tracks.

The spurt came again—and a soft clinking of metal. Then the mystery resolved itself. There was someone in the little areaway of the judge's house—someone with a flashlight, trying to do something to the cellar door.

The third time the spurt came, the Marquis saw that a girl was trying to prop the door open. Finally she succeeded and the flash went dark. The Marquis held his breath—and only by holding his breath could he have heard the light footsteps on the grass of the little lawn.

THERE WAS a creak as the girl negotiated the gate in the fence. Then she was on the street, flitting past the entrance of the alley, moving swiftly and silently toward Park.

Without a word, the Marquis and McGuire moved quickly in her wake. Their heads turtled together, and they got a swift glimpse of the girl—her heels tap-tapping now—as she passed under the street lamp at the corner of Park, turning the corner.

She was of medium height, graceful, dainty, slender. Her hair was auburn-black under a turban with a tiny veil and she wore a modish dark suit. The suit should have been mannish, but on her it was infinitely feminine, failing to hide the sweet curves of her body. She looked backward over her shoulder as she turned, and they saw the soft, small-featured oval of her face.

McGuire murmured, "What in hell?" as they strode silently after her.

She was out in the middle of the street, a half-block ahead, as they turned the corner after her, angling widely toward the strip of turf in the street's middle. They saw her gloved hand wave imperiously.

McGuire said: "Hey—she's taking a taxi. Jumping hell! Where are all the taxis?"

A sleek black car suddenly shot unexpectedly and silently out of the cross street, just as they reached the corner,
blocked them momentarily. When it had passed, they
hurried on, crossing the strip of turf. Their eyes were both
turned north where, a quarter block away, the girl was
climbing into one of three cabs before an apartment hotel.

Neither of them were conscious that the long, black
squad car had stopped just beyond the opposite corner—
until it suddenly shot backwards, almost running them
down. As they leaped to safety it stopped, almost touching
them. A voice in the tonneau said: "Marty!"

The Marquis swore. "Beat it, you dimwit, I'm bus...."
and then his lips clamped as the silvery haired, hickory-
straight inspector jumped out.

"Oh. Are you?"

His luck had run out and the Marquis knew it. Before
the angry inspector could get his breath the Marquis
clipped quickly at McGuire, "All right. Go on working on
that," and the redhead darted off into the street.

The inspector said stiffly: "The commissioner wants to
see you. We've been combing the streets for you. No—don't
stall. I'll have to pinch you if you don't come any other
way."

CHAPTER FOUR

ON THE COMMISSIONER'S CARPET

H E WAS a pale-gray, impeccable man—a civilian.
He was white with anger as the inspector ushered
the Marquis in, and he did not even wait till the door was
closed before he exploded.

"It will take years for the Force to live this down, Mr. Marquis. In all my time of office, nothing so disgraceful has come to my notice. This—this is abominable."

The Marquis stood, dapper, gloved hands flat in his pockets, his crisp, close-curling black hair bare. His somber blue eyes were attentive, interested.

The commissioner caught his breath. "And what makes it doubly damnable is your attitude!"

The Marquis said nothing.

"Good God!" the commissioner blurted. "Are you mad? I know—ever since I've been in here I've been told not to take too much notice of you and your squad—that you operated differently from the rest of the force. And this is how, is it? This—this monster, in his drunken frenzy, murders respectable people. And you—you have the infernal gall to back him up. Marquis—do you think this city is mad? Do you think the voters will countenance that sort of thing? Do you think we're living in the Middle Ages?"

"Just what complaint have you against me, Commissioner?" The Marquis' voice was soft.

"Complaint? That you're hindering Mr. Immerman's investigation! That you're publicly—at least so blatantly that the public prints cannot help take cognizance of it—setting yourself up as a defender of this beast Berthold—adding the final excruciating disgrace to the unspeakable thing your man has done, by defending, condoning him! But you won't, by the Judas, Marquis! You won't while I'm commissioner. You'll either come to your senses—stop this rotten effort to interfere with the man's just desserts, or—"

"Just a minute, Commissioner." The Marquis' soft voice cut across the other's words. "Before you state your alternatives, let me remind you of something."

He laid his hard hat on the desk, stared at the older man's angry eyes.

"I've been a copper all my life—twenty-one years this month. Eighteen of those I've been on the Broadway Squad. I've kept my part of town clean—so clean that it's a miracle to other people on the force.

"My men make money. They don't make a dirty dime. They make white money. You're not a policeman so you don't know what that means, but take it from me—it's a necessary thing.

"My men don't have very many cases in court. If we did—if we played the game strictly according to rules, do you know what would happen? I'll tell you. Every one of my twenty-two detectives would be in court permanently, and the section wouldn't be policed at all.

"We have the smartest, the most ruthless thieves in the world to contend with. There isn't a richer field for them in the whole world than Broadway. If I couldn't keep them in hand, you'd have a district that would make the old Barbary Coast look like a Sunday School picnic. But you haven't.

"You have a district that presents a respectable surface. There's damned little viciousness. There's shady business, right enough—but suckers only lose their money in my bailiwick. They ask for it and they get it. I've got to allow that much leeway.

"But vicious crime in my section is lower than it is in the swankiest sections of the city. It's so, because I know how to handle these rats. You don't. Nobody does—but me. All right, I've got a swelled head, but Marty Marquis' name means something in the underworld. Show me a crook who can face me!

"It's that way because I pay them in the only coin that they respect. I won't burden your conscience by going into it any deeper. Just take my word for this—they fear me. They fear my men. An order from any one of us is something for a crook to lie awake nights worrying about. You—the commissioner of police—can walk into my section. I'll show you men who want to commit murder—who've wanted to for years. *You* tell them off. They'll laugh in your face. *I* tell them off—and they'll go down on their knees to me.

"I can't do that sort of thing with regular coppers. I've got to have rare men—men who take my orders and who know how to represent me—to make decisions as I would make them—and to enforce my orders to the last ditch—or their orders."

THERE WERE high spots of color in his cheeks. He leaned over to the desk, laid black-gloved knuckles on the mahogany.

"Such men are hard to find. You probably know that my squad is made up of the outlaws of the department. All right. Maybe it's true, in part. I've got to have men who are ruthless, unhesitant. I'm bound to get some pretty grim characters from time to time. I've had men on my squad who would be capable of doing what Johnny's accused of doing—and doing it in cold blood.

"Johnny isn't. You've called him a pathological case. He isn't. He's a big, goodnatured overgrown boy, who has the necessary quirk in his heart to be heartless when he has to be. He's a physical giant—and I can send him after ten hoodlums and know he'll bring them back—probably carry them back.

"I need him. I need a dozen like him. They simply don't exist on this man's police force. What happened tonight is—at the worst—a terrible accident. But think this over. I don't believe now that Johnny killed your cheap political pimp!"

The commissioner jumped to his feet, his eyes popping. "What! You—you—have you any—do you mean to say—"

"I don't say anything yet—except that I don't believe Johnny killed Helwig. If you want it clearer—I believe that someone had a grudge against Helwig, was following him, keeping him in sight. When Johnny—I don't condone his being stewed, and I'll flay him alive for it presently—when Johnny came in and the fight started I think this enemy of Helwig was fast enough and shrewd enough to take advantage of the uproar to murder him!"

The commissioner gasping, held out a hand. "Wait, Mr. Marquis! This—this puts an entirely different aspect on the matter. If you can prove—if you can remove this frightful stigma from the force—Great Caesar! Who—who is it that you suspect of—of doing this?"

"I've no names to give you. I've nothing more to give you—except this.

"Immerman, who is in charge of the case for Homicide, is the brother of a man who once worked for me—Zeke Immerman. Zeke tried to cross me. He committed a murder—or instigated it—and tried to make it appear that I had done it. He wanted my job. In the payoff, he got himself shot to death. This kid, Tom Immerman, doesn't believe it. He thinks his brother was innocent—and that I had him killed for no good reason. Naturally, he hates me.

"That's where you got your reports, I know. The kid will say anything—do anything—to harm me. Consider them in that light. I'm not asking you for anything. I'm merely explaining why I'll fight to the last ditch for my men—in this case, for my man, Johnny Berthold. If you still prefer to believe other people's stories about me—you'll have to proceed according to your conscience. I'm in this fight to the last minute—on Johnny's side. The only way you can stop me, is to take my badge away—and I doubt that even that would be effective. Now—if you don't mind, I'll go back to work. I'm sure you've heard enough of my voice. Or do you want my badge?"

The dazed commissioner ran a hand over his pale gray hair, his eyes wild. "No, no," he said hoarsely. "My God— if you could prove that Berthold is innocent—"

The Marquis caught the inspector's jet eyes, nodded imperceptibly toward the door, turned on his heel and walked out, settling the imported hard hat on his crisp hair.

In the corridor, he waited for the inspector.

The gray-haired, black-eyed officer looked dazed when he finally emerged. "You ought to be with a medicine show," he told the Marquis.

"Yeah. Listen—what do you know about this Helwig who was killed? The more I think of it, the less I seem to know."

"You and everybody else. His father was a butcher in Brooklyn. He left home when he was about ten years old, sold newspapers in New York, graduated to hopping bells, got himself a stake and ran a little handbook for a while. I don't think he ever had any real friends—he was the closest-mouthed guy I ever heard of and strictly a lone wolf.

"He was probably mixed up somewhere in most of the big rackets in New York over the past twenty years, but not in any capacity that really counted. He had brains and he knew all the angles. God knows what he was after out of life, but he seems always to have made a bit of cash, lived by himself. He had women from time to time but they seemed to drop off him like water off a duck's back.

"Don't ask me how he got connected with the present administration. I know for a fact that he used to do chores for the old Wigwam, before the reformers got in. Anyway, Helwig suddenly popped up about six years ago as their unofficial payoff man. If anybody had votes that they could deliver, whoever they were, Helwig was the man to see. He picked up this little shyster, Curran, about two-three years ago—God knows why—and Curran's been his errand boy ever since."

"What'll happen to Curran now?"

"I hate to think. Your friend Immerman sent two men home with him, about half an hour—"

"He's out of the hospital?"

"Yeah. He wasn't badly hurt and he's got the jitters. He knew somebody, or heard of somebody, that got knocked off in a hospital, or something. He figured he'd be safer in his own place."

"Which is where?"

"I don't know, off-hand."

"What do you know that I don't about Joe DuVal, the private gumshoe?"

"Is he in this?"

"Maybe."

THE INSPECTOR hesitated, his black eyes searching the Marquis' blue ones. Almost under his breath, he said wonderingly: "By God, you've got me half convinced that you do know something. I was sure you were running a bluff—and I was kissing you good-bye. If you are—if that stuff you gave the commissioner doesn't prove out—you know you're in one hell—"

"I know all about it. What about Joe DuVal?"

The inspector shrugged after a second. "You know as much or more than I do. He's like half a hundred around town—how they get by is a mystery. They seem to go months without doing a thing and then damned if they don't crop up with a piece of legitimate business. How they get these clients I don't know, but they seem to."

A patrolman came scurrying down the hall just as the Marquis asked: "How is big Johnny?"

"They must have gone to town on him plenty. He was still unconscious when I talked to them last."

"Can you see that he's kept in the hospital?"

The inspector looked worried. "I don't know."

The Marquis swore between suddenly set teeth. "Damn it, you've got to! I wouldn't put it past those lugs on Homicide to get him down here and bend a few iron bars over his head."

The patrolman stopped respectfully and said: "Lieutenant Marquis—there's a call for you on the phone."

"All right." To the inspector he said as he turned toward a squadroom door: "There's a dozen ends to this business. I can't handle them all. I'm leaving Johnny to you. You've got to keep him safe—till I can get somewhere."

"I'll—try," the inspector said. "Wait! Listen—if that Curran gets knocked off too, it's going to double this stink."

"Isn't Immerman guarding him?"

The inspector's eyes were troubled. "Well—guarding lugs like that isn't all it's cracked up to be. If we knew who to guard him from particularly—"

"You'd like that, would you? I should tell you so you can drop it in Immerman's lap. Nuts. If all else fails I may even get my hands on the damned shyster and stick him out as bait. And I don't care if he does get killed—as long as I've got the killer."

He walked into the squadroom and had the call switched to a phone in there.

Asa McGuire said: "It's the break, chief. I followed the girl to Riverside Drive. She scurried around an apartment there and got a lot of clothes together. She sent them down the incinerator—*not* outdoor clothes. I think she was cleaning up traces of her ever having been in the place. Then she came back to where we first picked her up. I'm almost sure she's Dorinne Hoffman, the judge's wife."

"Where are you now? Meet me at that Riverside Drive number."

WHEN HE reached the mammoth, slightly out-of-date rookery high up on the Drive, McGuire was in the lobby, talking to an immense fat woman with sleepy oblique eyes and a brown complexion. She was in a wrapper and had curlers in her gray-brown mass of hair.

The redhead swung on the Marquis. "Look—" He held out a slip of paper. "The apartment was in the name of Joe Peterson. The rent bills were mailed to that damned shyster, Curran's, office. This caretaker is new and she says she hasn't seen anybody go in or out of the apartment yet. How many guesses do you need?"

They went up in a creaky elevator. The Marquis' eyes were liquid with thought. They went into a trimly furnished three-room apartment, closing the landlady out gently.

"You get it?" McGuire burst out. "Helwig had this place to meet Dorinne Hoffman. They were love-birds. Joe DuVal found it out and trailed along, maybe tried a shake-down."

"On Helwig? No private cop would have that much nerve."

"If he were hard up enough, he might take a stab at it. Probably Helwig gave him the icy stare—and DuVal lost his guts. Then maybe he figured the only way to keep Helwig from putting a finger on him—now that he'd made the play and failed—was to beat him to the punch. Good luck threw the chance in his way."

The Marquis shook his head faintly. "It could be," he decided and started through the apartment.

In the kitchen he found a stack of recent newspapers on the sink-board. They were all *Daily Sentinels*. From each had been cut a little square on an inside page. Some of the cuts were uneven and it was a simple matter to distinguish the heading on some of them—the astrological forecasts as made by "Neptune" daily.

"Hell," McGuire said. "This looks like it was Helwig himself who dropped that clipping in the restaurant. My God, imagine a guy like him going in for astrology. Or, hey—or else Dorinne Hoffman." Then he added dispiritedly: "I know. Don't tell me. She'd hardly be the one to jump into that brawl and conk him. I guess that lead fizzles."

It was broad daylight when they left the apartment and emerged again onto the Drive. At a service station, the Marquis found a phone and vanished in the booth. When he came out, he said grimly: "Big Johnny's still unconscious. Those lice must have hurt him."

"What's the next move?"

"Harry must have located DuVal by now."

"I told you he was the hand—that whichever one of the four folks in this picture was the brain—"

"Five, master-mind, five. Helwig, Curran, Judge Hoffman, Dorinne Hoffman, and DuVal."

"Well, getting DuVal will produce the answer. I told you that in the first place. All this running around—when all we had to do was sit and wait till Harry turned him up and then squeeze him—"

"You think Harry will, eh?"

"Don't you?"

"Some time, yes—but if I were DuVal, I'd be in a hole with the hole after me. Harry will dig him out—but it may be too late to do us any good. Nevertheless, we've got to pray he has luck."

The two or three members of the squad who were hanging around the little theater-ticket agency off Times Square when they walked in, crowded round anxiously, with a bombardment of questions. The Marquis said: "Skip it, boys. We're in a spot. We're waiting for a call from Harry Derosier which may get us out. Or it may not."

The call simply didn't come. They had food sent in, ate sitting at the Marquis' desk, far in the rear of the agency, but the telephone remained silent. Hours slipped away. The Marquis sat stolidly. McGuire paced the floor, sucking cigarettes. Noon passed. One—two—three.

The Marquis stood up, his face showing strain and said: "We can't waste time this way. Come on."

"Where?" McGuire said bitterly. "Where the hell is there to go? DuVal is the whole key to this."

"Maybe. But we haven't even talked to the shyster Curran. He's home at his hotel—wouldn't stay in the hospital. And there's Judge Hoffman. Maybe he'd have an idea *about* DuVal."

"They'd never let us get to Curran."

"We'll try the judge first. His court is just about due to close for the day."

CHAPTER FIVE

NEPTUNE'S HOROSCOPE

THE LITTLE pouter-pigeon received them in the library of the house just off Park. He sat, almost hidden by a huge walnut desk, fat little brown fingers playing with a fountain-pen set while his strange, shining brown eyes threw bright questions.

"Mr. Marquis—and Mr. McGuire," he said brightly. "A pleasure—and an unexpected one. You have a case in my humble court?"

"No," the Marquis said casually. "We're hoping to keep you from having a case in somebody else's court."

The fat little man chuckled. The chuckle became a shaking, silent, hearty laugh that lasted far beyond any reasonable time. The magistrate finally pulled a handkerchief from his pocket and wiped his eyes. "Ha! Ha! Very funny." He pulled pince-nez from a breast pocket and put them on. His round little dark face sobered and he aimed the twinkle of his glasses again at the Marquis. "I don't get it."

"Do you know a private detective named Joe DuVal?"

The fat little man blinked, frowned in puzzlement, cocked his small, glistening head and stared at the desk pad for a moment before saying: "No, no. I don't believe I have met the gentleman."

"You wouldn't know where he is now, then?"

"No. No. Definitely no. Why? If I may ask, why should I be likely to—"

"We didn't know," the Marquis said. "We found your name among his effects."

The shining brown eyes opened wider. "Effects? That sounds as though the poor fellow were—as though something had happened to him."

"Is going to," the Marquis corrected. "I want him for murder."

"What! Good gracious! And my name—"

"Probably has no bearing," the Marquis soothed him. "You never had any dealings at all with him, eh?"

"No, oh no—none at all."

"May I use your phone?"

"By all means."

He made a call to the ticket agency, spoke in monosyllables to the detective who answered, hung up. He stood up and said: "Thank you, Judge. I'll keep you informed."

"Do," the other said anxiously. "Please do."

"The guy's screwy," McGuire whispered when they were passing through the vestibule. "Any news on DuVal?"

"No. But big Johnny's come to. He tried to phone me. I don't want to talk to the lug. Izzy's buzzing around the hospital, trying to frighten the Homicide dicks with legal terms. He earns his dough, that one. I—"

They saw the girl again as they came down the little cement walk.

She was standing on the curb before the open gate, and even as the Marquis smothered an exclamation and strode swiftly toward her, a block-long limousine swung in to the curb before her and a chauffeur jumped out.

By the time he had the door open, the Marquis was beside her, bowing over his hard hat. "Mrs. Hoffman?"

IN THE light, her beauty was striking. She had long, blue eyes, the kind of milky-white skin that goes with red hair and her figure, in a green silk frock with green-and-white accessories was breathtaking. Yet she was fire and steel. Her long-lashed eyes looked at the Marquis coolly, imperiously. "Well?"

The Marquis murmured his name. She said arrogantly: "What of it. I am in a frightful hurry. Are you selling tickets or something?"

"No," the Marquis told her gently. "But we were trailing along behind you last night when you made your little trip. I thought we'd better kind of talk it over privately."

Her eyes seemed to become veiled, though her lashes did not move. "My dear man," she said exasperatedly. "I haven't the faintest idea what you are talking about. I was home all evening last night and I am sure that you can verify that if you wish to. You must have been mistaken in the identity of this—woman, whom you followed. I really haven't time to discuss it."

She stepped into the held-open door of the car, and the chauffeur, after a glare at the Marquis, climbed in behind the wheel and the car shot away.

When he could recover his breath, McGuire exploded into profanity. "She's it! She's a tough baby!" he insisted excitedly. "She could have done it."

"Because Helwig threw her over? I doubt it."

"Why couldn't she have?"

"She could. Any one of them could. Now I'm beginning to worry about that horoscope business."

"Why?"

"The horoscope last night was so damned urgent. If it did happen that our killer was a fanatic on the stuff, it would have made him do just as he did."

"Well?"

"Did you see today's little item?" As they walked toward Lexington, the Marquis took the horoscope he had clipped while in the theater-ticket agency, from his wallet.

The redhead finished reading it just as they reached the corner.

> Today is the gambler's day—even more so than yesterday. Everything should be pushed to a conclusion today—the stars favor the bold, even the desperate. Not for a long time have the heavens been so favorably disposed toward long chances.

The redhead stopped dead. He reread the clipping twice, as the Marquis whistled down a cab. He climbed into the tonneau, still reading it, his eyes troubled.

"Hey—what is this?" he grumbled.

The Marquis pocketed it, slowly and thoughtfully.

McGuire burst out: "Damn it—do you suppose—" He tightened his lips, but the words blurted out. "Damn it—do you suppose he's going to pull something else? If there's anything else to pull and he really does go for this stuff, he'll sure as hell—"

"We can't even guess," the Marquis said, "without knowing the situation that's going on between these five people. If we could get a line on that—"

"Damn that Derosier!" McGuire raved. "Why doesn't he find DuVal! If he's bearing down—"

The Marquis told the expectant cab-driver, "Drop us near the Hathaway Hotel—just off Broadway," and Mc-Guire's eyes were suddenly wide.

"You're going to try and see the shyster?"

"What can we lose by trying?"

WHEN THEY reached the dingy little hotel, there were at least six headquarters men in the lobby. That became less of a surprise when the Marquis learned that the dead Helwig, as well as the lawyer Curran, lived here.

Curran's two-room-and-bath suite was several floors above the one recently used by his protector. Surprisingly, when they left the creaking elevator, light shone from the wide-open door of the living-room of the suite. They strolled in. Shippee and Lear, both of Homicide, were playing rummy in the suite's living-room. They had only cold stares to give the Marquis, but neither of them said anything.

"Where's Curran?" the Marquis asked.

"Sleeping," Shippee nodded at the closed bedroom door.

The Marquis looked at it. "He'll have to get up, I'm afraid. I want words with him."

The two Homicide men exchanged glances, got up from the table. One of them moved casually in front of the bedroom door.

"Sorry, Marquis."

The Marquis' blue eyes blazed for just an instant, then were somber again. "Like that, eh?"

McGuire snarled: "You lugs ought to have your heads read. We won't forget this."

In the corridor outside, McGuire swore viciously. "I'm going to get those mugs later, if it's the last thing I do. Hey—look—there's another way in to that suite. Let's kick the door down."

"Behave," the Marquis said. "There wasn't much I could have asked Curran in front of those kids anyway."

And the idea hit him, just as they reached the ground floor again, were stepping out of the rickety elevator. He stopped in his tracks, grunting. His hand went to his pocket, whipped out the horoscope clipping and he stared at it. Then he cursed under his breath, jammed it back in his pocket—and then took it out again. He flung a glance at the clock, re-pocketed the clipping, took a step toward the door, checked himself once more, torn in indecision, half shamefaced.

Then he said between tight teeth: "Come on. I'm about to make a damned fool of myself." He swung toward the phone booths. "Don't bother asking what I'm going to do—it's too damn ridiculous. But it has one chance in a million."

Five minutes phoning brought him the information that the next edition of the *Sentinel* went to bed in less than an hour, that the Daily Horoscope was supplied by the Queen Syndicate and that the writer of the horoscope labored in an office in the Queen Syndicate offices on St. Catherine Street. The writer was, at the moment, in, and would see the Marquis.

Fifteen minutes wild ride in a cab got them to the building that housed the Queen Syndicate, and ten more cut through the endless red tape that was in the way of the Marquis' urgent request.

When the Marquis left the building, he had arranged that Neptune's Daily Horoscope, which would ordinarily have been repeated in the next edition, would be replaced by one which read—

> The latter part of today warns the native to check back—to examine recent enterprises for forgotten difficulties arising out of personalities. Particularly is this so after nightfall, when the whole aspect of the heavens changes from this morning's reading. Extreme caution and the most energetic measures should be employed to guard against repercussions from recent enterprises. There is another strange concatenation here. It shows success in any venture already started—provided no trouble with eyes interferes—and provided it is pushed to conclusion today.

"It's astrological hash," the bespectacled writer had moaned. "It means nothing."

"That's probably right," the Marquis admitted.

THEN, AS though he were not carrying enough, another blow struck him. When he emerged on to St. Catherine Street, Asa McGuire was gone from the fire-plug where he had left him.

Almost instantly, the chubby redhead ran out of a stationery store, almost directly across the street. When he saw the Marquis he waved urgently, ran out in the middle of the street to meet him. His face was pale with shock as he grabbed the Marquis' arm and hurried him back toward the stationery store.

"Big Johnny! He's gone! Ducked out of the hospital while Izzy was talking to the two detectives supposed to guard him! Nobody knows how he did it, but he's gone!"

He rushed the Marquis toward a pay-phone in the rear of the store, pouring out: "I started to think about big Johnny trying to phone you—thought there was a chance he might have remembered something from last night, drunk as he was, and I called him. I got Izzy—he wants to talk to you."

"Hello," the Marquis said hoarsely.

The pained, excited voice of the lawyer knifed over the phone. "Marty—they've pinched me—claim I conspired to help Johnny escape! You've got to help me—they're going to throw me in the can."

"Well, rot there!" the Marquis roared and slammed up the hook.

He whirled on McGuire and snapped: "We've got to find that big fool and get him to a safe place."

"Huh? Why? I don't get—"

"I wanted him in the hospital—not wandering around. In the first place—if Tom Immerman stumbled on him now, he'd rush him to headquarters and give him the works. In the second, I think I may have stirred up something— it's a chance anyway—stirred this damned killer, whoever he is, to something more. If that should, by any wild chance, happen while big Johnny is loose, he's done for. Come on—I know half a dozen places he might head for on the Stem."

They rushed back uptown to the blazing white-light district, hurried from place to place. In an hour, they had found no trace of him.

The Marquis snarled at McGuire: "Call the ticket agency. Put everyone you find there to work trying to locate the big fool! If they get him, put him in the back room of the agency and sit on him. I'll flay him alive. I'll break every bone in his head."

McGuire hurried to a phone—and then the break came.

The redhead flung headlong out of the cigar-store booth, jerked the Marquis wildly toward the street, babbling:

"Derosier called in! He's found Joe DuVal! Three minutes ago. DuVal was just leaving the Hathaway Hotel—or near there—Curran's hotel. He didn't go in—too many cops around—but he was hanging around. Harry's on his trail. He just hung up as I called in. Come on—the boys will look for big Johnny!"

They dived into a cab, raced into the side street on which the Hathaway stood, bore rapidly down on the dim-lit marquee. They were just in time to see the long, mustached Derosier hop nimbly into a cab, his eyes fixed ahead.

The Marquis snapped orders to his driver, and their cab shot up abreast of the stringy, English-looking detective's Checker.

"Where is he?" the Marquis called. "We'll take over here."

"The Bluetop—right there—turning up Broadway."

CHAPTER SIX
HIS HONOR—

THERE WAS no sense to the chase. They wound up Broadway, shot into the park, circled, wheeled, dipped. McGuire cursed in an undertone: "He's got wise to us."

"No. If he were, he'd be putting on speed. He's just trying to make sure he isn't being tailed."

They came out at 125th Street. The theater-time traffic was heavy, irksome, and half a dozen times they seemed to have lost him. The sun was down now and twilight fading rapidly. The private detective did not seem to be going anywhere—but somehow they were on Riverside Drive and, just when it seemed they would proceed north forever, the Bluetop vanished up a side street. Their driver trod hard on the accelerator, but the Marquis clipped: "No! Stop here!"

"What?" McGuire yelled. "Hey—he's getting away!"

"Don't be stupid. We're less than three blocks from Helwig's little secret love-nest. He can't be heading for anywhere else."

McGuire whistled.

They left the cab, walked unhurriedly the three blocks southward. They took up a position in the shade of trees across the Drive, while the last of the daylight faded.

They saw no sign of the private detective.

McGuire aghast, finally blurted: "My God—have we lost him?"

The Marquis suddenly started. "We deserve to, at that," he said in sudden flaring anger. "Who ever heard of a private gumshoe using the front door. He's probably got an in-and-out that we can't see."

They ran in the front door.

The creaky self-service elevator took them six of the eight floors and they hurried out, went up the rubber-treaded stairs, on almost noiseless feet—till they were at the top of the last flight.

In the exact instant that McGuire put one foot on the top step, the door of the three-room apartment they had visited earlier burst open silently and DuVal swung out.

McGuire stopped so suddenly that the Marquis, behind him, almost bumped into him.

For just a second, DuVal's long, horse-toothed face was turned toward them, bloodless, his gray eyes in panic.

His hand flashed to his hip—and McGuire dived.

The redhead's slashing fist caught the bony private detective under the chin, just as the other's pistol came free. The Marquis launched himself, lit on the private detective's arm, wrenched in instant torture. The detective groaned, sagged, and the pistol went sailing down the hall.

The Marquis pushed McGuire aside as DuVal, bleeding from the mouth, staggered back against the wall of the hall. The private detective's gray eyes were trapped, mad. "Wait, Marty—" he croaked.

The Marquis' black-gloved fist whipped squarely into his mouth, knocked his head back against the wall with a boom that shook the building. DuVal collapsed, dropped slowly to the floor, his hat rolling off and down the stairs.

The Marquis reached down and clutched the unconscious man's coat front. "Open the door," he told McGuire. "We need a little privacy here. Pick up his gun."

They dropped him in the living-room. He was groaning already. A bathroom opened from the foyer and McGuire got a glass of water, sloshed it in DuVal's face. It took three doses till the private detective opened fluttering eyes. Instantly, he closed them again.

The Marquis kicked him in the ribs. "Cut it out. Are you going to talk now—or after we've beaten the guts out of you?"

The detective made a sound that was almost a sob. "I—I swear I didn't do it."

"Who were you working for?"

THE DETECTIVE'S eyes were frantic. The Marquis kicked him again in the ribs as he hesitated and DuVal shuddered, cried out: "They—they'll kill me, Marty."

"Who?"

"The—the people downtown. I never should of taken it—but I was desperately broke—he offered plenty—" It was coming in gasps, as blood dripped down the bony man's chin.

"Who? What job?"

"Tail—tailing Helwig—getting the goods on him."

"For whom?"

"Why—why for the judge."

"You were getting the dope on Helwig and the judge's wife?"

"Yes. Yes."

"Did you get it?"

"Not enough for court evidence, but enough to—to be sure."

"When did the judge know about it—know that there was something going on?"

"Eh? Oh God, weeks ago."

"How much did he offer you to kill Helwig?" McGuire suddenly roared.

The trapped man's eyes flickered wildly. "No! No!" he croaked. "I didn't have anything to do with that. You're mad! That—that was big Johnny—"

The Marquis kicked him in the jaw, snarled: "That'll be enough of that. Who killed Helwig—you or the judge himself?"

The private detective's bloody mouth sagged and incredulous light jumped into them. "The—the judge? Was he—he wasn't at Lippertz' was he?"

"No, I guess not. I guess you did it."

"No, no—wait. There's an easy way in and out of that joint—through the kitchen and the building behind. He— the judge knew about it. I—I once brought him there to point out Helwig—but—but it doesn't make sense, Marty."

"Why did you duck out and go into a hole right after the killing?"

"I—I didn't know it was a killing. Lord God, Marty—I knew I was taking my life in my hands when I took a job that meant trouble with Helwig. He was a big shot downtown—could have had me framed and sent over—or could have had me knocked off. You know that. I was scared—I was scared every minute I was on the job. And after he was dead and I found that out, I was afraid I was in the grease anyway, so I ducked."

There was a second of silence. McGuire said finally, "What'll we do with him?" and prodded the wincing horse-faced detective.

"I don't know. Killing him, wouldn't be a bad idea." The Marquis looked down at the white-faced, shaking DuVal with thin eyes. "Judge Hoffman came to you weeks ago and wanted the goods on his wife and Helwig. You got him enough to convince him and were still trailing around, trying to get court evidence. Right?"

"That—that's right."

"Why haven't you gotten it? You've had plenty of chance."

THE PRIVATE detective licked his bloody lips and his eyes fell. "They ain't been going together the last two, three weeks. They had some sort of a bust-up. I haven't been able to find them together at all."

Intent lines jumped into the Marquis' forehead. "Helwig gave her the air?"

The detective squirmed with his eyes. "Not—not exactly. Look, Marty—I'm spilling my guts—coming absolutely clean with you. If it gets out that I was tailing Helwig, his friends downtown will get me. Give me a break, will you?

Let me have a little clearance—and slip me the price of a railroad ticket?"

"I'll slip you a session with the goldfish if you start stalling. Go on. Why didn't Helwig give her the air 'exactly'? How do you mean?"

The detective's Adam's apple bobbed. He said hoarsely: "I don't know for sure, see? But I think he slipped her the air—and then put the bee on her."

"Blackmailed her—you mean because of what he'd been doing with her?"

The detective nodded. The Marquis breathed softly. "A nice louse. By God, he—wait a minute. What would Helwig be playing about with a penny-ante racket like that for? He's making plenty—"

"He—he isn't making so much. At least he told a book-maker that. I overheard him in a phone booth. And there's nothing penny-ante about a hundred grand."

The Marquis' eyes grew round. "He was shaking her down for a hundred grand?"

"I—I think so. I heard him say something like that to her."

"And you kept quiet about it. Why? Hoping you could get a piece of it?"

"No, no," the other sobbed shrilly as the Marquis' foot caught him again in the stomach.

McGuire suddenly said, "Wait a minute," and wrinkled up his nose. He started sniffing the air around him. "Do you smell…?" He turned suddenly toward the bedroom.

In four long strides he was across the floor, had yanked the door open. He disappeared inside. Almost instantly, his hoarse voice said: "Good God, *Marty!*"

The Marquis jumped across the room, swung in.

THERE WAS a bed in the room and a wing chair beside the bed. Judge Hoffman sat in the wing chair. He did not sit erect. His little, shining head lolled on his padded shoulder in a way that no unbroken neck could possibly loll. The killer had not been satisfied with that. He had driven an ice pick into the front of the pouter-pigeon little magistrate's throat and there was blood all down the front of the broadcloth suit, all over the beige carpet and even some splashed on the counterpane of the bed. The Marquis' grab told him that the man had been dead at least two hours. He was almost cold.

Both the Marquis and McGuire gulped breath and whirled back toward the living-room in the same second.

Naturally, the private detective was gone.

They did not catch him. In ten minutes running through the apartment house, out into the street and through alleys, they saw no sign of him.

There was sweat on the Marquis' neck as they again stood before the dead man. McGuire said hoarsely: "God—what will this mean?"

There was even a touch of huskiness in the Marquis' voice as he answered: "A mere nothing. The newspapers will be only too glad to say nothing whatever about it."

There was a phone and he went to it. He called headquarters, got the radio control-room and put out a call for DuVal for "Urgent Questioning," warning the police force that the private detective might now be attempting to leave town.

"You're asking for trouble," McGuire moaned desperately. "That'll bring the commissioner down on us—wanting to know about DuVal! It tips our hand!"

"What hand?" the Marquis bit. "I had this little fancy judge pegged for the killing. We're on the edge of nothing."

"It could still be the judge. Somehow—by some miracle—he could have gotten into Lippertz', done the trick and got out again. He had the motive if anyone did. And DuVal worked for him—showed him his wife was cheating. Maybe they came here for the payoff—or maybe, even after Helwig was knocked off—the judge insisted on a clincher before he paid DuVal. When they got here, they got into a fight—" He broke off as the Marquis' head shook slowly, tautly. "Well—what's wrong with it?"

"I didn't say anything was wrong with it. But the crack at the base of the neck that Helwig died of, and this baby died of, isn't a blow everybody knows. The same party did for Helwig, and this one."

"That still fits."

"It doesn't fit that astrological-forecast set-up."

McGuire winced. "I thought that was settled—that Helwig was the one that read the stars."

The Marquis' jaw clamped. "If it's that way, son, we're licked."

"What?"

"Nothing. What time is it?"

"Twenty after six."

For a second, the Marquis hesitated, tense, driving thought behind his blue eyes. Then he said: "Let's get out of here."

"What! You're not going to report...." McGuire swallowed hard. "Marty—that would be the last straw. If they found us walking away from a corpse—they'd have real excuse to ruin us—"

"If we don't clean this mess—before the D.A. and a half hundred others can get organized—we're ruined anyway. And stalling around here—answering questions—while our last hour or two may be slipping away from us—won't help."

"Where are we going?"

"Somewhere where I can think."

NOT TILL they were in an obscure little tavern in the west Seventies, did McGuire blurt out suddenly: "Marty— are we overlooking Lippertz? That rat called the Riot Squad on Johnny. He knew how you'd like that."

The Marquis' blue eyes turned somberly. "You think Lippertz killed Helwig—*and* Hoffman?"

McGuire squirmed. "Well, why not? Nobody's checked him up. There might have been some equation there."

"What's the matter? Don't you think DuVal killed the judge?"

"You know damned well he didn't. The judge was killed at least an hour before DuVal went to that apartment."

"He could have been there before, and gone back after something."

"After what?"

"If I knew, I'd know everything."

"If DuVal did it, he was working for somebody."

"Maybe. Or maybe an angle cropped up. There's big money here."

McGuire brushed a lock of his red hair fretfully back from his face. "Then there's the girl, of course. Maybe she did it."

"She could hardly have turned the trick on Helwig."

"Maybe DuVal did that for her, or— Wait! Maybe DuVal did that for the judge. She guessed it and went and gave it to the judge today in revenge for killing her sweetie."

"Don't forget Helwig had cut her off at least two weeks ago and was blackmailing her. He wasn't her sweetie anymore."

"Well, my God—you're ruining your own argument. You've cleared everyone of the five people in the picture, practically. It must be someone outside. Lippertz, for instance."

For a long minute, the Marquis was silent, turning his lemon-and-seltzer slowly between gloved fingers, making little rings on the bar. Then he said softly: "There's no evidence against Lippertz. Maybe we've got a chore to do."

The redhead's startled eyes met the Marquis'. "You mean—make some?"

"It could be done."

A cab was parked at the curb, its radio muttering. As they opened the door to get in, the cabby hastily turned the dial to cut off the droning, jerky voice, brought in music.

"Turn it back," the Marquis told him. "We like police calls."

They were on Broadway, almost at the corner of Forty-fifth, when the voice of the announcer crackled sullenly: "Attention Cars 4281 and 4356! Proceed at once to Number —— Riverside Drive, Apartment 812. The body of a man has been reported in that apartment, believed to be Judge Hoffman! Signal 43!"

In the dark tonneau of the rumbling cab, the eyes of the two Broadway detectives met.

They said nothing.

CHAPTER SEVEN
TELEPHONE BAIT

THEY WERE out of the cab, on the dark side street, when the payoff came. The radio gave a preliminary crackle, then: "Attention all cars in the Central Park section! Go at once to Number —— Central Park West, Apartment 45. Detective John Berthold, escaped from custody in hospital this afternoon is believed to be in hiding at that address. He is wanted for homicide. Take no chances. Signal 30."

That was repeated. Then: "Attention all cars! Be on the lookout for Lieutenant Martin Marquis, of the Broadway Squad. Special orders from the commissioner, who has just walked into this room. He wants Lieutenant Marquis at headquarters—at once!"

The cab rolled away.

McGuire blurted, "My God—Johnny is in your apartment! We've got to get there before—"

The Marquis' voice was clipped, vicious. "You know damned well we couldn't get there before. Johnny won't fight. If they take him peacefully, maybe—"

"Maybe what? They'll give him the business—you know that. You can't go—your commissioner's evidently come unstuck. Let me go—I'll keep those—"

"It's no good. If they've got any connection in mind between the two killings—and they evidently have from the way that came over—they've got Johnny in a vise. We've only one hope—to turn up the real truth—and do it now. Come on."

"Where?"

"If we're going fishing, we'll need bait."

"What? What do you mean?"

"The shyster, Curran. The killer—whoever he is—can't be sure Curran didn't see him. Remember—Curran was inches away from Helwig when the blow was struck. The killer can't be sure the shyster was knocked out. And there's a wild chance—"

"Of what?"

"I put a bug in his ear. I'll tell you what I did downtown. This killer is evidently a sucker for astrology. I had them run a phony forecast. It was on the streets two hours ago. It looks like the killer was following slavishly everything that's printed. If he is—I worded the phony one so that it would fit perfectly."

"Fit—how?"

"The possibility of there having been a witness to the killing of Helwig. And that the killer ought to go out and knock him off."

"But—but, my God—Curran is under guard! How can we—"

"We'll snatch him."

McGuire gasped. "Are you mad? That'd be the end of us."

"Not if we turn up the killer."

"But—but it's a million-to-one gamble! Even using the shyster, the killer might not rise. My God, they'd crucify us—"

"They're going to crucify us anyway, you fool. Downtown has been waiting this chance for years. Our only hope is to blow up the job—before they get to us."

McGuire groaned, rocked his head in his hands.

"You said there was an extra door in that suite—one into the bedroom where Curran is?" the Marquis drove.

"Yes! Yes! But how are we—"

"Quit it! I know we've one chance in a thousand—but we've got to take it! You go in and talk to the two blood-hounds in the sitting-room. Make noise, pound the table—cover me while I get the bedroom lock open. Curran will be listening to your uproar, and maybe I can pick the lock without his noticing it. Once I get in, I'll have him out in a tick. I'll take him out the basement way and wait for you down there."

"It's mad," McGuire said hoarsely.

"It is—if there's still that mob of flat-feet around. But there shouldn't be. They should just have the guard on Curran on hand now."

IT WAS a perfect guess. When they strolled casually into the hotel lobby, there was not a soul visible—not even the clerk. McGuire, after a hasty quieting motion to the Marquis, hurried swiftly to the desk and stretched himself across it, head hanging down the other side. After a minute's fishing he came up with a pass-key. They hurried to the stairs, went up a flight, before taking the elevator. Incredibly, the mad project succeeded.

There were no detectives in the halls. Noiselessly, the Marquis made his way to the door that they knew opened into the bedroom of the guarded little shyster, Curran. McGuire walked boldly to the sitting-room door of the suite and, at a nod from the Marquis, went in.

After about a minute, voices started rising. McGuire made a good job of it. There was a crash as a tumbler was flung against the wall, the hollow boom of a kicked iron waste-basket. By then the Marquis had the key in the lock, had the spring lock turned fully open and had his gun under one arm.

He heard McGuire's hoarse voice, cursing, abusing the detectives in the other room.

In one smooth motion he was into the room, abandoning the pass-key, his gun covering the greasy, bald-headed little lawyer. The Marquis had maneuvered so quietly that Curran's back was still to him. The shyster was listening intently to the sounds in the living-room. He did not sense the presence, till the soft voice said in a hushed undertone: "One sound and you get it."

Curran whirled, stood trembling, his hands half elevated. He was in grimy shirt-sleeves, his black eyes white-ringed, his pasty, battered-and-patched, fat face and bald head gleaming with sweat.

The tirade continued in the next room. The Marquis jabbed his gun at the pudgy lawyer's coat, hanging over a chair-back and made motions. The greasy-faced Curran gulped, finally inched over and put it on.

The Marquis was at his side on the instant, hands running over the shyster's clothes for telltale bulges, but there were none. In Curran's ear, he lipped: "One crack out of you and I cut you down. No fooling. Got it?"

The lawyer nodded his fat head in panic. The Marquis picked up the green trench coat and homburg hat, jabbed the gun in the other's back, herded him silently out of the room, closed the door. He prodded him swiftly toward the stairs and not until they were two flights down did he hand the lawyer the coat and hat and snarl: "Get them on, rat. You might not live long enough to get over a cold if you caught one."

The other blurted in terror: "Marty—what are you going to do with me? What do you want—"

"Shut up. You'll find out soon enough. Keep that hat down over your face while we ride this elevator—and don't get recognized, or it will be too bad for you."

He told him nothing more till they were in the manager's office of the Joyland Dance Hall, high up on Broadway.

McGUIRE STOOD at the office door, his blue eyes threatening, stormy. The Marquis stood with one hip on the scarred oak desk. The pasty-faced, shivering Curran sat in the swivel chair, his frightened eyes on the phone. There was a sheet of paper with a few lines in the Marquis' neat handwriting on it.

"First you call Joe DuVal's office," the Marquis' grim voice explained. "He won't be there, but someone will answer and you give them that message. It's a Who-Called-While-I-Was-Out service. Got that?"

The other's Adam's apple bobbed. His scared eyes flicked to the Marquis' driving ones. "Ye—yeah," he whispered.

"Then you call Lippertz. Give him the same message."

The battered lawyer started, his eyes going round. "Lippy? Good God, did he have something—"

"Shut up. You do as you're told and do it fast. Then you call Dorinne Hoffman, and give her the same identical message."

The lawyer gasped, opened his mouth, but thought better of saying anything.

As the Marquis said, "Get going," he brought his manacled hands up from behind the desk, looked at the first of the jotted numbers on the Marquis' slip, licked his gray lips and began to dial.

McGuire strolled over to the small radio on the bookcase in the corner, turned the pointer over to the short-wave section and laid his ear against it, began to tune in, keeping the volume down to a whisper, as the clicks of the dial rattled in the loud-speaker.

"Hold the receiver so I can hear it, too," the Marquis cautioned the lawyer. "And keep to the script. One word more or less than I've given you and I'll cut your heart out and make you eat it."

He was right about Joe DuVal. A feminine voice answered, after three rings and said: "Mr. DuVal is out at the moment. Is there any message?"

The lawyer croaked: "Tell him Mr. Curran called." He spelled it out. "Tell him that I was a lot closer to Mr. Helwig than he may have thought, last night. And that it would be wise for him to meet me beside the wall on Central Park South, at eleven o'clock. The beech tree between Sixth and Seventh."

He had to repeat the long message to the puzzled girl, but she finally said: "Thank you. I will see that he gets it as soon as he comes in, or calls in."

Lippertz' reaction was a little surprising. When Curran snarled his message, the little restaurant owner fairly squealed: "What! What is this? A shakedown? I won't go for it, Curran! You can't get away with this—"

The Marquis took the receiver from the shyster's hand and hastily slammed it down.

There was considerable delay in getting to the widow—who had evidently just heard that she *was* a widow—of the fancy little magistrate, Judge Hoffman.

Vaguely, over the phone, the Marquis could hear sounds that he thought he identified as police sounds. Hastily, as they waited for the woman to come to the phone, he penned an addition to the script in front of Curran: "*If you say anything to the police, or if they learn about this any*

*other way, I will have to tell them everything I know—and
that means ruin for you."*

When the girl got that—and the rest of the bait—she
made absolutely no demonstration. The Marquis had
expected at least a gasp. Instead, she hesitated for seconds
then said coolly, "I understand," and hung up.

McGUIRE'S EYES were desperate and worried. He
twirled the dial of the loudspeaker as he left it, came over,
running his hand through his red hair. "Marty—what if
this killer is someone we don't even know? What if none
of these people had anything to do with it? God, we're
done for."

"I won't even think about that. It may be right—but
we'll never get a chance to prove it. Our only chance is
that it *was* one of them—and that we can nail him in the
next little while. I—"

The loudspeaker rattled with a sudden call for all cars.
Presently, the announcer's puzzled voice clipped out that,
"Lieutenant Marquis of the Broadway Squad is wanted
at headquarters for immediate questioning, regarding the
harboring of Detective John Berthold."

"They've got him," McGuire moaned.

Sitting impotently, waiting for eleven o'clock—the earliest deadline he had dared set with any hope of catching
all his fish in one net—the Marquis heard broadcast after
broadcast. In subtle changes in the alarms sent out for
himself, he could see the fine work of the myriad of jealous
and spiteful enemies he owned at headquarters.

McGuire swore viciously, ravingly, but the Marquis sat
dark-eyed, his jaw set.

Not till just before they were leaving, did the maddening one come over: "Officers on duty at railroad terminals and on main highways will watch for, and prevent, the exit of Lieutenant Marquis from town, should such be attempted."

McGuire raved: "The ————! They've torn you down. If we fail tonight—"

They both looked at Curran. The fat, pasty-faced lawyer had sweat streams running down his cheeks. He croaked hastily: "I—I'll do what you told me. I—I swear it."

"It'll all be over in an hour," the Marquis said stiffly. "Do as you're supposed to and I'll get you out of town afterwards. Flop—and God help you."

CHAPTER EIGHT
BLAST-OUT

THEN THE chips were down. Even the ride in McGuire's blue Stutz up toward the park was nerve-jangling. Twice, the grim-eyed redhead had to swerve down side streets to dodge approaching prowl cars or dollies.

Arranging themselves in the park was not too hard. The stone wall which ends the park is low, on the street side. Behind it, the ground drops down the side of a hill to the floor of the park. There was just foothold—a slanting ledge on which the Marquis and McGuire could crouch behind the wall.

Curran, the short, fat shyster stood on the sidewalk with his back to the wall. His hands were spread out on either side of him, on the stone wall. "Keep them there," the Marquis told him grimly. "If you make one move you're finished."

The lawyer's teeth chattered.

They crouched behind him, in the slanting shadow of a tree, their eyes just level with the top of the low wall.

The chill wind whistled down the street, swung the guttering blue street lamps on their standards. Only in the immediate vicinity of the two or three big hotels along the broad, tree-bordered street was there any motion, any human activity. The pavements were almost deserted.

"Where did you leave the car?" the Marquis asked McGuire.

"Around the corner, half a block down on Sixth."

The Marquis hesitated. "It could have been further away—"

He broke off, as, somewhere nearby, a bell tolled out the hour—eleven o'clock—and they were at the last ditch.

Nothing happened.

Minutes dropped away. The street became more lonesome. Far over on Columbus Circle, a trolley banged gloomily. A lone taxi chugged past, vanished. But no one came. Straining their eyes from concealment, the Marquis and McGuire saw nobody—no sign that there ever had been anybody. The whole wild gamble was a flop—a dismal, disastrous, blind-end failure. The chill that was in the bitter air began to creep toward the Marquis' heart.

As fifteen minutes dropped away—seeming like hours—he heard McGuire curse brokenly, half under his breath.

A lone figure suddenly hurried around the corner of Sixth and stopped dead, peering.

Pinpoints of sweat came out all over the Marquis' blocky little body—the sweat of relief. He cursed himself instantly, flaying himself for too-soon, mad optimism. Yet even this relief to his strung-tight nerves—the appearance of anyone—could not be denied.

He heard McGuire settling himself. In a whisper, he spoke in Curran's ear—"Remember those hands"—as the weedy little figure in dark topcoat and bowler hat opposite turtled his neck to peer across the street at him, evidently not seeing them—and then just as evidently spotting Curran.

Slowly, with the caution of a cat, the dark figure came forward and, as he glanced both ways in crossing the street, the Marquis realized that it was Lippertz, the restaurant owner.

Hands in his coat pockets, the collar turned up about his wizened face, he came forward, reluctantly, tentatively, as though ready to turn and run.

Then he was ten feet from the motionless Curran. He stopped. His grating, frightened little voice said: "Curran?"

"Yeah," the shyster said.

The restaurant owner licked his lips, blurted huskily: "What is this? A shakedown? Damn you, I won't pay it! You hear? You can't—can't shake me down now! You don't rate anywhere now!"

"No?" Curran growled.

"No!" the restaurant owner babbled. "I didn't do nothing! I got a right to protect my own property! I'm nearly bankrupt as it is! He—he's got to realize that—if I—if Johnny—hell, I'm ruined now. I was trying to save my last dime—"

With a sinking feeling, the Marquis realized that Lippertz was talking about him. The jittery little restaurant owner was thinking only of reprisals from the Marquis—reprisals for having called the Riot Squad on Johnny. Well, he had reason to—

IN THAT instant, the Marquis saw dim headlights, three-quarters of a block away, pull in slowly to the opposite curb, and go dark.

He spoke quickly out of the blackness, "Come here, Lippertz!" and warningly, "Those hands, Curran—don't move."

McGuire whispered: "Hey—what?"

"Throw that rat over the edge—get him out of the way—quickly!" the Marquis clipped.

"Wait! Wait!" Lippertz pleaded desperately as McGuire went over the wall like a cat. The restaurant owner tried to back away desperately, but the redhead, stuffing a gun in his pocket, got him with one leap. There was the sound of a fist spatting against flesh, McGuire husked, "One sound and I'll strangle you," a quick flurry of feet on the sidewalk, Lippertz' faint yell as the redhead pushed him over the edge. Then the sound as he hit the slanting dirt behind the wall and went cartwheeling down into the floor of the park.

McGuire was instantly back into concealment. "Hey—did you see that car pull—"

"Yeah. Shut up."

There was dead silence, for minutes. The car was too far away to see movement around it. Nor was there any movement visible to their straining eyes in the space between them and the car.

Then suddenly a soft voice spoke from under the tree in whose slanting shadow they stood. It snarled, "What sort of crap is this, Curran?" and the Marquis realized that DuVal, the private detective, had bitten on the bait.

Whatever moved the trembling, pudgy Curran, the lawyer did a good job of acting. Going only by a sketchy scenario outlined for him by the Marquis, he played it perfectly. He said: "I guess you know what it is, gumshoe. I want ough-day."

"Yeah? What for?"

Curran hesitated. The Marquis could almost feel the wily lawyer's brain trying desperately to guess what the Marquis would want him to say.

"To get out of town," Curran said finally. "I don't want the cops catching me. If they do, I might spill about you."

"What about me?"

"About how you were tailing Helwig, getting the evidence on him and on Judge Hoffman's wife—for the judge. About how Helwig suddenly got wise to you—and told you he was going to have you taken care of by the boys downtown—and how you realized you were in the grease. Maybe, if I had to, I could say I seen you start for Helwig's table when the lights went out and that big cop was slugging me around. And anyhow, the cops'll be damned glad to know you was in the joint, and ducked out the back way before they got there."

There was a second's silence. Then DuVal's voice came with a taut inflection. "The cops know that, smart guy—all that. Is that all you had in mind?"

For a desperate instant, the Marquis felt as though it had all gone beyond him. He could think of nothing to whisper into Curran's ear to drag out the conversation further—and he was suddenly afraid that he had missed the whole point in the tricky private detective's moves.

Curran said, with a stoutness that warmed the Marquis' heart: "You know damned well it isn't."

"Go on, then. Go on telling me why I should give you dough."

NO ONE saw the girl, till she was halfway across the street. Where she had come from was a mystery. She must have slipped around the corner from either Sixth or Seventh, hugged the building fronts till she was directly across from Curran. Curran, still maintaining his lounging position against the wall, in the street glow, would, naturally be the only one visible to her. The private detective, speaking from the dense shadow of the tree, was completely blacked out and the conversation had been conducted barely above a whisper.

It was not the girl's appearance, even then, that suddenly cut short DuVal's sentence. It was the black police car that went swiftly past them, out in the street, brakes whining slightly as they slowed to turn at the next corner.

The eyes of all four men were naturally jerked that way and so, when the car had whisked by, they all saw the girl, who might have sprung up out of the dark pavement in mid-street.

From the patch of shadow that hid DuVal came a sudden sharp sucking-in of breath.

The Marquis' eyes were hot with desperate question as Dorinne Hoffman came daintily, then rigidly, across and stepped up to the curb. She had on a pony coat, a small hat with a bow on one side, and she gripped a handbag, twisted between her gloved fingers.

Her voice was cool, defiant. "Mr. Curran, I presume?"

The lawyer almost stammered: "Ye—yes."

The Marquis, in that instant, was suddenly aware that another police car had just passed, was also slowing for the turn at the next corner. The devastating possibility flashed into his mind that someone had spotted McGuire's car in the vicinity and that cars were congregating. If it were so, he had only seconds left—seconds for the break to come—the break that seemed infinitely, disastrously far away.

Then it came—but it came so fantastically, so completely opposite from anything he had expected, that he was caught gasping.

The girl said, "I brought something for you, Mr. Curran," and fire and flame belched from her handbag.

She was an execrable shot. The bullet missed the suddenly leaping little lawyer entirely, kicked the Marquis' own hard hat sideways on his head. He was stumped, so startled that he was momentarily frozen. The lawyer squealed, flung himself aside, started to run wildly down the street.

McGuire roared at the fleeing lawyer, "Halt—you!" just as the girl's gun flamed a second time and the stone of the wall sang with ricochet. Then McGuire flung his gun across his arm, cursing and, perforce, fired. The girl staggered backwards, but the gun in her hand lanced out again. In a flash of street light her soft face was strained, tigerish. She whirled back on McGuire. The redhead roared, "Drop it, lady! I'll have to—" and the rest was drowned in a roar of thunder. The Marquis thought like lightning, whipped over the wall, risking his life on the hope that McGuire could handle the girl.

Curran, scudding away, was crouching over, running from side to side. The Marquis roared, "Curran! Come back here! I'll give it to you," and his gun shone in his black-gloved hand.

McGuire's gun thundered once more, and the girl moaned, stumbled again, and there was the sound of metal clanging on the sidewalk.

Curran, the shyster, down the street, looked back, flung himself to a shivering stop against the wall.

"Come back here," the Marquis shouted.

McGuire raved suddenly: "Marty—DuVal's got away. Watch that girl. I'll get DuVal. There he is, the—" and the gun banged again.

In that instant, as his head flung around, the Marquis saw the flash of white as it came from the inside pocket of the shyster, Curran, and went sailing over the edge of the Park wall.

McGuire was saying excitedly, "I brought him down. I got the dam' snooper!" but the Marquis had not heard him.

He was rigid, as light exploded in his brain with the force of dynamite. Curran, the hunched little lawyer, also was suddenly rigid, as he realized that the Marquis had seen his move. And then he wasn't.

WITH A speed and recklessness that would have seemed impossible to his bandy-legged plumpness, he suddenly flung himself over the edge of the wall, after the white square.

It took the Marquis only a split-second to get the full significance—to realize that the explanation of the whole nightmare tangle must be here, almost in his hands. He squirted light over the edge as he raced ten steps—and got one glimpse of the whirling fat lawyer bouncing down the side of the hill. The Marquis flung his light ahead of him—and dived over.

Even as he hit dirt, he heard the sudden keening chorus of police sirens pouring into the street above—and he knew his hunch had been right—that McGuire's Stutz had been spotted and surrounded. No other way could this many police cars be on the street in such short time.

Then he landed on the sliding dirt. The still burning flashlight ahead of him, by some quirk of fate, had lit pointing squarely at the lawyer below as he scrambled up.

The Marquis had one flash of his sweaty greasy face as he glanced up. Not five feet away lay the square of white. The lawyer dived for it—and the Marquis crashed down on top of him.

With the fury of desperation, the little shyster lashed up a knee, caught the Marquis in the stomach, drew a grunt and toppled the Marquis partly off him. The Marquis' eyes were shaded, somber. He drove a fist into the other's eye—there was no weight behind it, but it let him spring to his knees. There was plenty of weight to the two pile-driving blows that he drove straight at the fat man's jaw. With a little moan, Curran went limp, crashed on his side and lay still.

Then the Marquis had the letter. Sirens were screaming all around now. He could hear them coming in behind him in the Park, surrounding him. He had an envelope in his hand, addressed to Mrs. R.A. Hoffman, unsealed, evidently just written, judging by the freshness of the ink. It flashed into his mind that the lawyer must just have written it, while still under guard at the hotel—or rather, while his watchdogs *thought* he was under guard. Certainly, the possibility that he had been cooped up in that room all the time had been exploded now.

He scarcely dared read the letter, when he did have it open. Voices were yelling at him over the top of the wall to surrender, powerful torch beams centering him. Oblivious, he knelt there, eyes racing over the words.

> Dear Mrs. Hoffman:
>
> I regret to intrude on your grief at this time, but I am facing ruin—or worse. I was an acquaintance of the late Mr. Helwig. I may say that relations between us were rather unfortunate— that he exercised a control over me which made it impossible for me to refuse him any request.

He, within the last fortnight, explained the circumstances of the check which you had given him, and of the necessity for not presenting it for payment immediately. He forced—there is no use bandying words now that these ghastly things have come upon us—me to cash it for him. I may say that I had to mortgage everything I own, strain my resources to the utmost, to raise a hundred thousand dollars and I am now in desperate position. I appeal to you to relieve me.

Inasmuch as this horrible thing has broken and inasmuch as both of us seem in imminent danger of being involved, I hesitate to put the check through my bank for collection. Would it not be better if we transacted the business completely divorced from such institutions? I realize the securing of that much cash might be inconvenient for you at this time, but surely you have available securities, stocks, bonds, anything—which I would gladly take in payment. My own situation I reluctantly confess, is of such peril that I am in immediate danger of having control of my affairs taken from me. In that event, strangers would find your check—and the end result would be most distressing. I am not exaggerating when I say that, unless I can raise collateral within twenty-four hours, exactly that is going to happen. I urge you to meet me somewhere, exchange for this check which I hold, securities or some form of value, at once. I will make bold to call you on the telephone at midnight tonight, to make the final arrangements. I cannot tell you how I regret the necessity for this communication, but my back is to the wall.

Yours Respectfully,
Clyde Curran

The Marquis looked down with glowing eyes at the groaning little shyster. Through taut teeth, he said: "A shakedown letter, with the rush act, and you make them feel sorry for you."

Then a torch beam smacked him full in the face and the hoarse voice that he recognized as Immerman rapped at him: "Put your hands up, Marquis—up high."

"Behave," the Marquis said. "There's your killer—of both Helwig the politician and Judge Hoffman."

Immerman's voice was like a whip. "That won't help you. You're not framing any more—"

"Let's go down to headquarters," the Marquis said, "unless you want to lose that little badge of yours. The commissioner wants to see me. Take all these folks." He called up at Asa: "Are you there, redhead?"

The chubby detective put his battered, hatless head over the wall, said: "Just barely. Marty—where do we stand?"

"On top of the world."

THE HARASSED commissioner paced his office. The Marquis sat on the edge of his desk. "This Curran is a double-crossing lawyer. You've got to understand what that means. It means he can only go on for a certain time, before he gets caught up with. Dealing with criminals, when he does get caught up with, he isn't going to be sued—he's going to be murdered.

"He knew that. I can't quite believe that Helwig fully understood it, or he would hardly have taken him on. For a smart guy, Helwig was plenty dumb to befriend this vicious little rat. Anyway, he did.

"Helwig had nothing to recommend him on the score of morals either—oh, I know, he was big noise in the administration but he's dead now and you needn't get nervous. This will all come out. Helwig was gambling—and evidently losing. I heard he was stalling some bookmaker.

"He was playing house with Judge Hoffman's wife. Whether or not he made a play for her, knowing in advance that it was a cold-blooded shakedown proposition, or whether the idea came to him when he got hard up and tired of her, I don't know, but—he suddenly put the bee on her. He didn't fool. He demanded a hundred thousand dollars.

"I guess she figured it was worth paying, to save a multimillion-dollar husband from booting her out, so she gave in. But, apparently, she didn't have that much money. Helwig made her give him a bum check, which he held over her head, till she could raise the wind.

"Naturally, he took his lawyer, Curran, into his confidence, endorsed the check and handed it to him to collect. Here it is. We found it in his office safe. What? Yeah, it's a sappy place to keep it all right. It's not the only sappy thing Curran did, for all his smartness.

"Apart from being a sucker for astrology, which doesn't matter now, you've got to remember that he was in a panic. His past has been catching up to him and he's been scared out of his wits. After he skinned out of the policy dragnet by a hair—Helwig or no Helwig—the only thing that kept him from jumping town was that he didn't have a dime. I guess Helwig must have been shorting him. I assure you, he would have gone—despite the protection that Helwig was holding over him—like a flash, if he had had the money. But he didn't.

"And then, when Helwig handed him this check, two weeks ago, he did have. That is, he did have if he could cash it. Do I have to go any further?"

The commissioner burst out hastily, "Yes, yes—please go on."

THE MARQUIS crossed one neat, black-clad leg over the other. "All right. He took to following Helwig around, hoping. He was trying to get up his courage to kill his benefactor, so as to own the check. There was not much doubt that he could collect from Dorinne Hoffman—anybody could, in a spot like that. But, naturally, he didn't dare make a move as long as Helwig was alive.

"Remember, he has a brain like chain-lightning, or Helwig wouldn't have taken him on at all. When he went in that restaurant last night—it could even be that he was parked outside, waiting, for all I know, and just came in when he saw big Johnny in that condition—anyway, he saw the opportunity. He jumped at it instantly. Even if it failed, he wasn't laying himself open to anything, except a couple of cracks in the jaw.

"As he passed big Johnny, at the bar, he gave him the foulest sort of insult he could think of. Nobody else could hear it, and he kept his face in a smile. But Johnny heard it, and took a pass at him. Curran kept his head, took what Johnny handed him—and finally maneuvered to get knocked against Helwig.

"Stop to think of it, it was a natural. He knew Johnny would do just that—just what he did. And he knew Helwig would rise to protect him. The only open question was whether somebody would turn out the lights. I guess I'd gamble on that basis myself—a hundred thousand dollars if somebody would turn them out. A couple of pokes if they didn't. And, at that, he could almost bank on the proprietor doing it. It's the only infallible way those lugs have found to stop barroom fights.

"So—the lights went out. Helwig had obligingly drawn a gun and Curran had his hand on it. He knew the technique of that one blow to the base of the brain. He killed Helwig. Then he fired the gun, tossed it away, got in the way of Johnny, took one on the chin and went peacefully to sleep.

"The only way he tripped himself was by his astrology stuff. He dropped a piece of it at the scene. And he left some clipped papers where he's been hanging out the last week or two—the apartment he originally rented for Helwig and his girl-friend, which they no longer use. I guess he was even uneasy in his own hotel.

"Anyway—oh, yes, Judge Hoffman. Well, that's easy enough. Curran decided he couldn't wait for the payoff. Things were too hot around him. And the woman didn't have any way to get hold of the cash at once—because it all belonged to her husband. The solution to that—simple enough, isn't it? Murder her husband and then she'd own all that *he* had—which is just what he did, and so forth. Evidence? That letter will burn him twice over. Don't worry about evidence. Now, if you don't mind, I'd like to see Johnny."

The commissioner ran a hand over and over his pale-gray hair, looked from the dingy faced Immerman who stood with his fists clenched at his sides, to McGuire's chubby cynical face, to the inspector, and back to the Marquis.

"Yes, yes, by all means," he said, and then, drawing himself up, "Mr. Immerman—I would like to speak to you alone after the others go. Come to think of it, I would like to speak to a number of officers who have been unusually active in advising me this night."

The Marquis and McGuire walked out, started across to the jail.

"Do you think he'll remember about Johnny being bottled?" McGuire asked.

"It'll be lost in the shuffle, I think. There's only one guy who's going to remember that."

"Who?"

"Johnny. Let me take your sap a while. And you might get hold of that Lippertz when they turn him loose. Imagine the lug calling the Riot Squad on Johnny."

"*Tsk, tsk,*" McGuire said.

OLD WIVES TALE

IT WAS THE FIRST TIME THE LITTLE CZAR OF MANHATTAN'S MAIN STEM HAD HAD A CHANCE TO SEE THE OLD DOMESTIC TRIANGLE BUSINESS WITH REVERSE ENGLISH—AND HE FERVENTLY HOPED HE'D NEVER ENCOUNTER IT AGAIN. A JEALOUS MISTRESS, FURIOUS BECAUSE HER LOVER USED THE MONEY SHE GAVE HIM TO SPEND ON HIS WIFE, HAD TOO MANY INGREDIENTS FOR A MURDER BREW TO SUIT HIS TASTE. IT WAS NO WONDER THE THING ENDED WITH A BATTERED BODY ON AN ASH-HEAP AND A PHONEY CONFESSION FROM A LADY-KILLER.

KAVVELFOOT WAS the Broadway Squad's individualist—the lone married man. He was also the oldster of the squad—with a thin, aged face, pure white hair and the general air of an antiquated dodderer. More than one hustler, staggering up after being felled by a crack in the jaw from Kavvelfoot, had been unable to figure who had hit him.

The ancient detective looked sixty, was actually fifty, and on performance would have passed for forty. His thin, wan old face and humble, pale-blue eyes were just a plain—and eminently convenient lie.

He brought his wandering gaze back to the table at which he sat over the remains of breakfast with the Marquis.

THEY WERE almost alone in Harry's luxurious, blue-and-gold dining-room. There were a few drinkers at the bar, far up front, but at four in the afternoon the restaurant was at its lowest ebb of trade. Apart from their little corner, only one other table was occupied—in the third booth from the rear, along the wall.

"I wouldn't know," the Marquis said. "She's a little witch. She's crazy—but she stands on her own two feet and asks no favors. But whether she really can act I don't know."

Kavvelfoot glanced again. He was in position to see squarely into the occupied booth, out of the Marquis' line of sight. "Charming," he sighed. "If I had a daughter—"

"If you haven't a dozen, it's a surprise to me," the Marquis growled. "And don't start readying up that fatherly act for Marcia Lightlane. She's out of your class."

Kavvelfoot was pained. "Now, Martin! Now, Martin, now." Then presently, a curious light replaced the wounded one in his eyes. He cocked his head slowly. "Martin! By Hanna—don't tell me that you—that this little lady—"

"You damned old pack rat!" the Marquis said irritably. "I've known this girl a long time. I know a thousand girls. I like them—I like her. That doesn't mean I go around scheming how to get around them for— By God, Tecumseh, you're pathological!

"She's got looks, class—and the guts to paddle her own canoe. She treats her life the way she wants to treat it—and she doesn't cry uncle if she gets hurt. She's a genuine little personality and I take my hat off to her. That's all. She's one girl with dough that knows what do with it."

Kavvelfoot blinked. "She has money?"

"Plenty. Her dad made up some chemical that unkinks kinky hair. She collects royalties twice a year that hit with a thump—but she hasn't used her dough like most of them do. As far as her acting's concerned, she's been on the level."

"Eh?"

"She hasn't ridden on her money. She's trouped, worked in punk stock companies. She's done one-night stands and got stranded. She's put in seven years that I know of, trying to learn her business before cracking Broadway. Up till now, she's never bought herself anything."

"And now?"

He stowed her in the ash barrel.

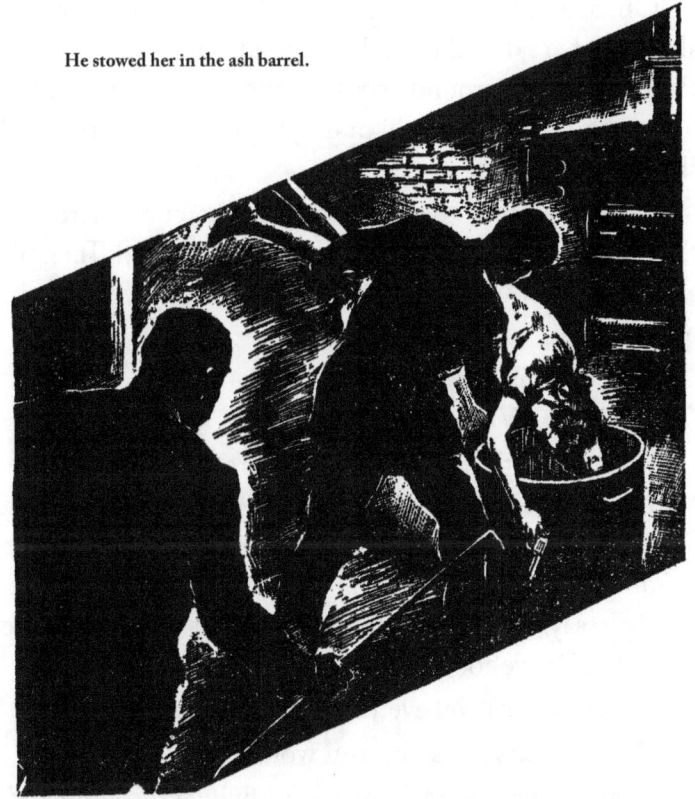

The Marquis shrugged. "I didn't say that. I have no idea."

"If Paul Donahue is starring her, that ought to indicate something. He's an experienced producer."

"Maybe so. On the other hand, she probably figures she's due for star rating by now. Maybe she's backed the show to get it. I don't say it's so—"

"I thought Donahue had plenty of his own. Or has he?"

"Don't ask me about Broadway producers. They're in and out of the money faster than horse-players. Furthermore, there are damned few of them who wouldn't rather use somebody else's dough than their own, at any time."

"But Paul isn't a grafter. Unless she's good—"

"Oh, hell," the Marquis growled. "There's a lot of gossip about that. Yeah—the kind you would think of. She and Paul have been around together the last year or so. Go on—make a crack and I'll brain you. Here—pay this and shut up."

He got up from the table, tossing the check across at the saintly looking detective. Kavvelfoot winced. Then his eyes shuttled quickly between the Marquis and the girl opposite.

"You're going to say hello to her?"

"Certainly. What of it?"

"Nothing, nothing. But it just occurred to me—ah—this *Said the Duchess* is opening the day after tomorrow—Friday. She—no doubt—will want to give you tickets to the opening. I thought—knowing you never go to openings—that is to say, Friday being my night off, it occurred to me that Mrs. Kavvelfoot and I—"

"My God, can't you even buy your own theater tickets?"

"On my salary? Martin, you wouldn't believe—"

"Salary? Since when did you start living on your salary? Every house in your section has been moaning that you take all the profits."

A pained look twisted Kavvelfoot's saintly features. "Martin! Such talk—even in jest—"

The Marquis made a disgusted noise in his throat, "Yeah. Very funny," he said sourly. "If she sends me a pair of Annie Oakley's you can have 'em. See you down at the agency."

THE GIRL didn't see the Marquis as he sauntered casually up to the booth. She was breathtakingly lovely—radiantly blond, with skin so transparent and fresh that it seemed almost moist. Her features were small, even, smooth, her lips ripe cherry and generous, her long-lashed eyes starry, as deep a blue as the Marquis' own. In a black afternoon frock that came high on her throat and had ballet-dancer's sleeves, slashed to give glimpses of her warm flesh, she looked desperately young and infinitely desirable. The little dab of black hat on her 'up' hair, and the wisp of veil did nothing to spoil the effect. The Marquis' black-gloved hand unconsciously touched the black silk muffler tight at his throat, tugged the front of his neat black Chesterfield into line as he edged up to the booth.

A man's voice—the girl's partner in the cubicle—was saying earnestly, quietly: "I mean it, Marcia—it's always been that way with me. What do you think I tagged around after you to all those tank towns for? Why do you think I'm in this hellhole of a city?" A barely noticeable southern accent rounded his words. "It wasn't accident that I dropped in on Paul when I knew he was doing this show. I—"

Then the girl's blue eyes noticed the Marquis' blocky little figure and flicked up quickly. "Marty!" she leaned back, smiled with real pleasure as he made a little bow over his hard hat. "Phil!" She held out a tiny gloved hand. "Phil—this is Lieutenant Marquis of the Broadway Squad—the little tin god of Times Square. Marty—this is Phil Gwathmey, our press agent."

The Marquis stood at the end of the table as the lean, good-looking youth stood up. He had a mop of thick, rich, dark-red hair, a young-looking, thin, tanned face and electric brown eyes, now a little clouded with embarrassment.

The Marquis said: "Pleased to know you, Mr. Gwathmey."

The youth muttered something, looked at the girl with reproachful eyes.

"Sit down, Marty, and buy me a drink—" she began, but the dark youth suddenly looked at his wrist watch, gave the girl a disheartened look and said stiffly: "I guess I'll run along, Marcia. I've some things to do, if you don't mind."

"All right, Phil. See you at the theater."

The youth grumbled that he was glad to have met the Marquis, strode off. The Marquis, looking after him dubiously, said: "I hope I didn't come at the wrong time."

Her laugh rippled up. "On the contrary—just the right time. Phil was getting a little too earnest. He was—what's the line? 'Paying me the greatest compliment a man can pay a woman.'"

"Proposing? He wants you to marry him?"

"Much more than that. He wants me to *re*-marry him."

"What!"

"Don't look so pained. We were married once—for six months. I was playing in stock down south—Charleston, South Carolina. He was the town's bright young lawyer, but he schemed around till he got to do the press work for the company. All for my beautiful eyes."

The Marquis' round face was serious. "And you gave him six months of you and dropped him."

Her eyes got tired. "Oh, Marty—are you going to lecture me again?"

The Marquis shrugged. "O.K., Marcia. It's none of my—"

"Oh, stop that. You're always criticizing my doings. I married him, didn't I?"

The Marquis grimaced. "What was the use of that? Nobody could have enough of you in six months, Marcia. It isn't human. You light up things in these gents and then check out while the fire's still blazing. Some day, somebody won't like it. You're a damned funny girl."

A waiter brought her a rum collins and him a coca-cola.

SHE HAD an exasperated look in her deep-blue eyes. She made a squirming gesture with her shoulders, cupped her drink in dainty hands. "I don't know why you always disapprove of my love-life, Marty. I enjoy living. I want love. I can't help it if I get tired of one man and get interested in another, can I? You pretend not to understand that. You'd think you were an old man yourself or something. You've had lots of different girls—and you'll have more. It's the greatest thrill in life, Marty—when it's new, and as long as it lasts—and then it's just nothing any more. I know it's that way with you and why should I be different? I'm nobody's property. I don't ask any favors. I'm not afraid to fall in love. And if it doesn't last—I'm not afraid of that, either. Maybe I've made some mistakes, but whom have I hurt?

"As for Phil—I married him one month after I started working in Charleston, and I divorced him two months before I left. He's a perfect lamb. His uncle was a judge or something in the town and Phil handled the whole thing for me, like the gentleman he is. He understood how it was, went out of his way to make things easy for me. I didn't even have to go to court. He did the whole thing—and nobody even had to know about it. I'm sorry he still feels the way he does, but—well, I adore him, and I was in love with him for six months, but it's gone now. It's just one of those things. And he's the only man who ever had a legal string on me. You know that."

"I didn't know that," the Marquis said wearily. "I haven't been keeping track of your goings-on for the last three years. All right, Marcia, you're too—intense for me. I guess you know what you're doing." He hesitated, then complained in a rush that startled even himself: "But I'm damned if I can get used to it. You sit there, looking like an innocent, unkissed, demure little schoolgirl. But you make a man—oh, hell, I've lost page two," he tried belatedly to pass it off.

Good humor was suddenly back in her shining eyes. She clasped her hands in mock excitement. "Why, Marty—you old rascal. I believe you're carrying the torch for little Marcia!"

"Cut it!" the Marquis growled. He stood up slowly, picked up his hat. "I've got to get back to work." He looked down at her obliquely. "What kind of a turkey is this *Said the Duchess?*"

"It's good, Marty." She was suddenly changed, intent. "The part was made for me. I'm sure we've got a hit. Paul thinks so too—really thinks so—and he's a terribly clever man—"

She had the grace to blush, as the Marquis eyed her quizzically.

"All right," she said defiantly. "So you heard about Paul. Well, *I* asked *him* to marry me and he wouldn't hurt his present wife by asking for a divorce. At least"—she hesitated and for a second, there was a shadow across her face, instantly gone—"he hasn't yet. What do you think of that?"

The Marquis looked at his hat. "Why should I think anything of it, Marcia? May I put you in a cab?"

"No." She jumped up. "The theater's just a couple of blocks down. You'll come to the opening, Marty? I'll send tickets to your place. I won't feel right if you're not there, Marty. You'll come—pretty please?"

"If I can," the Marquis grumbled.

He walked slowly down to the Times Square ticket agency that was the unofficial headquarters for the Broadway Squad, peculiarly conscious—and not for the first time—of the spell of her appeal.

The boy in the ticket agency was just inserting little white letters in the background of black velvet on one of the wall boards. The white letters advertised tickets for the opening night of *Said the Duchess*, with Marcia Lightlane, and he had that to look at every time he went in or out.

This was Wednesday.

ON FRIDAY, at eleven o'clock, when the Marquis strode quickly into the empty, lighted foyer of the Heyworth Theater, he had not yet succeeded in breaking the nostalgic spell. It was strengthened as he found himself surrounded by her photographs staring at him from frames from all sides of the lobby. The S.R.O. sign was up over the box-office.

One of the doors into the theater came open as he had his hand almost on it and Kavvelfoot—to whom he had turned over the tickets Marcia had sent—sailed out. The Marquis could not restrain an exclamation as he took in the big detective's get-up.

Kavvelfoot was resplendent in full evening dress, even down to silk-collared evening Chesterfield, opera hat and ebony cane. Hastily, he closed the door behind him, put a quick hand up against the Marquis' chest.

"Wait, Martin—wait just a moment. Look—Mrs. Kavvelfoot is here with me, you see? She—ah—seems to doubt that I have to work. Now, if you wouldn't mind assuring her that you need me on this case—"

"I'll tell her nothing," the Marquis said with feeling. "The last time I ran into your wife, she lectured me all afternoon about the hours you keep. What case anyway? What did you call me over here for?"

"Eh? Oh, yes—Miss Lightlane—the star—hasn't come to the theater. Paul Donahue mentioned it to me. I thought that I should call you—knowing that you—"

"What!"

"Yes, but Martin—regarding Mrs. Kav—"

The Marquis was already hurrying into the darkened auditorium. The play was in progress on the stage. He swung toward the manager's office, almost colliding in the dark with a dumpy woman about five feet tall who had the gait of a Bowery bouncer. The woman wore a white sequin evening gown. The Marquis lifted his hat as he hastily stepped around her. "Good-evening, Mrs. Kavvelfoot." Then, taking pity on the white-haired detective, "Come on, Tecumseh—hurry it up. Excuse us, Mrs. Kavvelfoot."

In the wall ahead a lighted oblong suddenly appeared and, emerging from it, the pale, worried face of the brown-eyed Phil Gwathmey, the press-agent and ex-husband of Marcia Lightlane whom he had met in the restaurant with her. His dark-red hair shone dully. He made an exclamation over his shoulder to someone in the office and hastily stepped aside. "Here he is now, thank God!"

He ushered the Marquis and Kavvelfoot in, saying in a worried whisper: "She's gone, Mr. Marquis—vanished off the face of the earth. Her understudy is doing the part."

Through the closing door the Marquis looked back and out at the distant stage. A blond girl in riding habit and a youthful actor in tweeds were in the center of the stage, surrounded by young people. The girl looked so much like Marcia Lightlane at this distance that it seemed impossible that it was not she. The young man was declaring love or something, and even as the Marquis looked she put her arms up and the actor in tweeds went into a clinch with her—just as the final curtain came rushing down. The house thundered with applause.

The closing door did not quite cut the noise off. The Marquis looked quickly at the slender, distinguished Paul Donahue, standing beside the walnut desk on the thick rug, nursing his wrist. He was slender, poised, forty-five or so with a sensitive face and gentle, understanding dark-gray eyes. His fine black hair was liberally sprinkled with white. For a moment, his eyes were on the door, as the thunder of the audience's applause swelled even higher.

The Marquis said: "What is this, Paul?"

The producer's eyes were worried. He ran a finger inside his collar. "We don't know anything, Marty—except that Marcia just didn't show up. She was due at the theater no later than seven. We've phoned her hotel—all her friends that we could think of."

"No indication that she might have been—no calls from anybody demanding money, or any of that nonsense?"

"Positively not. You're one cop I'd tell, Marty, in a case like that."

"When was she last seen—definitely?"

"She was in her dressing-room at three o'clock." Donahue's eyes went questioningly to the red-haired press agent's brown ones for confirmation. "Isn't that what Danny said?"

"Yes. She—" the intense-faced Gwathmey hesitated, then blurted: "She came to the theater to see you, didn't she?"

"Yes. We were talking over some last-minute changes. Then she had to get something from her dressing-room. Danny said he saw her go in there, after she'd left the office. That's the last we've been able to learn that anyone saw of her."

"No one saw her leave?"

"She probably used the stage door."

"Who's this Danny?"

"Danny Holden, my stage-manager."

"Where is he—and where is Marcia's dressing-room?"

THE PRODUCER led the way quickly to the door. The last of the excitedly chattering audience was just leaving the auditorium. Two or three men called out to Paul Donahue, congratulating him on a hit and he acknowledged them distractedly. The small, short-bodied woman in white sequin was parked just outside the door. With the house-lights up, her blazing eyed face was visible under piled-up hair.

She said: "Wilbur!"

The Marquis helped with, "Come on, Tecumseh!" and the saintly faced detective stopped only long enough to say hastily to the woman: "Now, Mother, probably you had best take a cab home. I'll come when I can, but you heard the lieutenant—"

Donahue led the way down the aisle and up onto the stage. From backstage, a circular iron stairway led to the second floor—the dressing-room level. Sounds of exultant laughter, noisy conversation of the young people in the show came from all the dressing-rooms as they mounted. The producer led the way to the room at the very top of the hall, stopped with his hand raised to knock, then let his hand fall as the Marquis stepped past him.

The door was open and a tall, broad-shouldered youth was standing with his back to it, staring down at the brilliantly lighted make-up table. He turned swiftly, at the

Marquis' first footfall. He wore gray slacks and a black coat over a black V-neck sweater. His white shirt was open to show his smooth throat. His skin was rosy, like that of a schoolboy, his blond hair a nimbus of fluffy curls, his mouth a dab of crimson.

Paul Donahue said: "This is Lieutenant Marquis, Danny. Danny Holden, Marty."

"Oh, yes. How d'ye do?" The youth's voice was the give-away. It wanted to climb, but vocal cords held it down to a nasal resonance.

The Marquis grunted. "You know anything about this disappearance?"

The stage-manager's baby-blue eyes were shining with excitement. "Yes, I do!" he said vehemently. "I know exactly—" He suddenly looked toward the door, over their heads. He sucked in breath, hit the air with an extended forefinger. "There! Right there! Right there behind you is the she-devil who instigated this! Yes, right there!"

The Marquis looked over his shoulder, turned. In the hallway, transfixed by Holden's extravagantly pointing finger, was a blond girl. She had on a camel's-hair sweater and skirt and held a comb in one hand. Her face was still shining from cold cream. She was obviously the girl the Marquis had seen on-stage just before the final curtain. Now, at close range, the little differences between her and Marcia Lightlane were apparent. This one looked a little older, a little more pinched. Her hair was not the same velvety blond but was obviously tinted and her eyes lacked the secret, melting depths of Marcia Lightlane's. Now, her cheeks flamed and fire was in her eyes.

She said carelessly, "You damned little trollop, what you need is…." and started into the room.

The blond youth drew backwards like a cat, but his pointing finger stayed extended. His voice was a squeal: "You! You! You knew the play was a hit! You knew the part was a godsend! You knew it would make a star, even of you! So you had Marcia abducted, knowing you were the only one who could step into the part!"

FOR A second the girl's eyes blazed and her lips tightened. It seemed that she would claw her way through. Then she relaxed, stood still and her eyes sought the Marquis with cold, calm defiance.

"Did you do that?" the Marquis' soft voice asked.

"No. This little specimen just happens to have taken a fancy to my fiancé, that's all."

"Oh, you liar! I wouldn't give a snap of my fing—"

"Shut up, all of you!" the Marquis snarled. Then, "I didn't catch your name, Miss...?"

"Gregory. Jean Gregory. And I—"

"Yes, yes, I know," the Marquis said hastily and, as the hallway beyond suddenly began to fill with startled, curious faces. "Come in and close the door please."

He asked the blond stage manager: "Do you know what clothes Miss Lightlane had on when she left the theater this afternoon?"

"Yes, I do," the other replied elaborately. "As it happens, her gown was one I noticed in DeVries and begged her to buy. It was blue lamé—flounced and shirred at the waist, with leg-of-mutton sleeves—"

"Is that blue silk?" the Marquis asked irritably.

"Yes, yes. Over that she wore a short Persian lamb jacket—black—and a little black pancake hat with a half-veil. Then she had on champagne stockings and black suede ties. She *was* wearing her diamond and emerald bracelet when she came, but I begged her to take it off. It spoiled the whole effect—"

"What kind of bracelet?"

"A very valuable one," Paul Donahue volunteered. "Graduated diamonds and emeralds."

The Marquis turned back to the rosy cheeked Holden. "You say she took it off—didn't wear it out?"

"I'm sure she didn't wear it out. She always took my advice in the matter of clothes. She probably left it in the safe in Mr. Donahue's office."

The Marquis looked questioningly at the producer.

"She might have," the producer said.

"Can she open your safe?"

"I—"The producer's gray eyes were suddenly tired. "Yes. Matter of fact, it was her own safe. We can soon find out."

They went back into the hall, down the iron stairs. The Marquis told Kavvelfoot, "Tell everybody to stick around," and the big white-haired detective nodded quickly.

On the way back up the aisle down in the auditorium, Donahue ran a finger inside his collar, swallowed and said in an undertone: "Marty—I'd like to see you alone a minute, without these others."

"Right," the Marquis said quickly, and when they had again reached the office, he told the red-haired press-agent and the sad-faced Kavvelfoot: "We won't want you two for a little while."

HE CLOSED the office door from the inside and leaned his back against it, slid his small, black-gloved hands into tight coat pockets. Donahue's sensitive face was strained. He took a cigarette from a heavy bronze box on the desk, snapped a lighter to flame, lit the cigarette and held it in his fingers, looking at the glowing end. He gulped. "You'll have to know sooner or later how things were between Marcia and myself. It was her money backing this show. Also *Say It Isn't So*, our resounding flop last season. I haven't had a dime of my own for two years.

"This safe"—he nodded at the cube of black steel in one corner—"is hers. To—spare my feelings, she kept a good deal of cash in there at all times. I took out what was needed, leaving chits there saying what it was for. She had a tab for the safe and I had one."

"How a tab?"

"To open the safe." He fingered out a small leather square from his watch pocket. It was spotted with rubber and copper studs, eccentrically placed. "The safe is electric. There's a slot here." He ran his fingers down the side. "Putting this thing in establishes certain currents and breaks others." He slid the tab into the invisible slot and the safe door swung silently open.

After a minute's squatting in front of it, pawing through papers, the producer said: "The bracelet isn't here, Marty."

The Marquis' eyes sharpened. "Then she left the theater wearing what? Twenty thousand—thirty—"

"Nearer thirty."

"—thousand dollar's worth of stones. That helps." He hesitated then asked the question that had been in his mind for some time: "Paul—is she much of an actress?"

The harassed producer's pinched face was miserable. "Not much, Marty."

The Marquis nodded thoughtfully, reached for the telephone and called Missing Persons. He gave a complete description of Marcia Lightlane and put the usual wheels in motion.

When he hung up, he sat on the side of the desk and said: "I'll have to ask you these things, Paul. You were in love with Marcia?"

The other's voice was husky and there was something odd in the oblique glance he shot at the Marquis. "Yes."

"How long has—well, you know."

"Since *Say It Isn't So,* Marty. About a year. I knew her two years. Why?"

The Marquis spread short fingers, examined them. "I've known Marcia a long time, though I've been out of touch with her lately. She—doesn't usually stay content with one person for as long as a year."

"What are you getting at, Marty? That she is changing her mind about me?"

"Not that, especially. That she had someone else on the string perhaps—someone who got tough with her."

"I'm sure you're wrong. I wish—Marty, I'm sure you're wrong. There's been no one like that in the picture. There's been no one at all. I'm not a baby. I'd know."

"You knew she was married once to this Phil Gwathmey?"

"Of course. She told me when she asked me to give him a job. That was just a crazy interlude—six months—hardly a marriage at all. I think he'd like to try again, but—Marcia wouldn't. It's just one of those things."

"Maybe so. Why are you so sure she's sticking to you?"

"I—to tell you the honest truth, Marty, she asked me today—not for the first time—about our getting married."

The phone on the desk rang—a single melodious chime that the Marquis did not identify till the other picked up the instrument and answered.

After a second, Donahue handed it over to the Marquis. "Somebody calling you."

The Marquis blinked, answered. A man's voice, obviously muffled by something said quickly: "If you want to know what's happened to Marcia Lightlane, go to Forty-six Driver's Lane in Garden City. If you get there within the next half hour, you'll see something—but you'll have to move like the wind." The receiver was hung up in his ear.

The Marquis said, "All right, Jack," and put the instrument down again. His face was somber, thoughtful, but there was instant, flying debate inside his dark head.

Finally he said, "How far—" and checked himself. He turned and went to the door, opened it and put his head out. "Tecumseh!" he called but the ascetic-faced white-haired detective—or, for that matter, anyone else at all— was not in the auditorium.

After another moment of quick debate, he went to the phone and ordered a prowl car from the precinct.

To the bewildered producer, he said: "I'm going out for a short while. Find Kavvelfoot and tell him he's in charge here. I'll be right back."

IT WAS a half-hour ride, in a prowl car with the siren going most of the way. The Marquis occupied himself with glum realization that he had a first-class tangle on his hands, and with worried hopes that nothing really unpleasant would be happening to the delectable little blond Marcia, who was—he had the phrase for it at last—who was trying to live her life too quickly.

Then he was in Garden City and at the bottom of Driver's Lane, where he left the prowl car and proceeded on foot to No. 46.

It was a charming, brand-new, miniature Colonial house, the conventional design modified by an artistic hand—a tiny masterpiece in red and white. It was set in the middle of a barbered lawn that was just the right size. Flower beds were arranged to give the maximum of trim beauty and there were a few trees on the lawn. A low, trimmed hedge bordered the property, with an opening for a driveway which, passing under a tiny porte-cochére at the side of the house, vanished into darkness behind, presumably to a garage.

There were lights on inside the house but the Marquis, momentarily entranced by the bright, chipper little house, hesitated a long minute, puzzled, before he decided to walk up the cement strip that led onto the little porticoed red-tile entrance stoop.

He bent to look for the bell, still uncertain as to a course of action.

There was a card in a little metal frame over the bell. In the semi-gloom he could not read it. He took out pencil flash, smothered its beam in one small, black-gloved hand and squirted a tiny ray, was surprised to read: *Mr. Paul Donahue.*

He straightened in bewilderment. So this was the producer's house. Strangely, facts that were in the back of his head—that the producer had a wife and a house somewhere—had not occurred to him before this.

Now they assumed sudden significance. A house—and a wife. Paul Donahue had a wife. This was where he kept her. Of course. Marcia had mentioned her. Paul Donahue—Marcia Lightlane—Paul Donahue's wife. The conventional triangle. Paul Donahue's wife, sitting at home—albeit in a charming little house—hearing, or knowing, about

Paul and Marcia. Paul Donahue's wife, jealousy-ridden seeking to hurt the woman who had stolen her husband.

It suddenly dawned on him that his list of people under suspicion was growing incontinently. Jean Gregory, the blond understudy, to whom Marcia's disappearance meant dizzy success. Phil Gwathmey, her morose, hungry, importunate ex-husband. There was no clear motivation discernible for him, but he warranted suspicion on general principles. Paul Donahue himself—though that took a stretch of imagination. Marcia Lightlane was his meal ticket, as well as his mistress, and he was no hot-blooded youth. He would scarcely want to do her a mischief. Bringing up the rear, the peculiar little effeminate stage-manager, Danny Holden—not for any good reason but because he seemed to be too excited about the whole thing, too effervescent.

Add to all those any casual thief, for whom, with a small fortune in jewels on her person she'd be a rich target—and now, Paul Donahue's wife.

On a sudden decision, the Marquis punched the bell.

There was, presently, a rush of feet inside, a hasty shooting back of locks and the door swung wide. A dainty little brown-haired girl almost rushed out into his arms.

"Oh, Paul—was it a succ— Oh!"

She caught herself in confusion as she saw her mistake and color flooded her warm little oval face. The Marquis stared, as the girl stammered in a small voice: "Oh—oh, excuse me. I thought it was my—husband."

SHE WAS supremely dainty, with a soft, little-girl face and big, round blue eyes, lash-shadowed. Her chestnut hair was softly waved to the back of her neck. Her simple, brown peasant dress almost, but not quite, concealed her perfect, curving little figure. She was lovely, very young, and either utterly unsophisticated or a far greater actress than Marcia Lightlane.

The Marquis bowed over his hard hat, casting desperately about for a conversational gambit. "I'm a friend of your husband, Mrs. Donahue. He's tied up and I was passing this way. He asked me to drop in and assure you that the play was a great success."

"Oh!" Her blue eyes lighted up with delight and she clasped her hands excitedly. "Oh! I knew it would be! I—" She checked herself, blushing, and her eyes got shy. "I—you must excuse me. You don't know how much it means to Paul...."

The Marquis smiled understandingly. "Indeed I do." Mentally he was scrambling. How to pry information—if information there was—from this child? How even to get into the house to do it? "I'm really one of Paul's closest friends," he groped. "That is—his closest Broadway friends. Though I suppose that's no recommendation to you. You must be pretty jealous of the people who monopolize so much of his time."

"I?" Her puzzlement was genuine. "Oh, Mr.—Mr.—"

"Marquis."

"Mr. Marquis. Do come in.... Oh, Mr. Marquis, how could I be jealous of Paul's career? Now tell me about the play. Was Miss Lightlane very good?"

For the life of him, the Marquis could see no disingenuousness in the question. She led him excitedly into a comfortable, tiny, colonial living-room. A log fire burned cheerfully on the hearth.

"Very good," the Marquis said.

"I'll make some coffee while you tell me about it. Will Paul be home soon?"

"Not very soon, I'm afraid," the Marquis said. "Please don't bother about coffee. I must—I have to get home myself soon. If I may just smoke a cigarette...."

She sat on the sofa's edge, her eyes shining. "This will make Paul a lot of money, won't it?"

"It ought to."

She laughed exultantly. "You know people think Paul is very rich—but he really isn't. He worried about it. I'm so glad everything is all right now."

"You're a remarkable woman, Mrs. Donahue, not to be upset over all the time Paul has to spend on Broadway."

"Unhappy? I? Oh, Mr. Marquis—I'm the happiest girl in the whole world. I know I don't see much of Paul, but he's explained that. It's only till he gets enough money. And I know I really have him, even if he isn't here. And now, with this lovely house and—and everything, how could I be unhappy?"

"Did you design the house?"

"Oh, no. A writer I knew built it for himself and his wife. Then he had to go out west and he wanted to sell it very cheaply. I—all my life, Mr. Marquis, I've wanted a real house—a real house to live in and own. In Detroit— I lived all my life in Detroit—my people always lived in apartments or boarding-houses and we moved around so much—always having to pay people rent and—and when I went to work in the photographic studio, it was the same. Only it was rooms, then—tiny little cubbyholes. Then, the first two years Paul and I were married, it was hotels. So when I set eyes on this adorable little house, it was like everything I ever dreamed of. We've been in it just four weeks now. It seems more wonderful every day and when— when Paul can come and be here all the time, it will be *too* perfect."

THE MARQUIS said good-bye, went outside and waited for something to happen. He prowled the grounds and the vicinity, found nothing. Or had he?

Gnawing wonder grew in his mind as the prowl car whirled him finally back toward Broadway. Had the anonymous phone caller sent him to find just what he had found? Was the whole business just a subtle way of calling his attention to Paul Donahue's wife? Or was there some other obscure clue that he was supposed to grasp from the odd little visit? Or had he missed fire entirely? Did something lie back of the anonymous call that he could not yet divine?

That answer came quickly—shockingly quickly—as the whole ugly, bitter little drama suddenly burst into the open.

The prowl car whirled into the now deserted street which housed the theater, just at half past one, set him down a few yards from the marquee. Hence he was able to get a swift glimpse of the lights and the dark forms in the stage alley as he piled out and started quickly for the lobby.

He checked himself, walked back to the mouth of the alley, ran down it.

Beneath the dull, round globe over the stage door, flashlights were burning, throwing light on the ground. Men's backs were between him and the chunks of light. A huge truck stood down at the outlet of the alley, a few yards beyond.

He ran up—and for an instant it was as though he had received a terrific blow under the heart. Little beads of cold sweat broke out on his neck.

MARCIA LIGHTLANE lay on the cobbles of the alley, half on her back, half on her side, one cheek flat on the stone. Her glorious hair was awry, her stony eyes peering, seemingly, along the ground. She lay in a little sprinkling of ashes. There were ashes smudged all over her dress, her face, her hair. One hand was turned upwards. The other gripped rigidly a small, silver-mounted pistol. An overturned ash barrel was a few yards away, spilling more ashes.

The uniformed D.S. employee sat on an upturned can, nursing his head in his hands. Two others stood with white-ringed eyes while the Latin-looking, slender man got up, wiping his hands to face the Marquis. The glow of light revealed him as Mercedes, assistant M.E.

He grunted in recognition. "Thank God you're here at last. That old man of yours has been preventing me calling the Homicide Squad."

The Marquis' throat was dry as he stared down at the thing on the cobbles, so dry that when he said, "What...?" his voice was a croak. He cleared it instantly. "What's happened?"

The doctor squatted, picked the dead girl's head up. Her whole body came off the ground. She was as stiff as a board. "Look here."

The Marquis bent. The whole side of the girl's blond head was a bloody pulp, beaten shapeless. Now it was a horrible mat of dried blood and ashes.

"When?" the Marquis asked softly.

"Around—well, somewhere in the last twelve hours. Somebody hit her with a blunt object, literally hammered her skull to powder. Your man—Kavvelfoot—say, how old is he, anyway?"

"I don't know. Go on, go on."

"Well, he was looking around the girl's dressing-room and found some ashes tracked into her rug. He prowled downstairs—down-cellar—just about the time that truck got here. When they started to roll that can across the alley...." He looked over at the huddled man on the up-turned barrel. "Tell him, you."

The man from the Department of Sanitation lifted his head. There was a welt across his left temple and his eyes looked bloodshot.

"I was down the alley taking out the ashes," he said hoarsely. "I didn't see that old goat around. I rolled the can out here and started to put it in the truck when all of sudden there he was behind me, making a grab for something with that cane of his—something in the can. I didn't see what is was, till he hooked it—a—a gun—in *her* hand—sticking out of the ashes...." He nodded at the dead girl on the cobbles. "I—his sneakin' around and all—I didn't know who he was—I didn't know what the hell was goin' on. I dropped the barrel and told him to wait a minute and made a grab for him." He touched his forehead with careful fingers. "Then I got this."

"Kavvelfoot thought, for a minute, when he saw the hand and pistol," the M.E. explained, "that maybe this young man was involved in the situation. When the young man got belligerent, that confirmed his feeling, so he blackjacked him. It was all a huge misunderstanding."

"How did you get here?" the Marquis asked.

"Kavvelfoot called me—twenty or thirty minutes ago—and he's practically prevented me by force from calling back my office or the Homicide Squad till you got here."

"Was that pistol fired?"

"No."

"Where's Tecumseh now?"

"He's got some of the people in the theater down in Paul Donahue's office, questioning them. Listen—my office and Homicide should be notif—"

"Go ahead and notify them," the Marquis said and swung for the stage door.

ONLY THE pilot light was burning on stage. A few house-lights were on in the vast, silent auditorium, as he emerged into the aisle.

He took just one moment to discipline himself, to crowd down the tearing ache that weakened him—to blot out the warm, poignant memory of Marcia Lightlane that danced in his mind. He drove it out till only a residue of dull fury remained.

No longer was there any mystery about the anonymous phone call. The killer—the cold-blooded, vicious butcher of the girl—had simply wanted him clear while the ash bins were being taken from the building—had evidently feared his prowling around, and had sent him to the first place that came to mind. Evidently the rat's nervousness had not extended to Kavvelfoot—or else he had disdained him.

Who? Who had made that phone call? Actually, anyone—including those in the theater—could have. The only person to whom it would have been impossible was the producer himself, Paul Donahue, who had been in the office with the Marquis.

There was no clue there. There was no clue anywhere. He was exactly where he was when he had started.

Then, as he was in the act of turning the knob of the door into the producer's office, his brain cogged and he saw the point he had overlooked.

He did not check himself. He stepped into the office—and into a moment electric with tensity and silence. He caught drama in the drawn, stunned ring of faces around him. Phil Gwathmey, the red-haired press agent, Danny Holden, the eccentric blond director, Jean Gregory, the slightly faded blond ingenue, were standing around the walls. Kavvelfoot was just inside the door. Every eye was turned on Paul Donahue, in the room's center, slowly taking a cigarette from the heavy bronze box on the desk. The Marquis' entrance was scarcely noticed.

He tried to catch the action, glanced from one to the other. Then Donahue's sensitive face, now grayish, but still poised and gentle, came up and his hollow gray eyes met the Marquis' blue ones. His voice was gentle, husky, but everything he had went into making it casual. He said: "Hello, Marty. I killed her."

Shock held the Marquis momentarily as speechless as the rest. Then he asked: "How?"

The producer picked up the heavy bronze cigarette box in one hand, but his poise was superficial. His fingers were too moist and shaking and the box eluded them, crashed down on the desk, then thudded to the rug, bounced and lay still, its cover flung back. Paul Donahue made no effort to retrieve it. He cleared his throat and said: "With that."

The Marquis' eyes whipped to a door across the office. "What's in there?"

"My secretary's office."

Kavvelfoot made a throat noise, suddenly stepped forward, jerking out manacles.

"Nix," the Marquis said. "Paul—come in here." He opened the door of the tiny office, told Kavvelfoot: "Keep these others here just a minute."

THE MARQUIS stood with his back to the closed door of the cubicle, small black-gloved hands tight in his coat pockets. Donahue sat uneasily, half on and half off the corner of the secretary's desk. His gray face was ashen and one gray-black lock of hair had slipped down across his forehead. His eyes were feverish, wracked.

"Why, Paul?"

The producer's jawpoints showed white. "Because I was trapped in a situation concocted by the devil himself."

"That doesn't mean a damn thing to me, Paul."

"Then maybe this will. She caught me embezzling some of her money—five thousand dollars."

The Marquis' forehead wrinkled.

"And so you killed her to prevent exposure?"

"No. It wasn't that. But she—when she found I had taken the money from the safe and left a chit saying it was for scenery, she knew it was a false item, and demanded to know what I *had* taken the money for."

"And?"

"I told her. She stood there and went perfectly white. She—she went out of her head, Marty. She became someone else—someone we never saw—a fiend incarnate. She called me everything in the catalogue. That was her right, of course. But finally she snatched a gun out of her bag. She was going to kill me, Marty—there isn't any doubt about it. I lost my head—panic—fright, whatever. I grabbed the first thing at hand and threw it at her to spoil her aim. The sharp corner of that thing caught her squarely in the temple. When I tried to grapple with her, she slid out of my hands like a sack of meal. Then I saw the little cut. When I touched it, I could feel the smashed bone through her skin and I—I knew that she was done for. She—she died—in the minute or two that I tried to think what to do. I could feel her pulse flutter out under my fingers. I tried to take the pistol away. She had it clutched in a death grip. I couldn't get it. I—then I—"

"How do you know she died?"

"I—I felt her die. I felt her go cool—"

"What made her go berserk? What was it you told her that sent her off? What *did* you do with the money you stole from her?"

The producer's haggard gray eyes fell, and he licked his lips.

Sudden startled light was in the Marquis' eyes. "Wait a minute. You stole her money to spend on your wife."

Donahue's, "Yes," was no louder than a breath.

"Go on," the Marquis said. "Explain. You may as well know I've just come from seeing your wife."

The producer's head jerked up, eyes stark with fear. "You—" he choked. "You told Una—"

"I told her nothing," the Marquis said. "Whatever she can be spared, she'll be spared. Go on telling me about you and Marcia. You never were in love with her? You— well, go on."

The producer's eyes did not lose their stark fright. His gray lips were warped as he said huskily: "You must understand. I was broke, down and out, two years ago, when I met Marcia. I was desperate. I—I had just been married a year then. I met Marcia and—she wanted to produce a play. I swear I didn't realize that she was in—that she had any personal thoughts towards me then.

"What could I do? You know how things have been on Broadway. I've played in bad luck the last few years. Better-known men than I have been walking the streets, unable to find a dime. And I had—my wife. She thought—

thought I was the greatest theatrical man on Broadway. She still does. I couldn't refuse to take Marcia's money. It was a godsend, till—till after the play failed and I was up against it again. Then she—well, I realized that she was in love with me and I simply couldn't let her go. She was the only angel anywhere in sight. I couldn't walk away and admit I was all washed up. I—I interested her in another play and—and, well, things happened.

"She—I sort of took the line of least resistance, I swear. Marcia didn't know how broke I was but she knew I didn't have much. She did everything possible to make it easy for me to take her money. Like keeping currency in the safe—I told you about that. I swear I didn't design these things. They just went along from moment to moment. I—God, Marty, they weren't as cold-blooded as they sound."

"I know they weren't, Paul. Go on—the five thousand."

THE PRODUCER licked his lips. His gray eyes were tortured and his voice was sunk almost to a croak. "I—Una wanted something. She—Marty, I love her better than life. She has never questioned me, never asked me for anything. She's had it plenty hard and never stopped smiling and loving me. She—saw something she wanted—something that really meant a lot to her. I won't attempt to explain it to you, but it was something that she has a complex about. She asked me to buy it for her. She's so straight and decent and sweet—I knew she wouldn't have asked if it hadn't meant the whole world to her. I thought of the—the nights with Marcia and I—couldn't turn her down. I took the five thousand and paid it down, gambling that this play would go over and I could meet the balance when it came due."

He hesitated, and all the starch went out of his body. "Marcia—asked me—and I told her. I—what made her so furious was that she—that I—God, Marty, I'd rather burn than tell you this. This morning—well, I let her think that I was going to—to divorce Una and marry her. She—she's been wanting me to for a—well, a long time. Of course, when she found out about my taking her money, she knew I'd been lying.... I guess she's never had anyone—prefer another person to her. I guess her vanity was—well, bigger than other people's. I guess she just went out of her head."

The Marquis' eyes were burning. "It's a new twist to the old triangle, anyway," he said. "What did you do after she was—after you decided she was dead?"

"There—I didn't think there was anyone else in the theater. I couldn't take her outside. I thought of the ash bins—of getting her out. If—if she were found in the city dump, no one would know where she had come from."

"You're not a damn fool. You must have known a good lawyer would make it self-defense."

The producer raised sick eyes. "Could a good lawyer explain it to my wife?"

The Marquis was silent. Then he took a long breath. "I like your wife, Paul. I think she deserves a better break than having you burn—whatever you deserve. Come in here and keep your mouth shut. I think it can be fixed."

"Wha—what?"

"You heard me. You keep your mouth shut. Come on." He opened the door and walked back into the larger office.

Four pairs of eyes were glued to the slender, stumbling Donahue, as the producer followed at his heels.

"Close the door," the Marquis said.

He faced the three members of the company and slid his gloved hands deep in his coat pockets.

"Miss Lightlane—I am satisfied—was killed by accident. It was self-defense. I'm quite sure we can prove it in court but if we do it will mean trouble to people who don't rate it. I want you all to forget what you heard Mr. Donahue say a few minutes ago. We're going to tell the Homicide detectives—when they come—that it was an accident and I don't want any mention of this confession—or alleged confession—of Mr. Donahue's."

For a second there was a strained silence. Slowly, the Marquis' eyes traveled round the room. The blond girl, Jean Gregory, lines hurting her still-pretty, pale face, her cornflower-blue eyes trying to read the Marquis' with a desperate intensity, sat on the arm of a club chair. The thin-faced, electric, red-haired press agent, Phil Gwathmey had started up from the edge of the desk, horror in his eyes. Danny Holden, the blond, pink-cheeked stage manager, no longer looked so young. Vicious little lines had come into his cherubic face and his pale eyes were glittering.

Jean Gregory was the first to speak. She said huskily: "All right, Lieutenant. We'll say what you tell us."

Danny Holden broke the spell. He flung himself away from the wall, beating the air with one fist. "I won't!" he shrilled. "I won't say that!"

THE RED-HAIRED Phil Gwathmey's eyes flamed. He jammed his hands in his coat pockets and his face was white and twitching. He said through suddenly clenched teeth: "I won't say it either! He killed her—and he's going to pay! If it was self-defense, he can prove it! You must be mad, Marquis! He killed my wife—"

"Your ex-wife."

"My ex-wife, then! But I never stopped loving her. She was an angel. This—this monster debauched her—and then murdered her. And you—you, a powerful police officer, conspire to cover him up—to conceal his rotten crime—to let him get away scot-free!" The youth's face was as though lined with black crayon now and his breath was coming faster. He said, in sudden excess of fury: "Why, damn both of you! I'm going to tell the truth—or I'm going to make sure the world knows the truth! I'm going to tell you something...."

"What, for instance?" the Marquis voice cut like a dull knife. "That you were never divorced from her? That the divorce she was supposed to have received in Charleston was a phoney—fixed up to pacify her while you tried to work on her again?"

The youth gulped, and for a second, his eyes were frightened. Then he caught himself, railed wildly: "All right. That's true! I loved her too much to give her up! I thought I could make her love me again! I could have, too—except for this monster. And I'm supposed to let him go scot-free for murdering her! Murdering her because she wanted to marry him."

The Marquis' eyes snapped. "She told you that? Today?"

"Yes, damn you! And he—the swine—said he'd do it—but he lied! He has a wife and he took the rotten way out. He killed her! But he's not getting away with it! He's going to pay! By God, he's going to pay *right here and now!*"

The nickeled pistol was a shining streak of light as the wild-eyed Gwathmey whipped it from his pocket, swung it to Donahue's heart.

The Marquis fired through his pocket, sent the pistol flying into the air, sent the red-haired Gwathmey reeling and cursing, sobbing with pain and exasperation, into the wall.

Paul Donahue stood like a ghost, not moving. Little rivulets of sweat ran down his face from his forehead.

The wounded Gwathmey screamed: "Damn you! Damn you! You won't stop me! I'll tell the truth! I'll tell everything."

"Will you?" the Marquis said, and somehow there was suddenly electric silence. "Will you tell the truth, you filthy little rat! Will you tell that you're just one of these lazy, worthless southern loafers, trying to trade on your manners and looks? That you married Marcia because of her money and that, when she wanted to call quits, you pacified her with the phoney divorce, thinking you could get her again? Will you tell them that when she told you today that she was going to marry Paul Donahue—which wasn't true, incidentally, but was probably just her way of getting rid of you—that you went berserk? That you saw her fortune slipping out of your hands—saw the fraudulent divorce exposed and yourself tossed into the gutter, if not the can? Will you tell them that you murdered her after overhearing the fight in here, and sneaking along behind Paul while the poor dope rushed to the conclusion that she was dead, lost his head and stowed her in the ash barrel? That you saw that she wasn't dead—but that you made damned sure she *was* before *you* left her? No, you won't have to tell them, you little rat, because I will! Tecumseh—take him!"

The red-haired Gwathmey had finally gone over the edge. With a wild sob, he tried to fling himself, injured hand and all, toward the nickeled pistol that had fallen on the rug.

He landed on it—but the huge, saintly, white-haired detective in evening dress dived with incredible speed. His hard fist smacked under the press agent's ear almost in the instant that the youth got his frantic fingers on the gun. Again and again, Kavvelfoot drove the fist into the screaming southerner's face, till the other slumped and lay still, blood streaming from mouth and nose.

PAUL DONAHUE stammered hoarsely, in the minute's stillness: "Marty—good God—how did you—where did you find out all that stuff was true—that the divorce was only a fraud? Who told you?"

"Nobody told me," the Marquis said casually.

"You—you mean it was a guess? Just a wild guess? That you were just—just groping?"

"Groping nothing. I knew she wasn't dead when you left her—if you were telling the truth. Otherwise, there would have been no purpose in the frightful beating she got—afterwards. As soon as I realized that the divorce was a fake, that made the other half clear."

"But—but how? How did you know that it was fake? Good God, are you a mind-reader?"

"No, I'm no mind-reader. But South Carolina has no divorce law. You can't get one in that state."

He turned his back on the gasping producer and told the rest: "Don't make any mistake, you people. The quarrel in this office that Mr. Donahue refers to, never happened. You don't know anything about it and it's best you don't. You won't any of you have to go on the witness stand and run the possibility of getting some bad publicity.

"For your own information, I'm about to tell the Homicide Squad that Phil Gwathmey—you all know that anyhow—was desperately trying to win Marcia back because of her money. That he had made her think she was divorced and as long as that stood, he was free to work on her. Today, she gave him the idea that she was going to get married again and he saw her money going away from him so—he lost his head and killed her.

"That's the whole story—and if you, nance—or you, Miss Gregory—ever contradict that, I'll go after you. If you don't know what that means, ask somebody who does. You'll have to go up to Sing Sing to do it—or to a grave-yard. Do what I say—and you can always ask favors of me and the Broadway Squad. You've got that?"

They nodded, full understanding in their frightened faces.

Paul Donahue stammered huskily, "Marty—Marty—" as he followed the Marquis out the door.

"Here comes Homicide." The Marquis nodded at a swarm of men sweeping down the aisle. "Tell your story the way I outlined it—and get over to that little spot in Garden City as fast as you can. And get out of my sight. I don't like to think of luck slopping all over one person the way it has over you."

To the Homicide sergeant he said: "You get the pinch. A nice big murder conviction positively on your record. Tecumseh's holding the killer down inside. He's trying to make up stories to drag other people in with him, but there's nothing to them. Come on. I'll give you the whole story. You'll fry him with your eyes shut."

AN HOUR later, as the Marquis walked slowly down the black little street, away from the theater, Kavvelfoot lumbered along beside him.

"Ah, Martin," he said anxiously. "I—it seems to be only about two o'clock. It happens that I—that a certain busi-

ness matter—one which I am—er—I've got to take these
clothes back tomorrow morning and—as a surprise for
Mrs. Kavvelfoot—that is to say, *now* would be an ideal
time to attend to it. Would it be all right if I told the boys
at the agency, in the rare event that Mrs. Kavvelfoot should
call up in the next couple of hours, to allow her to believe
that I am still working on the case? A perfectly harmless
bit of deception—"

"Yes, yes. Go away," the Marquis said. "Beat it."

The saintly faced, white-haired detective opened his
mouth, closed it, looked sharply down at the Marquis.

When he spoke, there was real, unobtrusive sympathy
in his soft voice. "I'm damned sorry, Martin. I was foolish
enough to believe right up till now what you told me about
that girl. I wish—well, there's nothing to say except that
it's a tough break, my boy."

"What is?"

"She—well, this having to happen to this particular
girl."

"Don't be a fool," the Marquis snarled. "I know a thousand girls."

"So you do," Kavvelfoot said softly. "That's right—so
you do. I'd forgotten. Well—I'll take this cab, Martin, here,
if it's all right with y...."

"I said so, didn't I?"

After the cab had rattled away, he looked back once at
the dark marquee of the theater, eased the Chesterfield
higher on his blocky little shoulders, trudged on toward
Broadway.

DEATH FOR TWELVE MONTHS

A NEW NEON SIGN WENT UP OVER THE FACADE OF THE HOTEL TRUMBULL—JUST IN TIME TO ILLUMINATE FOR THE LITTLE CZAR OF MANHATTAN'S MAIN STEM THE CRIMSON RAIN THAT POURED DOWN FROM ABOVE. LIEUTENANT MARQUIS WOULD HAVE BEEN ABLE TO PLAY WEATHER MAN A HELL OF A LOT SOONER AND NIP THE TORRENT IN THE BUD IF HE'D ONLY STOPPED TO REMEMBER THERE ARE STILL PLENTY OF PEOPLE WHO WON'T LIVE ON A FLOOR THAT'S NUMBERED "13."

CHAPTER ONE
RED RAIN

BROADWAY WAS almost dark. Warm spring wind swept down the canyon, vaguely sweet on the thinly populated sidewalks. Only a few red-and-blue neon signs still burned at three in the morning.

Lying flat on the cement sidewalk before the towering, yellow-brick Trumbull Hotel, the mammoth electric sign began to lift. It came up on its side—almost half as long as the Broadway block on which the hotel fronted. A myriad cables were strung along it, from end to end. High up on the building's face a splash of light showed a scaffolding on which three men in overalls knelt, directing with their hands as unseen winches inside the hotel exerted pressure on the cables that laced through half a dozen windows.

A knot of overalled men on the sidewalk spread out, to block the few pedestrians who would have walked within the danger limits.

The Marquis, dapper in dark, meticulous clothes, black-gloved hands in the tight pockets of his Chesterfield coat, leaned against the building on the corner opposite, his China-blue eyes on the huge sign as it was rocked upright and slowly borne aloft.

Beside him, the redheaded McGuire sucked a toothpick. It was pure chance that the Marquis' companion happened to be McGuire, the acknowledged camera-eye of the Broadway Squad, rather than another of his twenty-two hand-picked individualists who policed the white-light district under his orders. McGuire's allotted section simply happened to be unusually quiet at this moment.

Foot by foot, the huge sign went up. McGuire spat out his toothpick and said: "That thing must have cost a couple of grand, at least. This dame Coveleskie is all right. She's on her toes."

The Marquis said, *"Mmmm."*

"In all the time I been on Broadway," McGuire said, "this is the first Broadway Hotel I ever saw go uphill. When old man Brandon had the dump, it was in the red all the time. This old lady is coining money—and in these times, too. She knows just how many high-class grifters she can let in at fancy prices and still keep the respectable stage people

The unknown assailant stole three police whistles, a book of traffic tickets, a toy microscope and half a pint of whiskey after killing Old Man Hift.

and such from walking out. She hires talent for her dining-rooms just before they become smash hits, and she knows exactly how much funny business to put up with. She's a damned phenomenon. And she was never in the hotel business before, was she?"

"No."

"How the hell does she do it?"

"She's smart—and maybe she's got just the right background. She was the madame of the highest-class house in San Francisco for years. Then she ran Hadley's Casino in Detroit for a while, and Harry was saying she used to supervise the commissary for all the Federal women's jugs. Maybe the combination is just right."

"Damn right, if you ask me. She's turned the drum from a headache into a gold-mine in—how long? Can't be more than two years since she bought it, can it?"

"She didn't buy it. She won it in a poker game with Brandon."

"Well, anyway, it isn't more than two years."

"I guess."

THEY STOOD and watched, while the mammoth T-shaped sign rode up ten stories. It was finally pulled in against the stone front of the building and the spotlight widened to show half a dozen more windows, teeming with men. In half an hour the two-ton sign was firmly bolted in place, and in fifteen more minutes, the crews of electricians had swarmed over it, screwing in bulbs, cementing connections, testing.

The cables began to disappear, snaked upward or slapping down to the sidewalk. The trestles and scaffolds were, in incredibly short time, emptied, pulled in, until finally the huge sign stood alone and untended.

There was a three-minute interval when nothing at all happened and then the sign blazed light.

HOTEL
R
U
M
B
U
L
L

It was a new light on Broadway and, as such, a part of the Marquis' business. It was a smart move. The bustling hotel had needed it. It threw enough light downward to shine on the now empty sidewalk before the three revolving-door Broadway entrances, and it gave a brisk cheery look to the whole place.

It was coincident with the lights flashing on that the door at the far end of the hotel—the hostelry occupied the whole block-face and had entrances on two side streets as well as Broadway—swished open to let out the hatless blond youth.

Hatless blond youths with cameo-like profiles who wear belted camel's-hair coats, gloves and spats, are no great novelty in the world's greatest theatrical center. This one would not have claimed their attention if it hadn't been for his actions.

He skipped swiftly along the front of the hotel—and promptly ducked back inside the minute he reached the door closest to where the Marquis and McGuire stood.

Even that would have been of little moment, were it not for the tall, stiff-shouldered man in the black fedora who burst out of the far entrance, obviously in pursuit, and stood a moment irresolute, looking swiftly in both directions.

A frown was suddenly on McGuire's chubby, deceivingly boyish face as light caught the features of the dark-hatted man. He said: "Wait a minute, chief."

The tall man with the stiff shoulders hurried along to the corner of the hotel opposite them, peered down the side street, cursed audibly and plowed quickly back into the hotel.

"That's Louis D'Astuma," the camera-eyed redhead said quickly. "You know—the Chicago dice-and-wheel man."

"What's he doing? Playing hide-and-seek?"

They waited for a minute but neither of the two reappeared.

McGuire said: "That D'Astuma is a dangerous gee, chief. If he's after that blond kid, it might mean trouble. Wouldn't hurt to have a little talk with him."

They started across the street.

McGuire said: "I don't make the blondie."

"I've seen him somewhere. An actor. I've seen him in a spotlight somewhere."

THEY PUSHED into the warmly lighted, cream-and-blue lobby. Even at this hour there were little groups of people seated in alcoves, a sprinkling of others passing to and fro. McGuire and the Marquis saw neither the blond youth nor the dark Chicago gambler.

The huge, squarish desk of the hotel was set in the middle of the rotunda. They threaded their way around it, scanning the faces in range carefully without result. Behind the desk ran a corridor between the two largest side-street entrances, and behind that a mammoth cigar-and-news stand used up the rest of the space. Behind the stand there was another corridor, but a narrow one. Smaller doors to the side streets also opened from this corridor and there was a bank of elevators just inside each door. The executive offices of the hotel were a row of ground-glass-paneled doors along a short hall that divided the elevator banks.

The Marquis strolled over to the bell-captain's pulpit-like little niche opposite the newsstand.

"Tommy, do you know Louis D'Astuma from Chicago, or is he a guest here?"

"I don't know him, Marty. Wait a minute, I'll ask if he's reg—"

"No. He must have just walked by here, chasing a blond guy who looks like an actor. D'Astuma is tall, dark, heavy-set, with a kind of glowing face and black eyes. His shoulders look stiff, sort of, and he wears a black fedora hat—"

"Oh, yeah—I saw him—and that blond guy, too—just a minute ago. They went back there." He pointed to the rear traverse, rubbed his chin. "Maybe he—or both of them—took the elevators or went out the side doors."

The Marquis said "O.K." and continued on back, then, as the traverse was deserted, turned right and went out one of the small side doors. McGuire followed at his heels.

The side street, as far as they could see, contained neither of the two they were seeking. They back-tracked, heading for the side door at the opposite end of the narrow corridor, again stepped out into the night.

The block between where they stood and Sixth Avenue was utterly deserted—save for one figure. Even as they looked, the hurrying form reached Sixth Avenue, turned a white face over his shoulder under the corner street-lamp and vanished around the corner. The street-lamp glinted on hatless blond hair.

They stood looking after the actorish youngster. The Marquis slid hands in his coat pockets and growled: "The hell with this merry-go-round. We'll do it another time."

"Well, look, we can at least see is he registered," McGuire urged as he tried to get in front of the departing Marquis.

Then the blood came down.

There was a sharp spattering of drops on their hats and the pavement round them. McGuire cursed, looked up quickly—and ducked back as more hit him in the face. Swearing roundly, he wiped his chin with his bare hand, glanced down at it mechanically.

His blue eyes went wide.

"Hey! Wait!"

The Marquis turned back, stopped as McGuire whipped out a flashlight, sprayed light around the sidewalk.

Ruby drops were scattered here and there, with one gout the size of a saucer. "Marty—look! For God's sake! Blood!"

Sharp interest replaced the irritation in the Marquis' eyes as if by magic. As one man they looked quickly upward, and as one man, they backed quickly across the narrow little side street, still staring up at the broad side of the hotel.

More windows were lighted than were dark. The patrons of the Trumbull were not early retirers. The Marquis' head and McGuire's might have been on the same pivot as they ran their sharp scrutiny slowly up the face of the building, on a straight line from where the blood had fallen.

McGuire said excitedly: "Look—that dark window— there's a curtain blowing out of it! It's about the only open window." His crooked finger came up and his lips moved silently as he started quickly again at the bottom and counted upwards. The Marquis' head followed the chubby-faced McGuire's in exact unison, and they both checked together—"Seventeen!"

THEY WENT swiftly back into the hotel, punched the elevator bells along the nearest bank of three. When the ornamental bronze door slid open the Marquis said over his shoulder, "I'll go up. You stay here," and strode aboard.

"Huh? What the hell for...?"

The closing door cut off the redhead's plaintive question as the Marquis clipped at the operator, "Seventeen—no stops!" and was rocketed upwards.

Before he was deposited on the blue carpet in the cream-colored corridor, he had estimated that the room they had spotted would be around the corner from the elevator bank and not more than two doors down the corridor. He stepped out, reached the corner in three strides, his eyes automatically jumping ahead to the door he had in mind.

He stopped so suddenly he almost lost his balance.

A man was backing out of the room, keying the lock. He was tall, in Broadway-cut gray clothes, a blue shirt, gray hat. Thin salt-and-pepper hair showed under the brim of his hat. He gave an impression of catlike strength.

The Marquis unbuttoned the bottom button of his coat and took the pistol from his hip pocket just as the other turned away from him and walked quickly toward the stairs, further down the hall. The Marquis took a quick step after him—got sufficient look at the other's blue-black chin and rocky face to identify him as Hemingway, the house detective. He hesitated in bewildered indecision as the other strode swiftly, but not with any particular urgency, to the stairs, and down, without once looking back.

A sharp line creased the Marquis' forehead as he dropped the pistol quickly in his side pocket, took out a flat black leather case of steel picklocks. He tapped once at the door and, receiving no answer, worked the lock quickly open. Then, the pistol in his hand, he slid into the room, closing the door instantly behind him.

Even before the fact that two standing lamps glowed in the room registered on his brain, his eyes were on the windows. There were two of them in this, the living-room of a small suite.

The windows were closed, locked. He stepped swiftly over to peer down at them and realized that the thin coating of soot on the windowsill had not been disturbed in some hours.

He swore softly, fretful at the obvious fact that both he and McGuire must have made some mistake in estimating the floor.

HIS EYES went to the door in the wall of the living-room. There was a crack of light under this door, too. He stepped across, opened it and was looking into a bedroom, equipped with twin beds done in gold-and-ivory. Here, too, the windows were firmly closed.

A girl lay asleep in one of the beds, her tawny-gold hair a fan on the pillow. The bed-table beside her was littered with bottles, pill-boxes and glasses. There was a pile of magazines and papers on the floor beside her, and the light came from the reading-lamp on the other of the twin beds.

Then he caught the faint smell of laudanum. He stepped over till he was directly above the sleeping girl's lovely blond head.

Enough of her shoulders was bare to show that she wore a wispy white night-down. She was breathtakingly young and fragile-looking, with even, small features, her long lashes shadows on her cheeks. She was a little pale and so utterly still that she gave, even while sleeping, the impression of weakness.

Hesitant, unable quite to believe that both the red-headed camera-eye and himself could have made a mistake in counting windows, the Marquis wasted a minute in trying to argue around it. Then the nub of the matter finally occurred to him.

Like most New York hotels, the Trumbull had no thirteenth floor, in deference to superstitious guests. The seventeenth floor up would actually be numbered 18.

He strode back out of the little suite, swearing, closing the doors behind him, trotted down the hall and up a flight of stairs, and was again before a closed door, identical with the one he had forced downstairs.

There was no need to force this one. It opened under his hand and he felt cool night air in his face as he stepped into the darkened chamber.

This time his eyes, going to the window were not disappointed. Against the faint light from the street he saw the curtains blowing out the window. And atop the radiator under the window was a shapeless dark blob.

His gloved finger snapped the ceiling lights on and the dark blob became a wizened little bald-headed man, half sprawled across the radiator, his throat cut from ear to ear, blood lying in dark pools on the enameled radiator cover. Some of it in little veins ran out toward the windowsill, dripping sluggishly in a dozen places, already viscous, drying. There was a huge dark stain on the floor by the end of the radiator, showing where the man had lain before making his desperate effort to pull himself upright.

The Marquis dived to his side, whipping off a glove, gingerly got fingers on the blood-soaked man's pulse. There was not even the flicker of pulse.

CHAPTER TWO

LAUDANUM LADY

THE MARQUIS stood up slowly, let out a pent-up breath. He had a sinking feeling inside. In eighteen years on Broadway, he had learned to dread hotel murders like no others. Hotel-dwellers were strangers among strangers and it was always easier to find more suspects who had no alibis than guests who had.

He looked closely at the dead man, but he remained a puzzle—just a nut-cracker-faced, baldheaded little man with staring brown eyes, a vaguely dirty look about him. He wore quiet brown clothes of cheap quality. His hat and coat were on the table in the center of the room.

Moving toward the door, the Marquis saw the spilled apparatus on the floor beyond the table, but he did not stop. He walked back to the elevators, jabbed the bell.

When the door slid open he told the operator: "Go downstairs. You'll see a chubby, redheaded man standing near your car. Bring him up here—tell him the Marquis said so."

The Marquis walked back into the death room and around the table. He knelt, studied what was on the floor beside it. It was a minute before he recognized it—a microphone, similar to that used in broadcasting from the commercial studios—but with a plug in the base. From this plug, a pair of earphones dangled.

Reluctant to touch it, the Marquis had to kneel to inspect all sides of it. It was oblong in shape and all its sides were smooth black—rubber, it looked like—except one. That one was indented in the center, making a sort of cone.

It dawned on him that this was one of the newly invented listening-in devices which would permit an eavesdropper to tune in on any conversation, even through brick walls. Whoever had been occupying this room—the wizened little dead man?—had been listening to the talk in one of the rooms around him!

The Marquis felt a surge of hope. That seemed, at the moment, to narrow the whole thing down. He stood up just as McGuire hurried into the room and came to a sudden stop, looking at the dead man.

"Oh-oh!"

The Marquis said quickly, "See if you can identify him. Go through him as best you can," and stepped over to the phone. His black-gloved fingers avoided delicately any part of the instrument that might carry fingerprints. He asked for the desk and inquired, "Who is registered in this room—seventeen-ten?" then added, "This is Lieutenant Marquis of the Broadway Squad. Hurry it up. And don't tell anybody I'm calling."

After a second, the clerk stammered: "No—nobody, sir. That floor is closed. It's being renovated."

"Nobody on the whole floor?" the Marquis said incredulously.

"N-no, sir. Nobody."

AS THE Marquis hung up in consternation, McGuire suddenly said: "Hey! I know this guy! This is Dirty Charlie, the penman. How did he ever get mired in murder? He had a holy horror of rough stuff. I thought he was in McNeil's Island for paperhanging."

"A check-forger?"

"Yeah. Hey—his pockets are half inside out! The labels are cut out. There's nothing on him— Oops! Wait a minute."

In the act of fingering the dead man's hanging breast pocket, the redhead paused, squeezed it and got a crackle. The inside end of the pocket had not quite been turned inside out. McGuire plucked out a crumpled newspaper clipping. One edge was stained with blood, but he unrolled it carefully and read it, in growing curiosity.

"Hey!" He passed it over to the Marquis.

GEORGE HIFT PASSES AWAY
Lifelong Anstable Resident Succumbs to Fractured Skull
Suffered in Firehouse Robbery Three Months Ago

George Hift, seventy-one, passed away today in the Darlington Memorial Hospital, victim of a brutal attack suffered last February from the unknown robber who prowled the otherwise empty fire-hall while the volunteer brigade, and Policeman Mike Hale, were fighting a fire at Dangler's Wharf. So far, the identity of the cowardly assailant who struck him down is unknown, but it is believed that he is the same marauder who, last December, struck Dad Berman down, in a previous attempt to loot the municipal offices above the engine-house.

Policeman Mike Hale believes the thief to have been mentally unbalanced, owing to the peculiarity of the loot which he took, and later abandoned. This consisted of three police whistles, two books of blank traffic tickets, a half-bottle of whiskey, and a toy microscope.

Mike has been communicating with all upstate insane asylums, in an effort to identify the unknown with a patient who may have escaped from one of those institutions.

The sympathy of the *Observer* goes to the bereaved… etc.…

"Where the hell is Anstable?" McGuire asked.

"About eighty miles upstate."

The Marquis stared at the clipping, discomfort in his somber eyes.

"You think that has something to do with this?" McGuire wanted to know.

"I hope not," the Marquis said fervently.

They went at the rest of the room—drawers, closets, shelves. There was nothing else in the room, nor had the bedroom been touched. There were no mattresses or bedding on the beds.

"What's that thing?" McGuire asked, when they came back to the living-room.

"A detector. The gadget that replaces wire-tapping."

"Oh-oh. He was listening in on somebody next door?"

"There isn't anybody next door. Look—pack that dingus out of here. Then call up Homicide and let them struggle with this stuff."

McGuire's bright eyes were startled. "You're going to lug out evidence on them?"

"Why not?" the Marquis growled. "It's not the first time."

"It'd be the last time, if we get caught."

"I'll take a chance. We've got to beat that crew on this one."

"Where'll I take it? How am I supposed to get it out of—"

"Wrap it in your coat and take it over to the ticket agency. Get Charlie to go over it for fingerprints. Hurry it up. I'll phone downtown."

"Hey, if there's nobody next door, who was he listening in on for God's sake? Somebody up above, maybe?"

The Marquis hesitated a minute. "Maybe. I want you back here in ten minutes, so get moving."

He picked up the phone again, while McGuire hurried out, called headquarters and reported the dead man's presence, letting it go at that.

Then he walked to the stairs and went halfway down, stood looking hesitantly at the door of the suite behind which he had found the sleeping girl.

He was reluctant to believe that the parts of this little drama should be falling so neatly into place—to credit the weird little string of developments that were helping him forward. Yet—if the eavesdropper in the death room had not been able to listen in on anyone beside him, it must be someone above or below. And that smell of laudanum plagued the Marquis' mind.

He started down the rest of the way and hesitated suddenly as the elevator around the corner of the corridor clanked open to discharge a passenger.

He flattened himself in the shadows of the staircase as the passenger hurried round the corner and stopped, fishing out a key, directly before the door of the suite the Marquis was observing.

The Marquis stared. The passenger was the actorish youth with the curly golden hair, the youngster Louis D'Astuma had been chasing on the street.

EVEN AS the Marquis blinked incredulously, the youth took hold of the knob, jabbed the key at the keyhole. Then, as the door came open without the key, he gasped. He dived inside, crying, "By God—Martha!" frantically, half under his breath. He did not even bother to close the door and the Marquis hastily slipped down the rest of the flight, watched through the broad crack, while the youngster burst into the bedroom, dived out of sight in the direction of the bed which held the beautiful blond girl.

A moment later he backed out of the bedroom, swabbing his neck with a handkerchief, his face bewildered, frightened. The Marquis stepped inside the door, closing it softly behind him. The blond youth turned slowly, his blue eyes darting around the baseboard of the room as though seeking something. He did not become aware of the Marquis' presence till he saw his feet, and legs. He gasped, jumped backwards, one hand going to his coat pocket.

The Marquis said: "Don't fret yourself. I'm a policeman."

The other stood tense, half crouched, little splotches of flush on his cheeks. He was not as handsome in this full light. His nose was a little pointed, his eyes without much luster, a little vapid. Again the Marquis had the memory picture of having seen him in a spotlight.

"A policeman!"

"Uh-huh. How long have you been out of here?"

"About three hours."

The Marquis eyed him carefully. "Are you sure? Didn't I just see you downstairs a few minutes ago, coming out of the lobby?"

The other's Adam's apple bobbed. "Yes, but—yes, but I—I had a little business I suddenly remembered I hadn't finished and I had to go out again. I didn't come up to the room."

"You mean you hadn't shaken off Louis D'Astuma?"

The other's face paled a little and he licked his lips. His blue eyes were gaunt. "I—I don't know what you're talking about."

"This is a bad time to lie, son. A man was killed right under here, not half an hour ago."

The youngster's eyes seemed to bulge. "Killed!" he croaked.

"Yeah. His throat was cut. There may have been a tussle or something and maybe you or your wife heard it going on."

The youngster's stunned eyes did not leave the Marquis'. He shook his head tensely, crazily. "No. No, we didn't."

"How do you know she didn't?"

"She—she's been asleep. I have to—she's not well, and she has to take sleeping medicine at night."

"What's wrong with her?"

"She's had brain fever. She's been in the hospital in Chicago for a year and a half. She's still under doctor's care."

The Marquis' eyebrows went up. "Chicago? That's where you met Louis D'Astuma, eh?"

The other's eyes shrunk but his lips tightened defiantly. "I don't know anybody by that name."

"What's your name? You're an actor, aren't you?" the Marquis cut in.

"Dick Tanneman. What if I am?"

"Louis runs a few night clubs out there as well as his gambling spots, doesn't he? Employs a little talent, eh?"

The other did not answer. His eyes were sunk in his head, frightened.

The Marquis said, soothingly: "You'd better give me the story, son. Otherwise I might have to pinch you for this murder."

The actor's face went starch-white, and his hand crept up his throat. "Me? Me?" he choked. "Good God! I didn't—I don't even know anybody on the floor below. I—you—"

"Just tell me all about why D'Astuma was chasing you with blood in his eye. I'll see he doesn't touch you."

FOR A second, the other drew up in defiance—and then he broke. Once started, he seemed eager to get it out. He blurted in a rush: "I—it's Martha! My wife—he wants her. We—she came from New York after her father committed suicide two years ago. D'Astuma was a friend of her father. He gave her a job in the club I was working in. Then she—well, we realized she was sick. He wanted to keep it quiet and he had me take her to this sanitarium in the country and I—I stayed there to give him reports.

"We fell in love and got married. I didn't know he—that he wanted her himself, until I told him we'd had it done. Then a friend of mine called me and told me he was coming out to kill me. The doctor said I could take Martha away as long as I made sure she got plenty of sleep and no worries. I—I had a few dollars and we ran out and came here. We had a chance of making something here. But he found out somehow. I—he caught up to me, today." The youth swallowed desperately. "I—I don't know what to do. I was afraid to lead him back here."

The Marquis nodded.

"When you came in just now, what made you suddenly bolt into your wife's room as you did?"

"I—the door was unlocked. I thought he might have—"

The Marquis' eyes were curious. "You're sure you locked it when you went out?"

"Oh my God, yes! Positive."

A picture floated into the Marquis' mind—a picture of Hemingway, the rock-faced house detective, backing out of this door, keying it closed.

He said: "All right. Lock it again now. And don't tell anybody you've talked to me. I don't think anybody will ask you. I'll look after Louis D'Astuma for you."

He stepped quickly out into the hall again. From the head of the stairs he could hear the sounds of a number of men, moving around in the death room below. The Homicide Squad had arrived.

He did not join them. Instead, he rang for an elevator on the floor where he was, rode down to the lobby again.

He hung around the lobby till he saw the redheaded McGuire returning, then nodded him into a corner.

"What goes on?" McGuire wanted to know.

"The blond kid was working for D'Astuma in Chicago. So was some girl D'Astuma had his eye on. The girl got sick and had to go to a sanitarium. D'Astuma sent the kid along to handle things and the girl married the kid. D'Astuma evidently wants to tear his heart out."

"What's that got to do with Dirty Charlie having his throat cut?"

"I wish I knew. Nothing, apparently, except that either Charlie or the person who killed him may have been listening in on the actor and his wife. They live right above."

"And what's that got to do with this crazy clipping about the robbery in Anstable?"

"I don't know. I want you to get on the phone and put out an alarm for Louis D'Astuma. I want him picked up and held for me personally on any charge that comes into your mind. Then I want you to get on long-distance to Anstable and see if you can dig up any information that will give us a lead. Call the town clerk or somebody. Meet me here when you're through."

CHAPTER THREE
MISTRESS OF THE INN

THE MARQUIS left the redheaded McGuire, walked to the rear of the lobby and into the little hall of ground-glass-windowed doors. The last of five bore the small, gold-leaf lettering—*E. Coveleskie.* He tapped—twice—and received no answer.

Through the ground-glass he could see the glow of the green-shaded desk-lamp within. He tried the door and it opened, showing him an office almost in darkness, save for the downward beat of the desk-lamp on white papers. Apart from the flat-topped walnut desk that held the papers, a swivel chair and a club chair flanking the desk, the room looked utterly bare. In the dimness beyond the desk, the vague shape of filing-cabinets presently emerged and—surprisingly—a man, standing motionless beside them.

The Marquis blinked, stepped in, reached a gloved hand out and tilted the oblong lampshade to shine on the figure.

Hemingway, the house detective, blinked stolidly into the light, brought a lighted cigarette from behind him and sucked at it.

The Marquis said: "Well, well. Am I interrupting a game of puss-in-the-corner? Didn't you hear me knock?"

"This ain't my office, Marty."

"Where's Eleanor Coveleskie?"

"Upstairs. The Homicide Squad is up there, too. They found a guy dead in one of the rooms."

"Very interesting. And you, the house snoop, hang around down here."

"I work for her. She told me to wait here for her."

The Marquis again felt a faint surge of irritation. This was definitely wrong. The question that had been on the tip of his tongue regarding the house detective's furtive exit from the actor's room upstairs, he stifled.

Instead, he asked: "Do you know Louis D'Astuma, from Chicago?"

The house detective's face was muddy, as he frowned. "I know *of* him. Yeah, come to think of it, I know him by sight."

"Is he in the hotel?"

"Eh? Wait a minute. I'll find out for you." He stepped over, lifted the receiver of the desk phone quickly and asked for "Registration." He made the inquiry and hung up. "No, he's not registered."

"I didn't ask you that. I asked you if he was in the hotel."

The other looked blank. "Not that I know of. You mean under another name or something?"

"Or something."

"Hell, I haven't seen him, Marty. Seems like I would have if he'd been here any length of time."

"Yeah." The Marquis stared absently down at the desk, nodding. "Well, thanks for the effort. If you should see him, give me a ring at McCreagh's Theater Ticket Agency, will you?"

"Huh? Sure. Ain't you interested in this killing upstairs?"

"Oh, in a way."

The Marquis went out, closing the door behind him. The office just across the narrow hall was dark and he tried the knob. It opened and he looked into a dark little room similar to the one he had just left, save that everything was under cover for the night. He left the door on the latch, walked quickly back across the lobby to the long row of telephone booths, peering in one after another till he found McGuire. He slid open the booth door as the grimacing redhead was saying irritably into the mouthpiece: "What? What? All right. I'll call him then."

"Come on," the Marquis said. "I want you to plant yourself on Hemingway's tail. He's in Eleanor Coveleskie's office now. Hang tight to him. I think he's sour. What did you scare up?"

"Nothing more than we had. Anstable is a one-horse dump—used to be a county seat till fifteen years ago. Population nine hundred. Last December a prowler caught the watchman out for a breath of air in the middle of the night and slugged him. He prowled the offices—the police department, water company, town clerk—all the municipal offices—they're all crowded into a couple of rooms. The crook didn't steal anything. That watchman quit. Then, three months ago—February—practically the same thing happened, only the crook walked off with that silly bunch of junk. The cop says I might try the town clerk in the morning."

"What about D'Astuma?"

"I put out the alarm for him."

"All right. Get behind this Hemingway."

"What the hell? Do you think the house dick's mixed in this knifing?"

"I don't know just what I think. Plant yourself here and ignore me."

HE LEFT the redhead across from the mouth of the little hall, walked noiselessly to the dark office opposite the hotel owner's, and stepped inside. He found a seat on the back of a chair that enabled him to close the door to within an inch of the jamb, let him keep watch through the sliver of opening.

He had to wait twenty minutes before the white-haired, stiffly erect, tall woman in black swept down the little hall and pushed into the office across from him.

As the Marquis stepped silently out of concealment, the hook-nosed old woman threw a quick look back toward the rotunda, a look which completely missed the Marquis behind her. She stepped into the office saying in a bitter, low voice, "So, after chasing him all over town, you have to run him to earth in my own hotel!" and would have closed the door behind her on the last word, save for the toe of the Marquis' shoe which checked it.

The woman spun around, her gray eyes shining bits of ice. The Marquis continued on into the dim office, his eyes gentle, somber. He said: "I think that statement needs a little explanation, Eleanor."

He closed the door softly. "So the gumshoe here tracked him down and you cut his throat? Or did your errand boy do that part, too?"

She faced him stonily, hooked her thumbs in the top of her black skirt as a man would hook them in his belt.

"Don't be stupider than you can help, Marty. I wasn't talking about the man who was killed."

"Who are you talking about, Eleanor?"

She eyed him through thin lids. "I don't think I can tell you, Marty."

"I think you can, Eleanor. Do we need this"—he nodded sideways at Hemingway—"or can he go about his business?"

The old woman hesitated a long minute. The Marquis looked over at Hemingway and said: "All right, Sherlock.

Miss Coveleskie and I are going to have a little private chat. On your way."

The sullen-eyed detective looked anxiously at the grim old woman, started toward the door. She did not look up and he faltered on, his eyes questioning her. "Shall I…?"

"Yes. I'll see you later."

When they were alone, the Marquis said: "If I turned all my newshawk friends loose on this killing, I don't think even your genius would be able to keep the place from getting a black eye. Come clean, Eleanor."

She looked him in the eye. "It has nothing to do with this killing, Marty—nothing whatever."

"If it hasn't—you know I'll never repeat it."

"All right," she said wearily, finally. "The fact is that old man Brandon's daughter has turned up."

The Marquis blinked. "Brandon? The old soak who used to own this hotel?"

"Sure. You know how I got the place?"

"In a poker game."

"More or less. I took it off Brandon around five o'clock one morning. He gave me a note for it that wasn't legal. I was to meet him later in the day and get the deed and so forth. Only he blew his brains out at seven A.M."

"And?"

"That made it his daughter's property. I got hold of her, showed her what I had and she made good. I gave her a couple of thousand out of the goodness of my heart and—legally—bought the hotel from her for one dollar and other valuable consideration."

"So?"

"She's turned up, married to a guy named Tanneman. Evidently she went a little batty after she left here and she was in a sanitarium in Chicago.

"Well, this husband of hers braced me Thursday and said she had to have more money. She's evidently still sick and can't do her own business. He's got all her powers of attorney and so forth and he seems to think I really gypped her. He won't listen about the poker game."

"So what? She's got no claim on you, has she?"

The old woman's lips were a thin line. "That's the hell of it, Marty—she has a damned good one, legally, and this husband of hers has dug it up."

"How?"

"When she signed the place over to me she was just under twenty-one. It wasn't a gag—she really thought she was a year older. She just found out different. Legally, she can still cancel the sale, because she was a minor. I've got every dime I own sunk in the place and I've made it a property, as you know. This damned kid can pull the chain on me and toss me out on my ear."

"What's he asking from you?"

"A hundred thousand dollars. Maybe I can raise it, maybe I can't. He's not fooling. He says *he'd* take the hotel away from me, if it were his own affair, but that she only wants the hundred thousand."

"You're going to pay it? Have you checked on the claim?"

"Of course. I have her birth certificate—or a copy of it. Solly—my lawyer—has gone into the whole thing. I haven't a leg."

"And you've had Hawkshaw trailing this Tanneman all over town?"

"Yes. I wanted to check up on him—you know, make sure he was her husband and all that. Maybe—well, maybe find something I could fight him with. It took the dope three days to find out they were checked in to my own hotel, under their own names."

The Marquis eyed her thoughtfully. "It's a good thing it wasn't the girl who had her throat cut, Eleanor. If it had been, do you know what I'd do?"

"What?"

"Throw you in the boob so fast it would take your breath away. You're a lot tougher than you seem, and I know how much this place means to you. Somehow, I can't make up my mind that you're in the clear here."

"All right," she said wearily, "go ahead and think what you like. I've got worse troubles than your goofy suspicions."

The Marquis was constrained to say, "I guess you have, at that," but when he was again out in the lobby, he had an uneasy moment of wonder as to whether he had not been neatly hoodwinked by the grim old woman. He had the maddening feeling that he had been on the very point of discovering something of vital import, only to be smoothly steered away from it.

McGuire was sitting on a settee behind a cornice in the lobby. Hemingway, the house detective, was leaning against the auditor's window thirty yards away, and the Marquis saw his green eyes slither sideways at him.

He waited till the tall catlike house dick had strolled away, in a roundabout route toward Eleanor Coveleskie's office, before he sat down beside McGuire.

"Stay with that guy," the Marquis said. "Don't interfere with anything he does—short of murder—but stay with him. There's something wrong for sure."

"All right. Listen. McBain was down here looking for you. He's in charge of the Homicide party upstairs and he's raising hell to know where you stand? After all, you found the body. It wouldn't hurt to go up and give them a little information."

"Very little," the Marquis said.

CHAPTER FOUR

DEATH FOR
TWELVE MONTHS

WHEN HE again reached the lobby the dawn was breaking and he realized with a queer, almost panicky feeling, that he had run himself out. With a dozen questions clamoring in his head, he was hung up, at least until he could lay his hands on D'Astuma—and something told him that this was no time to be hung up. He searched the lobby for McGuire. There was no sign of the redhead.

He walked out onto Broadway, crossed over, almost reluctant to leave the hotel for even a minute, stared up grimly at the vast oblong pile of yellow brick. Its brand new sign was still blazing.

He walked on down to McCreagh's Theater Ticket Agency—the Broadway Squad's unofficial headquarters—spent an hour on the phone, spurring the search for Louis D'Astuma.

He found himself waiting for something but he didn't know what. The feeling of expectancy grew more worrisome with the passing hours. He could not sit still. At ten o'clock, he phoned the suite on the eighteenth floor of the Trumbull and got Tanneman, the blond youngster, on the phone.

"Have you a gun?" he asked him.

"Why—why, yes."

"Keep it around, and don't let anybody in unless you know who it is. Just to be on the safe side."

The other's gasp was audible. "But—you mean D'Astuma is…?"

"I think D'Astuma's gone into a hole and pulled the hole after him," the Marquis said. "I've no special reason for what I said. Just be careful, that's all."

He hung up, wondering why the hell he had made the call. He sat drumming his fingers on the desk-edge.

The hours wore away. There was no word whatever of the missing D'Astuma. Evidently the Chicago gambler had heard that the alarm was out for him and had gone to earth. The Marquis chafed.

He was cheered only slightly when the newspaper editions containing the Homicide Squad's reports reached him. The headquarters detectives had apparently made even less progress than he had.

He had some food, strolled back to the hotel, saw no sign of McGuire, returned to the ticket agency. The badgering feeling of something stuck in the middle hung over him, and grew during the early afternoon.

It occurred to him to phone the town clerk at Anstable. He questioned him painstakingly, groping blindly for a clue—any sort of miscellaneous information that might light the picture, but had to hang up not having advanced an inch.

He slept a few hours on a couch in the room at the rear of the agency, was awakened to be told McGuire had phoned. The redhead wanted to know if he were to spend the rest of his life watching the rock-faced house detective.

"Tell him, yes," the Marquis said.

The day was long gone now. Broadway was blazing, swarming with crowds, when he strolled out. He stood staring with worried eyes, northward toward the hotel.

He could not down the gnawing feeling that inside that blank-faced block of stone and brick, things might even now be happening, working furtively toward some obscure climax.

He told the detectives in the agency, "If you want me, try the bell-captain at the Trumbull Hotel," and had almost succeeded in working himself out of his anxiety by the time he was across from the towering pile.

Cursing his nerves, he looked up at the corner suite on the seventeenth floor—the suite of the young Tannemans.

And in the instant that he segregated the window, the light suddenly blinked out, leaving only vague luminescence.

He stopped dead in his tracks. Without thinking, he flung a swift glance at a clock in a window, saw it was barely ten o'clock—and the feeling of premonition that had gripped him all day suddenly squeezed at his heart.

HE WENT quickly across the street, trotted into the lobby, walking swiftly, threading his way through the crowded lobby toward the elevator bank.

He had one foot inside the door of an open car when his arm was jerked from behind and he half stumbled in a circle to face the worried bell-captain.

"Marty, listen—McGuire phoned about three minutes ago and again just now. He's in nine-seven—got it to sleep in. He wants you to call him immediately."

"Tell him I'm up in eighteen-ten—the Tannemans' suite. I'll call him in a minute," the Marquis clipped.

He shot up to the eighteenth floor, flung out into the corridor, hurried around the corner.

His heart came up in his gullet. The door of the suite stood slightly ajar. He jumped for it, flung it open, his gloved hand half drawing the gun from his pocket. The door hit an obstruction and he jumped inside—and looked down at the unconscious figure of the blond actorish youth. Blood was trickling from a lump on the side of his temple. There was a leather blackjack with a torn wrist strap on the floor beside him, and a nickeled pistol lay by the window. The Marquis snatched at his pulse, found it beating strongly. He ran into the bedroom.

The bed that had been occupied by the girl was empty, bedclothes flung on the floor. A trail of newspapers led from the doorway to the bed and the reading lamp at the bedhead had been torn from its moorings, lay smashed on the floor. Beads came out on the Marquis' forehead. He had been watching at the very instant that the struggle.... The phone on the beside table suddenly pealed.

For a split second, the Marquis' roiling thoughts kept him from answering. Then he scooped up the instrument.

McGuire's excited, husky voice fairly screamed at him: "For God's sake, come down here—room nine-seven—the whole thing's going off...." The receiver banged in his ear.

The Marquis stared at his own handset, dropped it and ran from the room. He was sweating as he waited for the elevator. When it dropped him to the ninth floor and he piled out, the redhead was waiting for him.

He grabbed the Marquis' arm, ran him down the hall, rattling in his ear: "I been nearly crazy. You told me not to interfere with that rat. About half an hour ago he goes down to the basement, me behind him. He goes to the freight elevator. It's down in the sub-basement and he beats it down there. The door's propped open at the basement level. I stay up and see him go down and get in. I had the bright idea to take a perch on top of it. We go up—past seven, where he lives—right on up to eighteen. I'm stuck on top, not knowing whether to get off and come down or what to do, while he gets off at eighteen. He's gone about five minutes. I decide to stick. Then he comes back—with the girl on his shoulder! He's gagged her with her nightgown and he's got her wrapped in newspapers. I don't know what to do. He closes the door and we start down. I get the emergency trap open and I get the drop on him—but I don't know what the score is. You told me not to interfere."

"Where is the girl now?"

"He took her in his room—it's that room right there—beside the freight elevator!" The last words were in a hoarse whisper as they checked their pace turning into the final corridor.

The Marquis said, "All right. Follow my lead," and they ran to a silent stop outside the door at which the redhead jabbed urgently.

THE MARQUIS put his ear against the panel, slid the safety catch off his gun with a gloved finger. His forehead was flushed, his eyes shining.

Inside, he could hear a hoarse voice. It was raised almost to a shout in pleading, or the sound would not have penetrated.

The voice said: "Martha! Martha! Listen—I just want to talk to you, is all! Answer me! Can't you hear me? Listen, Martha—what kind of dope has that guy been feeding you? Martha—look, honey—tell me you're all right!"

The Marquis' hand darted into his pocket, snaked out the case of picklocks. Beads of sweat were on his forehead as he carefully, noiselessly, eased one into the door. The pleading voice swelled, died away, swelled again, inside the room.

The Marquis exchanged a head signal with McGuire, suddenly turned the picklock and marched into the room behind his gun. The redhead, snatching the instrument case from the lock, was a step behind him, closing the door instantly.

"Stand just where you are," the Marquis snapped.

Louis D'Astuma, his swarthy glowing face covered with a day's growth of beard, jumped up from beside the bed. The blond girl lay glassy-eyed on the bed, still wrapped in newspapers, her nightgown a twisted rope on the floor beside her. Hemingway, his hands automatically half lifting, stood with his back to the bureau. A thick roll of greenbacks was clutched in the doughy-faced sleuth's hand.

McGuire stepped over, jammed his gun in the house detective's belly and said into his terrified face: "Open up the paddy, gumshoe, or— That's the spirit." He palmed the roll, stepped back again, inspecting his take. He whistled. "Wow! Look at this!"

"Shut up," the Marquis said. Then to the fiery black-eyed D'Astuma: "All right, Louis. What's the story? It'd better be good. You and the snoop here are cold for a kidnaping rap at the very least."

The swarthy-faced man seemed to swell. In his excitement, his perfect English utterly deserted him. "Kidnaping! What's you say! I'm love this girl, Marty. I'm give her job when she come to Chicago. I'm send her to hospital when she's sick—pay bills a year and a half. I'm send this snake-in-the-grass, Tanneman, out to see she gets the best. I'm hear he's marry her. I'm go out—but somebody's tip them off. They run away. The doctors say no good—she not strong enough. I come looking for them—find him and he's give me the run-around. My head, she's busting of worry—I'm afraid he's kill her. He's keep her full of dope—not good. I catch *him* here"—he jerked his shaggy black head at the house detective—"get him and pay him to tell me she's here. Then somebody sets coppers on me. I have to duck—I'm pay him some more to keep me here and finally to bring her down so I can see she's all right—talk to her—make her see that snake-in-the-grass—"

"Why'd did you set up the listening apparatus in the room under them?"

The Italian's fiery eyes turned toward the house detective in a pained way. "That's a his idea. I don't know nothing."

The Marquis looked at Hemingway. "So Dirty Charlie caught *you* at it and *you* cut his throat?"

The house detective licked gray lips. "Marty—for God's sake—I didn't...."

The door burst open so suddenly that it cracked McGuire in the back of the head, sent him pitching across the room.

The blond, actorish Tanneman staggered in, almost fell, caught himself against the wall with one hand. His face was a mess of blood, his eyes wild, groggy. They fastened with difficulty on the tall D'Astuma. He cried out brokenly, "You damn murderer!" and whipped up the nickeled gun with startling speed.

THE MARQUIS fired instantly into the point of the actorish youth's shoulder, slammed him sideways against the wall, knocking him from his feet. The pistol skidded across the room. The youth slid down, half on his knees, his face contorted with agony as he clutched at the shattered shoulder. The last trace of haziness went out of his eyes and he looked at the Marquis aghast.

"You—you shoot me!" he blurted out between pain-racked lips. "You shoot me—to protect that murderer? He was going to kill her—her and me—and you shoot me down—"

The Marquis shook his head slowly. "No, chum. I didn't exactly do that. I shot you to get that gun out of your hand before you knocked off all the witnesses against you!"

McGuire, up on his feet again, stopped rubbing the back of his head and squatted, open-mouthed. "Marty—you mean he...."

The Marquis looked down at the actorish, sharp-nosed face. It was mottled with red splotches now and a dingy look was creeping over it. "Yeah. I just remembered where I saw him—under a spotlight. Only it wasn't a spotlight—it was a droplight. He was one of your roulette croupiers, wasn't he, Louis?"

D'Astuma croaked: "Yes."

The blond youth groaned. "My God, are you mad? What difference does it make? What are you talking about?"

"It makes quite a difference. I thought of you as a simple soul. If I had thought of you as a wise-guy before, I might have seen through your little racket."

"Racket!" McGuire echoed.

"Why not? I don't know why I was dumb enough not to see it staring me in the face. Angel-face here spends a lot of months in the sanitarium with the girl. He learns all about her—about the sale of this hotel. He finds out the hotel is a gold-mine now. He works on the girl—she's still a little hazy—and gets her to marry him. Then he finds out where she was born. Nobody's told me this, but I know it was in Anstable, New York, wasn't it?"

Again D'Astuma croaked, eagerly. "Yes. Yes. How you know—"

Feet were running down the hall outside, vaguely audible on the soft carpet. The Marquis finished, "My God, do you have to be told the rest?" looking at McGuire. "The office of the town clerk in Anstable was prowled—not once, but twice. Nothing of value was taken either time. Plain enough, isn't it? The first time, angel-face here stole the girl's birth records and brought them away so that he could get Dirty Charlie to forge them in such a manner as to make the girl's birthday a year later than it actually was. The second robbery was to replace them. Then all he had to do was wait a few months, come down here and put the squeeze on Eleanor Coveleskie, keeping the girl half doped to take her out of the play. It was a smart gag—or would have been, if he hadn't hit the watchman upstate too hard, and if Dirty Charlie hadn't had such a horror of murder that he threatened to blow the works when he found what had happened. Angel-face was wise to the listening-in business below so he knifed Charlie, left him down there. Am I boring you?"

The actorish blond youth was a crouched, cornered rat now. His teeth showed between his lips and he was breathing quickly. The Marquis looked at him dully. "Don't start acting up now"—and the door flew open.

Eleanor Coveleskie stepped through the entrance, her seamed old face granite-hard, a small automatic pistol in her bony hand. She looked quickly, anxiously around. "What's the—"

The blond Tanneman sprang from his crouch. He dived, hands clawing, for the old woman's gun-hand.

With the expression of a person brushing away a fly, the old woman coolly jabbed the gun-muzzle outward, between the youth's clawing hands, drove it into his mouth with a crunching of teeth, dropped him sobbing to the floor.

"Well, what does this mean?" she asked the Marquis grimly.

"Not a thing, Eleanor. Just that you own your hotel. The girl was twenty-one when she signed the bill of sale—and don't believe anything different." He looked over at McGuire. "Better call Homicide and tell them their little mystery is cracked. And—uh—I'll take that evidence you took from Hemingway here."

McGuire looked darkly up. "You'll take half and like it."

"I can't quite understand how I got that mixed up," the Marquis said, half an hour later as they walked down the hall. "I probably would have cracked the whole works right away if I hadn't thought that blond rat was an actor. I would have sworn it was a spotlight I saw him in."

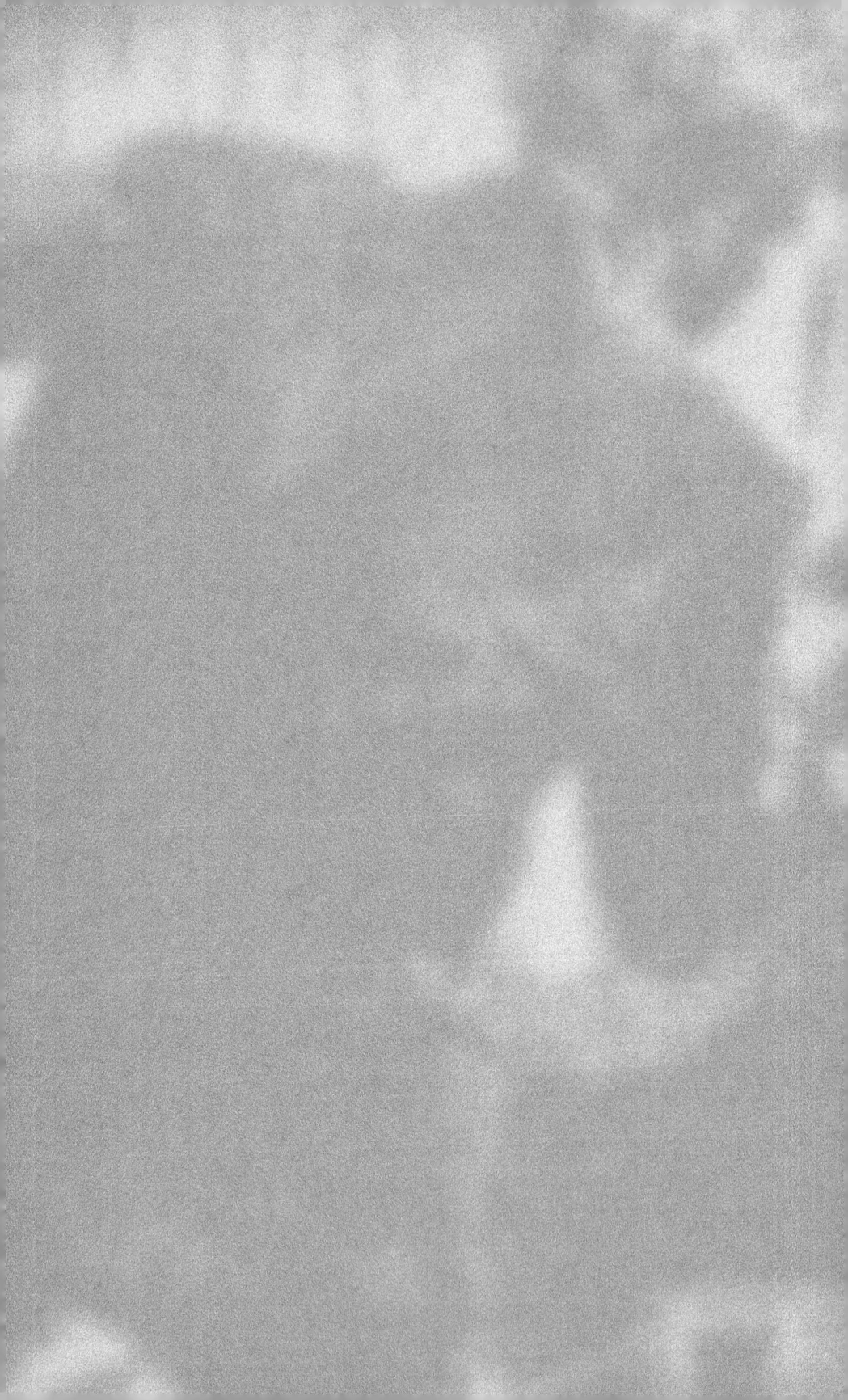

MAN HUNT

BIG BELLA, QUEEN OF THE
HONKY-TONKS, HAD SAVED
THE LIFE OF THE LITTLE
CZAR OF THE BROADWAY
SQUAD ONCE UPON A TIME,
AND THOUGH THE PAST MAY
HAVE BEEN DIM IT WAS DAMN
WELL NOT DEAD WHEN SHE
DEMANDED PAYMENT IN KIND.
"KNOCK OFF A RAT FOR ME,
MARTY," SHE ASKED. AND
HE HAD TO ANSWER, "SURE,
BELLA, I'LL KILL HIM FOR YOU
IF THERE'S NO OTHER WAY." IT
TOOK HIM ONLY FIVE SHORT
MINUTES TO LEARN THERE
WAS NO ALTERNATIVE—THAT
MURDER WAS HIS ONLY OUT!

CHAPTER ONE
QUEEN OF THE
HONKY-TONKS

THE MARQUIS' first thought was that Big Bella was ill. In ten years he had not seen her anything but cheerful, clowning. When he walked into the vast, luxurious, Chinese-red, yellow-and-black living-room of the apartment, she was standing rigid before the fire, her raddled face as sharp as a scythe, her big body smart in throat-high black, her shining little brown eyes almost sunk in a sea of mascara. There was no greeting whatever. Her eyes burned and she drove crazily at him in a shaking, husky voice: "You're my last hope, Marty. Will you kill a man for me?"

The Marquis cocked his head, slowly sat his blocky, neat little body on a sofa-arm. "What?"

"You heard me. Will you knock off a rat for me, if you have to?"

He searched her eyes, her burning face, opened his mouth.

"I'm not kidding, Marty!" Her voice had a slaty note. "Believe me, I'm not kidding. I think I want a man killed." Her brown eyes burned hollowly and she licked her paint-cracked lips. "What do I have to do? Remind you that I killed my husband for you, sixteen years ago—or held him while you killed him?" Her big bosom heaved rapidly. "He had you cold. If you had taken one more step into that

Then hell broke loose as the jittery
gunman spun as though stung.

area-way and I hadn't run out and jumped him, made him shoot wild, held him while you emptied your gun—you would have died then and there, Marty. You know it. Tim Hays was a worthless thief and killer when the drink was on him, but he was all I had. When you killed him, it put me on the street. I've been fighting up out of the gutter ever since. You told me then that there was nothing I couldn't ask you—ever. Now I'm asking. Or doesn't the promise of Marty Marquis in his first suit of plainclothes bind the great Marquis of Broadway?"

"Of course, Bella, but let's talk...."

HER TEETH were set. "Talk? This is Big Bella, Marty—
the queen of the honky tonks. I don't need any talk. You

either will go all out for me as I did for you sixteen years ago—or you won't. Don't give me any holy-horror stuff about killing. I grew up in the same Avenue A tenement with you, Marty. I know you. Maybe you don't go out with a gun in your own hand and blast. Maybe you scheme around and manage it without showing. Who cares? You couldn't run Broadway with slaps on the wrist, and I know just how tough you really are under those vice-president's clothes. I mind a certain Frankie Rao that got dead....All right, but don't let's kid each other. This is cold turkey, Marty. I want to know if you'll come through for me or not!"

Her skinny hands came up and pressed her burning forehead. "Oh, God, Marty—I don't know whether I want killing or not, but if I do— Some crawling louse has got hold of Sylvia. She's half out of her mind. He ought to be killed and you—hell, Marty—plain talk—does the promise still hold or do you laugh me off?"

The Marquis eyed her worriedly. "I couldn't laugh you off, Bella. Whatever you need, you can have."

"Even killing?"

"Even that, I guess, if there's no other way. Who is the guy, Bella?"

"I don't know. Sylvia's been in a Broadway line the last three years. Not that she didn't go through school—the best of them—"

"Wha-at? How old...?"

"Nineteen. She's nineteen. Time doesn't stand still, Marty. She's grown up and she's a dream." For the first time the brittle note in her voice broke. "She's beautiful—and refined—everything I'm not—everything I wanted her to be. I didn't want her to get in the business, but you know how it is. And it worked out. Anyway, she's got her man and she's quitting it. She's engaged to a wonderful boy—a rich boy, Marty—this Carleton Druitt. I don't know if you ever heard of...?"

"The stockbrocker's son?"

"Yes. He's a honey—a clean, swell kid, Marty. If—"

"Does his family know about...?"

"Me? Yes. Everything. I had a talk with the old man. They're the salt of the earth. They've seen Sylvia and they love her. It's everything I've prayed for for her, Marty—and now this guy's crawled up to wreck everything."

"What guy?"

"She won't tell me. I've nearly talked myself crazy trying to find out. Some guy—and some police trouble, Marty. That's all I can get. I've gone down on my knees. I've promised her my heart on a platter, if she'll tell me. I've promised anything else I could think of. I thought of you and promised that you'd go to bat for her—that you'd do anything for her—get her out of anything. That was the only thing, so far, that's reached her. She knows you're the little tin god of Broadway. At first she wouldn't believe that you'd help. I—I never told her what happened to Tim, Marty, and you mustn't. But I told her you were a friend— that you'd do anything for us—forget you were a cop, if necessary—fix up absolutely everything and anything for her. She said if that were so, you were the one person who could help her. But I've got to know, Marty—now! Where do I stand? Am I out of line or did your promise really mean something? Cold turkey, Marty—no sliding around it, and no halfway business. Will you pay me back for your life by getting her out of this? And I mean anything—absolutely anything—to get her clear?"

After a worried minute the Marquis said: "My promise is good, Bella. Where is she?"

SHE WAS a dream. Small and dainty, lusciously curved, with skin like blue milk and deep, starry-blue eyes, small hands and feet, she came with hesitant little steps from the bedroom. Her shining blue-black hair was piled on top of her head. She looked about fourteen rather than nineteen save for the sweet roundness of her body. There were fever spots in her cheeks and her eyes were sick with fear. She was grinding a handkerchief in her trembling hands.

The Marquis made no attempt to patronize her, take a what's-this-childish-nonsense attitude. The dark terror in her eyes was too real for that. Suddenly the Marquis' impersonal attitude vanished in an uncontrollable wave of sympathy and a poignant urge to help her for own dainty sake.

Bella was saying: "I've told Marty all that you've told me, baby. He'll help us—believe mother, he'll help us."

The girl's hollow eyes were on the Marquis with a terrible intensity that presaged hysteria.

"Suppose Sylvia and I talk it out alone, Bella," he suggested mildly. And when she had left and the door closed behind her, "Just forget I'm a cop, Sylvia—except when it might help us to remember. I'm going to take care of this for you."

She sat down rigidly on a chair-edge, her hands locked in her lap. She had to try twice before she got out huskily: "What if I—if I've done…?"

"Something wrong? Who hasn't? Think nothing of it. I'll take care of it in short order. Depend on it. There's some guy, your mother said. Tell me who he is and I'll give him the beating of his life. If that isn't enough—"

She was on her feet in panic. "Oh, no, no! It's—it's—no, no, nothing like that. It's just that he—he has something—

some Leica film—something terrible. I have to get it back—"

"Film? What—who…?"

"I don't know. He called me a week ago. He gave me till today to get five thousand dollars. Mother got it. He—he's going to call again today, any time now. That's why I asked mother if you *would* help—if you would take the money and—and see that they did give back the pictures."

The Marquis blinked. "Is that all?"

"All? Oh, my God—"

"I mean all you're up against? A simple blackmail racket?"

"Simple? It's the most terrible—it means that I—"

"I know, I know. I meant simple for me. You just want me to get back these pictures for you?"

"Yes, yes. Take the money. Arrange to meet them when they call—oh!" Fresh, sudden fear filled her eyes. "But will they? Maybe you being a police officer—maybe they won't—"

"Don't worry about that. If they're professionals, they'll be glad enough to deal with me. You let me talk to them when they call—and stop worrying about anything. I'll get your pictures and there'll be no five-thousand-dollar payment either."

"Oh, God—you mustn't try to trick them! We don't care about the money—or anything. Oh, you've got to promise—"

The Marquis' eyes were troubled. "We don't have to do that."

"Oh, you do—you do! Believe me—you've got to swear that you won't do anything—that you'll go through with it—or I can't ask you to help me at all! You've got to!"

The Marquis opened his mouth, shrugged. "All right. But it's insane—unnecessary. When are they calling?"

"Any time now."

"These—uh—pictures. Will I recognize them without your having to tell me what's in them, or had you better…?"

Her cheeks were flaming, her head down. "You—you'll recognize them."

CHAPTER TWO
DEATH OF A SOLDIER

EVEN WHEN the Marquis saw O'Near it did not jog him. He had already taxied up to Harlem, was within a few blocks of Baisley Street and was loitering away the last fifteen minutes before midnight. O'Near, tall, Indian-faced, with his wide-brimmed black hat, went by with his partner, a squat blond detective named Soldier. They were out of headquarters—homicide squad—and O'Near was high on the list of the Marquis' departmental enemies. They did not see him on busy Lenox Avenue, although they sauntered by within a few yards, apparently on no very urgent mission.

Baisley Street—two blocks long—was far west, desolate, lined with ramshackle cottages, some of them in decay. Sickly trees lined the curb. One distant street lamp sent vague flickers through the leaves. Otherwise the street was smothered in blackness, silent, when the Marquis reached the sagging, one-story frame building whose paintless clapboard front bore the shiny metal numbers 35, and a cracked wooden sign which still vaguely showed the legend: *Horse-Shoeing Done.*

He took a careful look over his shoulder before he stopped at the shack, saw not a single moving thing. He squinted his eyes to find the handle to the wooden door, got out his pencil flash and squirted light inside his black-gloved fingers.

A voice from the corner of the building told him in an undertone: "Keep that thing burning. Take out your gun and throw it inside."

The Marquis straightened, stared dully toward the corner. He could not make out any form in the blackness. After a second he took the gun slowly from his hip, opened the sagging door a foot and tossed it inside.

The muffled voice said: "All right. Go on in."

He stepped through, leaving the door open behind him, let light slip through his fingers a little more freely. He was just in time to see a wiry figure kick at the plain dirt floor, and to see his gun go flying across to thump into a corner of the wooden shed.

There was nothing in the barn-like structure except a rickety table in the center, on which someone had eaten a meal, ages ago, and left cans and oil-paper to collect dust—and an ancient, half demolished Model-T in the center of the left-hand wall. Piled in front of the car's radiator were two tires and, atop them, the two seats and two rotten, dirt encrusted blankets.

There was the sound of the door being closed at his back, a wooden catch being shot, then heavy breathing. A nervous voice said huskily in his ear: "All right, copper—get this! If this is a trap, or you pull anything fancy, you'll regret it, see?"

The wiry little man who had kicked his gun scurried around the table, to be on the opposite side from the Marquis. Even in the faint light, the Marquis could see drops of sweat on his wizened, dark face as he said fretfully: "I didn't hire you to do the talking, Dan. This—the Marquis wouldn't pull anything like that."

With his nervous, whining, half-whisper, the Marquis recognized him. His name was Boering—a cheap, crooked little private detective with the courage of a rabbit. He held a gun in his hand, as did the big swarthy-faced youth who presently stepped around in front of the Marquis.

The Marquis said dully: "So you had to hire this big goof to give you the guts to make contact."

The heavy-bodied young thug thumbed a lock of hair out of his queerly-shining eyes and said huskily: "Never mind the guff. Where's the dough—and don't let too much of that light out. There's boards on them windows, but—well, come on! Get it over with."

The Marquis said, "Where's the stuff I'm buying?" and Boering's gulp was audible in the musty, dank silence.

"I—I've got one print and the negative. You can look at the print if you want to. I—I hold the negative till…." He fumbled with a small, square box in his hand, fingered out something and put the box on the table.

AS THE Marquis stepped across the lumpy dirt floor, the wizened Boering retreated hastily. The big, vicious-faced man stood unmoving, the gun in his hand steady on the Marquis.

The box had a prescription label on its top—had had, rather, for all but a scrap of it had been torn off. It was a hinged box. Inside was a tiny roll of film.

"I've got to see what I'm buying," the Marquis complained. "Can't we have some more light around here?"

"No."

"Then you can go jump in the lake."

Boering whined hastily: "Be quiet, Dan! No, wait, Marty. We can't have anybody seeing light coming out of here. If you want to duck down between that car and those seats—see. Dan—that'll shield it from the windows."

The Marquis glanced at the boarded window low in the center of the rear wall, then at the glassless sash—also boarded—adjoining the front door. "I'm not any more anxious than you are to have company," he growled, and went over and kneeled in the little niche.

Even there, he could not make much of the tiny film, though he held it right against the full glow of the pencil-flash. Three of the six squares were blank. Three of them had pictures—sharp, clear pictures—but they were too small. He could just make out a girl, naked from the waist up, in three different poses. The poses seemed extravagant, like a dancer's. In one she seemed in the center of a room, her arms up over her head, with other heads in the background. In one, she was arched backwards over a table or desk. In one she was on a couch or bed.

"Where's five thousand dollar's worth in this?" the Marquis wanted to know.

Boering's excited whisper trembled. "The middle one. Maybe you can't see it, without a glass, but there's a perpetual calendar and a clock on that desk. It shows ten minutes after eleven on the first of June."

"So what?"

"So it places her in Janisse's studio, at exactly twenty minutes after eleven."

Horrible light broke on the Marquis.

Janisse! The millionaire sculptor—according to the headlines. Janisse—whose amazing bronzes and marbles had rocketed him into international prominence, whose cunning productions were fought for, at fabulous prices, by collectors, museums and, strangely, by architects for inclusion in building decoration. Janisse—whose statues were always the same—the figure of a woman—but whose electric fingers somehow imbued them with the very animal essence of woman, so that no man could look at them unstirred. Janisse—whose models—all who had posed for him—rose to fame with him because of what he had disclosed in their bodies.

Janisse—whose seven-day-old unsolved, midnight murder in his Jane Street studio was barely out of the headlines now!

Time, date, details, were not in the Marquis' mind—but he did need them to see the thing that must be here. No mention of Sylvia Hays had been made in connection with the case. Of that much he was sure—or Bella and her daughter would have had to tell him. And certainly no one needed to tell him that these pictures, by the ghastliest coincidence, had been taken on the murder night—maybe close to the time of murder. He was shaken. The girl was innocent, of course—but what a wreck the tabloids would make of her life with this. What hell a publicity-seeking district attorney could cook up for her.

The petulant whimper of the livid-faced gunman bit suddenly, fretfully: "I don't like this stalling. What's going on here? You copper—if you're pulling something, I swear I'll give it to you!"

For the first time the Marquis realized exactly what made the gunman's eyes shine so queerly. He said flatly: "All right, cokie. Here's the money. Let me have...."

Then somebody rattled the front door and the incredible trap was sprung.

THE COKIE'S sudden throat sound was animal as he swung toward the door, the gun whipping up. Boering whimpered and they both stood like crouching statues. The Marquis was numb, his heart in his throat.

A scrapy voice that the Marquis recognized as O'Near's partner, Soldier, said harshly outside the door, "Open up in there! It's the law!" and in one flaming fraction of a second, the full picture of what he had walked into etched itself in the Marquis' brain. He suddenly saw himself, trapped cold on a felony-compounding charge—the damning pictures of Bella's daughter in the hands of a sniveling coward and a nerve-jumpy dope addict—a matter of minutes, after the homicide detectives got them, before they blabbed every last thing they knew. It was impossible! He could not have gotten himself into this! Why—how— Sweat came out all over him as he realized his own helplessness—even his gun taken....

Nails screeched as a board was ripped off the rear window.

O'Near's dark Indian face showed for just an instant behind a blazing torch; "Just take it easy in there!"

Then the hell.

The jittery gunman cried out as his nerves twanged. He spun round as though stung. Boering's terrified squeal, "Oh, God, no...!" was lost in the thunder of his frantically crashing gun. O'Near vanished, cursing, while lead ripped and pounded the boards.

Boering squealed, "Dan—good God—they're cops!" but the half-crazed gunman had snapped his control. His voice cracked shrilly.

"So what? —— all cops!" He flung round on the Marquis, his eyes mad, beyond reason. "And you—you lousy double-crossing ——————!"

ONLY A miracle freed the Marquis' numb brain in time to let him fling himself aside. He dived into the narrow slot between wall and car, while lead thundered, clanged deafeningly against the metal. He pinwheeled over the mudguard, down, a wild flurry of arms and legs.

Somewhere out back, O'Near yelled hastily, "Keep back, Ben—the rats!" but the warning came too late. The thick-bodied detective had already launched himself in a bull-like rush. There was a crackling, splintering, as the door went down before him and he was framed for an instant stumbling in the vague luminosity of the doorway. The gunman in the blackness sobbed, "All right, you—!" and his gun laced crashing flame—once, twice, Soldier, diving forward, was stopped, half-turned and hammered backwards, a sobbing, *"Ahhh, God!"* dying in his throat.

The gunman blubbered through his chattering teeth at the whimpering Boering: "Get that dick's gun! Here give me that one and get out, will you?" There was a smack and Boering cried out, went stumbling after the Marquis' pistol.

From behind the frame structure O'Near's hoarse voice yelled, "Ben! Ben!" and he was suddenly pounding around toward the front.

"Out!" the gunman shrilled—and the wildly scrambling Marquis heard them run out, heard their flying steps on cement—and his gun went with them.

The panting O'Near burst through the front door and there was a sudden catch in his throat. He swore brokenly, dropped down a split second beside his partner, and the Marquis heard him moan—and then the Indian-faced detective was gone.

His gun banged as he raced away and he was crying in a tight, choked voice: "Come back, you cop-killing ———— ————!"

The street came to life with a roar. Lead hammered at the wooden blacksmith's shop as the Marquis got free. Red flashes cracked the street as he plunged out. It took him a hot second to make out the running forms—the two fugitives—almost at the corner street lamp above, O'Near racing after, shooting.

The big gunman, even as the Marquis stared, suddenly ran out in the road to hammer three shots back at the homicide detective—and O'Near's gun spit flame and lead. The big man's legs buckled.

He tried to fling back to the curb, but O'Near's gun pumped twice more thunderingly, and the big man piled down in a screaming heap—but the little rat-faced private detective had reached the corner and was gone! Even as the thick-witted O'Near put his head down and sprinted, the Marquis' heart gave a leap. Out of positive, final disaster—there was suddenly one whisper of hope. The sniveling little Boering had wriggled clear. If only he could keep ahead of O'Near. If only he had a car waiting—or some means of escape.

O'Near pounded around the corner, and the Marquis held his breath, scarcely daring to hope.

Then, as seconds dropped away with no more shots, he realized that Boering was away—and suddenly his own decision was clear. He must duck, slip away himself—rather than stay and brazen it out, pretend he had just happened to be in the neighborhood.

For once he had to do the thing he knew was not smart. He had to get clear here and throw his own private little machine into frenzied activity—throw out a net quickly into which the little private detective might stumble, before the headquarters machine beat him to it.

He sweated, his ears strained, as he scrambled over back fences, stumbled through back yards. And still there were no more shots. The screaming of the shot gunman in the street had died. The shrill rising whine of a police siren was the only thing that reached him. Another spurt of hope! If only O'Near had not recognized Boering.... He flagged a taxi.

In the cab, riding south, the Marquis clipped at the cabby: "Can you get police calls on your radio?"

"Sure."

The set crackled—as the Marquis juggled the rising hope. O'Near had had only a second, peering in the rear window, in which to recognize the private detective. Maybe he didn't even know him by sight. In minutes, the entire force would be combing the five boroughs for the cop-killer. If they only lacked his identity—if only the Marquis could claim that one advantage!

The droning voice of the announcer came on, driving another knife into him. "... private detective named Boering, height etc... wanted for the murder of Detective Soldier a few minutes ago. He is believed to be in Harlem, vicinity Lenox Avenue....

The Marquis cursed huskily. Even that hope was gone. The headquarters machine, too, knew exactly whom they wanted. The issue was clear-cut now. The rat-faced little Boering was loose, crawling somewhere in the city's shadows, holding in his rotten hands disaster for both Big Bella's girl and the Marquis. The vicious dragnet reserved for cop-killers would be scouring every alley for him. Somehow, the Marquis had to run through it, snake out the little rat first....

He checked the cab, ran in and phoned McGuire to meet him. He was the one member of the handpicked

Broadway Squad whose loyalty and brains the Marquis rated on a par with his own.

CHAPTER THREE
THE MARQUIS
GRABS A STRAW

THE MARQUIS sat in McGuire's car at the edge of the Park and clipped out what had happened. The chubby redhead piled out, ran in and phoned. His face was white and set when he climbed back in the car.

"Every man on the squad is going to work on it—but my God, Marty, he'll be in a hole with the hole in after him. The downtown boys have a hundred chances to our one."

"I know it."

The redhead ran a finger inside his collar. "What if they get to him first. God knows where you'll get off. With your gun to confirm what he'll tell—you're cooked. And if you ask me, that girl not only faces arrest for killing Janisse—but a damn good chance of conviction."

"You think I don't know it? What's this Janisse set-up?"

"It's still unsolved—plenty. This Janisse—if you've seen his work, you know what kind of a guy he was. A big, handsome pup with a lot of black hair and snapping black eyes. He went through women like a prairie fire. Homicide's working on that angle—if they're working on anything.

"He lived with a little old, half-blind guy, named Hazelton, who was a sort of secretary. Janisse picked him up at a race track somewhere, where the old man handed him a good tip or something—just a goofy fancy—and he worked for Janisse for years. Did whatever finagling was necessary to keep Janisse's women straight, looked after the house—that sort of thing. They didn't get much out of him. He has sort of a dumb loyalty to Janisse, though why I don't know. Janisse kept him, but he didn't leave him anything and he's out on the street now.

"Janisse sent him out that night, to see a spick named Ronola. This Ronola was the one they tried to hang the killing on at first. He has a previous narcotic conviction—and Janisse had a big supply of reefers in the house. They tried to tie it together, but unfortunately the spick had an alibi. As it happened, he met the old man in the lobby of his building at exactly ten minutes before the murder time. The murder time was exactly eleven thirty—the watchman in the building next door heard Janisse scream. Either this Ronola really was clean, or damned clever. It seems he called the old man's attention to the time—and also a porter who was mopping up the lobby. Anyway, they couldn't break him.

"And the old man wouldn't give out the names of Janisse's women. Oh, they checked on all they could. Half the showgirls in town were nuts to get to pose for him. Seems they got famous that way and got better jobs or something. And then, the guy had sex-appeal in a big way. Anyway, they checked until they ran out of women."

"But the killing?"

"Well, this watchman heard the yell and a crash at eleven thirty but he didn't pay it much attention. Then the old man, Hazelton, came home about twelve—he never did give out what he was seeing Ronola about, although—and here's another angle they worked over—this Ronola was being seen around town with one of Janisse's former flames—a Nina Porter.

"Anyway, the old man came home and found Janisse sprawled out on the floor, in his shirt-sleeves, with a broken woodworking chisel driven into his neck and blood all over. The place stunk of marihuana and the windows were all open wide, but the cops have an idea that the old man may have done that to get the smell out before they got there."

"Was there anything about a candid camera?"

"Huh? No."

"Let's get the murder pictures downtown."

FIFTEEN MINUTES later, at headquarters, they stared at a glossy print of a vast hollow studio. It was a duplex, its ceiling two floors high. A gallery ran along the back wall midway up—evidently the living quarters opened off this at the rear. In every corner of the studio, floodlights blazed down, and there were one or two half-finished statues whose shoulders sparkled in the eccentric lighting. A board of switches and a huge master switch were bare against one wall. Half the studio floor was bare, the other half covered with an immense thick rug, as though to divide the working area from the social.

The body of the sculptor lay in the social area—at the foot of a desk. The desk contained the perpetual-calendar-and-clock device. Heads and busts peered from shelves and bookcases. Turntables, armatures, various modeling paraphernalia littered the room in the working area. A huge couch was before a stone fireplace in the social end and hanging from the arm of the couch was a thrown-open camera-case, its camera plainly visible within.

"Listen," the redhead burst suddenly, "if we could clean up this murder—put the finger on the real killer—then even if the headquarters guys do catch Boering and get the pictures, they won't have anything to hang on the girl."

"Who handled the killing for homicide?"

"It's on the back here."

They turned the photo over and read: *Detective in charge: William O'Near.*

For a second, there was electric silence.

McGuire breathed: "Good God—what a coincidence!" Then, "Well, isn't it? What's the matter?"

The Marquis said nothing. He was hunched in the seat, his round little face expressionless, his deep-sunk eyes burning in slow enlightenment.

McGuire burst out: "Well, what about it? Will we take a crack at it? If we could nail the real killer...."

The Marquis took a good ten seconds before he said dully: "I think I know the real killer."

"What? Who— Oh, my God, you mean...?"

"Drive up to Riverside Drive."

TWENTY MINUTES later he faced Big Bella again in the red-yellow-and-black living-room. As she let him in, hastily closed the door, her brown eyes were wild, her skin pasty-yellow under the rouge. "Oh—what happened? You—"

"Happened? Your blackmailers murdered a cop. I was an accomplice to compounding a felony. I think that makes me equally guilty. One got away—with my gun. The first cop that gets him—both Sylvia and I are through. Where is she?"

The bedroom door opened and the girl came out, her hands to her cheeks.

The Marquis said: "You killed him, didn't you?"

Her wild eyes stared at him crazily a moment, then she suddenly buried her face in her hands, and deep racking sobs shook her. Big Bella flew to her side. "My baby!" She folded her in her big arms, and her eyes were like piercing fire over the sobbing girl's shoulder.

"All right," her raspy voice screamed defiantly. "All right, so she did kill him! What of it? Does that let you out? You owe me a life—your life. Now you can pay me. Or does the big act come now? Are you the righteous cop...?

"Shut up, Bella," the Marquis' dull voice bit. "I'm in this up to my neck. I couldn't get out, if I wanted to—and every minute means something. I want to know what happened." And to the girl, "Don't get frightened, Sylvia. I'm still your friend. I'm fighting for you. But we're both in a terribly dangerous spot. I've got to know what happened."

Through the sobs that shook her, the girl blurted desperately: "I—I don't know what happened. He offered me a chance to pose for him. The girls said it would make me famous. I went down there. He—he made me strip to the waist and pose, while he gave me a cigarette to smoke. There was something funny about the cigarette. It made my head spin—made me feel crazy. I found myself dancing, stumbling around. He was snapping pictures of me with his camera. Then I felt his hands on me. He was loathsome—I hated him. Then everything went blank and I woke up—woke up with him half sprawled across me and that—that thing in his neck. I had my hand on it. I didn't know what to do. I grabbed my clothes and ran. Oh, God—" She buried her head in Big Bella's bosom, sobbing.

The veins stood out on the Marquis' forehead. He said, "O.K. kid," and turned toward the door.

"Marty!" the shrill, raspy voice leaped frantically at him. "Marty! Wait! You—you're going to—"

"Yeah," the Marquis said. "I'm going to—while I last."

When he climbed into the car downstairs part of him was sick and shaky. The wise McGuire was silent. The

Marquis said grimly: "I don't recall ever having done this before, chasing around trying to save a guilty killer, at any cost. Maybe I have, but I don't remember it. And you don't have to, Ace. Better bail out on me."

"Don't be funny. She did the trick, huh?"

"The pup evidently had a yen for her and fed her loco weed. Then he tried to make her—only the weed kicked back and he got the chisel in his rotten neck. But the courts don't recognize marihuana as a defense. She'd fry—without a chance. Even the defense-of-honor would sound fishy in court. She stripped for him herself—and she ran away afterwards."

"Hell fire!"

The Marquis hesitated. "This may sound funny to you, Ace—but, I'm going to save that kid, if I go down trying. I know—I'm in the grease too, but even if I weren't I'd go all out. She doesn't deserve to burn—and she's going to—unless we make it. We've one chance in a thousand. That's to find Boering before—"

He stopped suddenly, as an expensive cream-colored convertible swirled into the curb behind them and parked. A tall, curly-headed, good-looking young man jumped out.

The Marquis swung around in his seat, his eyes intent, as the young man closed the driver's door and told the car's other occupant: "All right, Dad, but it's got me worried. Who could know anything dangerous about Sylvia? And why call me up anyway? I've got to ask her."

McGuire stiffened. "What...?" and the Marquis clipped him to silence.

A slow, drawly voice inside the car said: "Carleton, you're crazy. In my time, I've had probably a thousand anonymous phone calls offering to reveal secret information about this

one or that one of my friends—sometimes for cash, sometimes for nothing. There's a certain type of unbalanced
person who delights in these little fancies. At any rate,
why not let it go till morning? If Sylvia was feeling too
badly to go to work—"

"But—but he said he'd call again in a couple of hours.
I don't know what to do. Oh, if she's asleep or ill or anything,
I won't worry her with—"

"Exactly what did this man on the phone say—again?"

"Just this man's voice. He said he had some deadly information about Sylvia and would I pay money for it, if
it were as he said."

"Typical crank, I would say. Pure—"

"Get going," the Marquis whipped in McGuire's ear.
"Get to a telephone before they can reach Big Bella."

They shot away, whirled round the corner. A drug store
was in the middle of the cross-block. "There!" the Marquis
clipped.

He ran in, fishing out a nickel, jammed into a phone
booth. Sweating, he whipped the mechanism round and
the phone began to ring. Again and again it rang, while
the Marquis swore in mounting apprehension.

When finally Big Bella's voice did come on, he threw
words at her. "This is Marty. Sylvia's fiancé is on the way
up. He's received a call from somebody offering information. For heaven's sake don't let her peep about anything.
Laugh it off. Tell him to laugh it off. I'm taking care—"

"Will you wait!" Big Bella's voice raved frantically. "Give
me a chance to say a word. He just came. I did exactly
that. I wouldn't even let him in. Oh, God, Marty—what
are we going to do? If Carleton finds out the truth—"

"You sent him away, told him nothing?"

"Yes, yes, of course. What else—"

The Marquis clipped down the hook, ran back out to the car and threw at McGuire: "Back up! Get that yellow convertible in sight and follow it."

"Hey! It just went by here like a bat out of hell, around that corner." McGuire sent the coupe leaping forward. "Maybe we can catch...."

The street into which they skidded was bare and empty. There was no sign of the convertible.

The Marquis swore, jumped out again and ran back to the drug store, flipped a phone directory. When he climbed back in the car, he snapped: "Over to Number Two Fifth Avenue."

"Is that where they live?"

"Yeah."

"My God—what is this?"

"That was the girl's fiancé. Somebody just phoned him, apparently. Go through the Park."

THEY SWEPT over to Fifth Avenue, flung to a stop across the street from the skyscraper, block-long, exclusive apartment house. The Marquis piled out, trotted in to the lobby.

The switchboard attendant assured him that neither Mr. Druitt, Junior, nor Senior, was in, and he returned to the car.

"What now?" McGuire asked.

"Sit here and wait."

"Marty—you don't suppose this rat Boering is shoving his nose up again? Where would he get the guts to...?"

"No, it couldn't be Boering. That one is sulking in some sewer, shaking his teeth out. He isn't thinking up new people to put the shake on."

"Well, who then, for the love of heaven?"

The Marquis hesitated in the darkness. "Maybe the guy who hired Boering."

"What!"

"Stop and think. There's got to be someone. Where would a strictly sewer rat like Boering get that film? Where would he fit into this picture? Look at it.

"Janisse gets the girl down there and feeds her marihuana and it winds up in murder. He's sent his only servant out. Somebody comes along and grabs that film—don't ask me why—I don't know—but somebody who knows the ins and outs of the set-up. You know damn well Boering wouldn't be the one. In the first place, he wouldn't have the nerve to walk in on that scene and calmly hunt around for a chance to make a dollar."

"Then—"

"But somebody did. Somebody walked off with the film and hired Boering to make the contact and collect on it. Now that Boering has muffed it, this wise guy is looking for fresh meat. Maybe he's desperate for money or something. Only now he doesn't mention the pictures, because he hasn't got the pictures. Boering has them. But that doesn't mean he won't have them."

"Huh? You mean...?"

"I mean that Boering, with the town on fire for him, is damned liable to run to his head man as fast as he can, for protection. That may be our chance. If we can nose out who that head man is and get on top of him, we can be waiting for Boering when he comes running."

McGuire's eyes were bleak. "It's just as tough that way. How do we locate this boss?"

"If these Druitts will cooperate when that call comes...."

THEY SAT and waited. After an hour McGuire said: "Listen—maybe they went in some other way, put the car up and went in through a rear entrance."

The Marquis reentered the lobby, went to the switchboard alcove. "Have Mr. Druitt, Senior or Jun…."

The uniformed attendant said: "They won't be home till two o'clock. Mr. Druitt, Junior just called…. No, I have no idea where they could be reached before then."

"All right," the Marquis told McGuire grimly, back in the car. "I'm not going to waste any more time. Get down to this Ronola's place on Horatio."

"Ronola?"

"Yeah. We can come back later."

As they shot away McGuire asked: "What do you expect to do with this Ronola?"

"He could be the master-mind we're looking for, couldn't he?"

"How? He wasn't prowling around that murder scene. The homicide squad have covered that ground."

"In this case, that means O'Near—and O'Near is a stupid oaf. I know that for a fact. Covering ground that he's already been over isn't useless."

"But Ronola's alibi covers the time the films must have been taken."

"That's another thing I don't like—that alibi. I don't like alibis where people notice the exact time at the exact moment. And I don't like alibis supported by old men with weak eyes."

"And porters."

"Porters notwithstanding."

"You think you can crack it?"

"Think? My God, man, I'm clutching at straws! If I could crack it, it might give us a hold on Ronola. That might get us Boering and the pictures—and my gun. A miracle could happen—even to us."

CHAPTER FOUR

RONOLA

THEY STOOD looking up at the modest apartment house. It was on a flatiron-corner, its lower street-level floor ringed with stores. It was eight or ten stories high, of yellow brick and was a little more exclusive-looking than most Village apartments.

They went through a small foyer and into a large, many-pillared, tiled lobby. No one was at the desk, no one at the switchboard, no one anywhere else in sight. There were two or three club chairs, a couple of couches around the lobby. The rug was rolled up against one wall. The Marquis' eyes were intent, darting as they moved forward five paces and stopped, five more and stopped when the telegraph company's clock on the wall became visible.

Also visible became a small corridor crossing just beyond the clock. The Marquis strode forward and peered along it.

A porter was mopping this corridor. Beyond the porter was a side door, opening onto another street.

The Marquis' eyes shone. He glanced at McGuire's startled face. "That alibi isn't worth a damn. The old man probably came in, went up, came back and sat on one of those front couches, out of sight of the clock. Ronola could have come in this side door, seen the old man, climbed on a chair, run the clock back as far as he wanted to, gone out again, come in the front entrance and walked the old man over here. While they waited for the elevator, he could have pointed out the clock."

"But it's a telegraph-company clock. How can you set them back?"

"They're regulated every hour. That would be an advantage. You can set them back, and then they correct themselves at the next hour. There's no worry about the clock being found wrong later."

"I still don't know why he'd want an alibi, if—"

"Behave. He's got a criminal record. He's had some dealings with Janisse—or Janisse's ex-girl-friend, this Nina Porter. He's just walked in on a murder scene. An alibi would be his first thought, if he's as shifty as I think he is."

The indicator buzzed sharply in the propped-open, lighted elevator. Down the hall, the old man stopped his mopping, wearily leaned the mop against the wall and came plodding slowly towards them.

"I think we'll go up and have a little talk with Mr. Ronola," the Marquis said, and they followed the old man into the car.

"What floor is Mr. Ronola?"

The discouraged-looking, yellow-mustached porter said dully, "Seven," and set the car into motion.

The car shivered to a halt at the seventh floor and the doors slid open. A youngish, swarthy, black-haired man in a wine-colored bathrobe, his white silk shirt open at the neck, stood there. His dark glowing face was hard and rocky, despite the pencil-line mustache. He had a letter in his hand.

He gave the Marquis and McGuire an uninterested, contemptuous look and handed the letter to the ancient on the elevator. "Mail that for me right away, will you, Joe?"

The Marquis moved forward as the Latin turned on his heel. McGuire started to follow, till the Marquis drove his elbow in the redhead's ribs, and sent him gulping back into the car. The redhead's bewildered, "Yeah, down," came as the door slid closed behind the striding Marquis.

The swarthy, hard-faced man turned back, in the act of entering an open apartment door, eyed the Marquis dully.

"Mr. Ronola?" the Marquis asked.

"So what?" The glowing dark eyes thinned. There was a touch of red around the eyelids and the swarthy face was a little drawn.

"Lieutenant Marquis—Broadway Squad. Like to have a few words."

The man's jaw locked. "My God, aren't you ever going to get through with this? All right, come on in."

He turned his back and walked through the little foyer into a cheaply-furnished living-room, saying: "More cops, Nina, hide the liquor."

THE MARQUIS bowed over his hard hat. Evidently Nina Porter, the dead Janisse's former flame, was on intimate terms here. She was in salmon-colored silk lounging pajamas, sitting with one leg under her on the couch, smoking. She was small, brittle, with black hair and a carefully made-up small, doll-like face. Black bangs hung over her forehead and she might have been Chinese. Her agate eyes regarded the Marquis spitefully.

"Well?" Ronola asked wearily. "Have you figured out some new way I could have killed Janisse?"

The sound of the stopping elevator came through the open door. The Marquis said quickly: "I think it might be better if Miss Porter let us talk in privacy. It's for your sake I suggest it."

The swarthy Ronola looked at the girl, shrugged. She got up and walked through a door in the far wall, closing it.

"I—" the Marquis began and turned round at McGuire's cough. He said, "Excuse me just a minute," and walked out into the hall.

"The letter?" McGuire whispered. "Is that what you wanted?"

"Certainly, you dope. Let me have it."

He ripped open the special-delivery letter, addressed to one William Harder, in Philadelphia.

It was handwritten.

> Dear Bill:
>
> Can you possibly let me have a grand and a half till the tenth? I am in a hot spot here. A couple of joints have got me on the cuff—and these New York gamblers are tough. I am sure I can collect something on that Janisse matter in the next few days, but I am going to be in real trouble unless I get something on the line right away.
>
> Yours,
>
> Don Ronola.

The Marquis let out breath. "Come on."

He walked in, holding the ripped-open letter in plain sight—and Ronola's swarthy face lost color.

"My assistant, Mr. McGuire—Mr. Ronola. I seem to have made a little mistake. Maybe we can fit you into that little killing after all."

Ronola said hoarsely: "You guys can't do that. That's tampering with the U.S. mails."

"We'd tamper the door of the Treasury right now. Sit down and—"

"You can't rig me for that killing. You know damn well I didn't do it."

"What we think and what a jury would think might be different, just bear that in mind."

"You're crazy. I've got an alibi—"

"Stop it. With this letter, I could make that alibi look sick. Let's see. You're desperate for cash. You went to Janisse to try and get some. He won't give and you start arguing, finally stick a knife in him and run. You come in the side door, see the half-blind old gaffer that works for him sitting in the lobby. You run back the clock, go and brace him. Sounds kind of good, don't you think?"

There was sweat on the Latin's swarthy face. "I didn't kill—"

"Maybe not. But you did pick up some film—out of a candid camera, didn't you?"

"What?"

"Film. Little pictures. You better had, greaseball—or we'll have to hand this to homicide."

"Listen—I don't know what the hell you're talking about. I swear—"

"Then what *do* you know? Wait a minute. Our time's valuable. Frankly, we don't care who the hell killed Janisse. We do care about catching a rat named Boering and some films that he has."

"Films? Of what?"

"Of a certain party that was in the house before the killing—shortly before. Janisse was snapping pictures of this party—and they might be embarrassing. That's all we care about, Ronola—getting those films. And you're elected. Take your choice of either of these two pictures—

"One: we spring this letter on homicide, point out how you could have faked the alibi—and you go to the can.

"Two: something like this. You went to Janisse's that night—why I don't know. You got there before, during, or just after the killing. You go in. You're up against it for dough. Somehow, you spot the films in the camera. Maybe you smell dough in them—or maybe you've just got a dirty mind and know Janisse had one too. Anyway you duck out with the films.

"You get here and see the old man waiting. You know you're going to get dragged into the murder inquiry. With your record, it's a cinch you'll be in hot water. So you cook up the alibi, do your talking to the old man, get rid of him. Then you develop the films and find you've really got something.

"You find out or maybe recognize the certain party in the picture, and you see the time-clock-and-calendar that places her there close to the murder time. You know you can cash in. You need dough the worst way. You hire this scum Boering to collect for you—only it goes wrong. Boering goes into the ground. You were counting on the dough—and now you're really in a squeeze. You rack your brain, think of the girl's boy-friend and make a desperate attempt to put him on the shake yourself.

"Meanwhile—and this is where we come in, Ronola— you're half expecting Boering to come running to you as soon as he can run the gauntlet. And that is exactly what we're waiting for, too. It's too bad about you needing dough, greaseball—but that's out. What's going to happen is that you're going to turn Boering and those pix over to us, or we hand homicide a case that even O'Near's thick head can understand."

THE LATIN'S face was stiff, shiny, his eyes sunk. "I—I don't even know this Boering. You got me wrong," he insisted.

"You better hope we haven't."

"I didn't kill him. I didn't see any pictures."

"Don't be silly. Where do you expect to make dough out of the 'Janisse matter' then?" He waved the letter.

The Latin licked his lips. He started to speak, swallowed, licked his lips again. "All right. You've got me in a spot. I'll tell you exactly what's what. Janisse took Nina Porter on a trip. He—he hurt her."

"How?"

"He—well, he was brutal with her and things went wrong with her. Besides that, he gave her the air, after she'd been his girl for quite a while. She—I happened to meet her and she hired me as her manager. I thought Janisse ought to be sued. He offered to settle for twenty grand.

"I said O.K. and he was to send the dough. Only he didn't. That was a month ago. He's been giving us the royal run-around. He's always 'out' when I try to get in touch with him. Once, we were told the check's in the mail—only it ain't. Then he winds up sending that old rat of his over here to try and settle for half." He ran a finger inside his collar. "That—that was what he was doing the night I went over to his place to have a showdown. That's what Hazelton was here for that night, not for the first time either. I—I didn't crack about it to the cops because it would have put me in a worse-looking spot—on account of it was the night he was killed. The old weasel that worked for him never peeped about Janisse's business and I gambled that he wouldn't pop off about this."

"And?" the Marquis drove. "You went over there around the murder time. You saw what?"

The Latin's eyes crawled. "You—you won't believe what I say."

"We'll try."

"I—all right—I swear this is God's truth. I got into the yard and somebody conked me. When I come to, a few minutes later, I looked in the door and saw Janisse and a half-naked girl all tangled up together and that knife stickin' out of his neck. I got one look and beat it."

The Marquis grunted. "Let's try that last bit over again. It stinks."

"My God—you think I'd go prowling around in a spot like that? You think I'm crazy?"

"No, but I think you're slippery enough to do it—and I don't think it'd bother your nerves any. And—you're desperate for dough."

The sweating Ronola spread his hands. "I can't tell you any more. That's on the level."

"You did fake that alibi."

"Well, yes. Wouldn't you in my...?"

"I'd do a lot of things in your shoes—but lying to us isn't one of them."

The Latin sagged, turned palms outward. "I swear to God I've given you the straight dope."

The Marquis eyed him carefully a long time. "I hope you have. And I hope you've got the sense to be more scared of us than of those debts of yours."

The anxious-eyed Latin said nothing.

"We'll be back," the Marquis assured him, and turned and walked out.

Crossing the lobby, McGuire said: "What does it add up to? He isn't your master-mind after all."

"I wouldn't bet a dime on it that he wasn't putting on an act—half-truth and half-phony," the Marquis growled. "He's hard and he's got a mind like lightning. You wait here a minute."

"Where are you going?"

"To phone one of the boys to come down and keep watch over him."

He went into a drug store down the block, called Kavvelfoot, the squad's oldster, at the theater ticket agency on Times Square that was the unofficial headquarters of the squad. "Get down here as fast as you can. I want you to keep an eye on this Ronola. There's a possibility that Boering may run to him. If he does, I want you here to jump him."

Back in the lobby he told McGuire: "Where is this Janisse's place? I've a mind to check up on this spick?"

"One block over and two blocks down. You can't miss it."

"As soon as Kavvelfoot comes, you join me there."

HE WALKED over and down Jane Street. The sculptor's studio sat at street level, an immense black-brick building, two stories high, flanked by a wooden fence. There were no windows in the wall that faced the street—only the vast skylight in the roof. The board fence that masked the little side yard was ten feet high.

In the gloom, the Marquis bent to look for a bell by the fence's gate—and suddenly realized that the gate was ajar. He pushed into the little yard. It was bordered on the end opposite him by what seemed a factory building, on the side to his right by the rear of a tenement, and on the left, of course, by the low, black studio building. It was Moroccan in architecture, a silled door in the middle. He stepped uncertainly toward it—and a voice sent a chill through him.

It came through a tiny, scroll-work-grilled window beside the door, and it was the voice of O'Near, the Indian-faced homicide detective.

He was saying: "I got reason to believe there was a camera in this room that night Janisse was killed, with some film in it—some pictures Janisse was taking of a jane. What I want to know is—was the film in that camera at the time I was here?"

The Marquis stepped quickly to the window. The huge statuary-filled studio was lighted by blazing corner floodlights. A shrunken little white-haired man was standing over by the panel-block of switches at the far side of the room, one spidery hand on a chair-back, his bright blue eyes tired and sick and discouraged.

"I'm sure I don't know, Sergeant. There's Mr. Janisse's camera there. I've taken nothing out or put nothing in. Didn't you examine it that night?"

"I didn't think of it," O'Near grumbled.

"What's the importance of the film?" the old man asked dully.

"Huh? Well, that—that's police business so far. Hey, listen—" O'Near's voice became fretful. "Why'n't you tell us what woman Janisse had here that night? We been pretty patient with you, up till now. But we got to know sooner or later."

The old man stood up wearily. He was short, shabby, and his lined old face was dog-like in its sagging tiredness.

"I've told you before—I don't know. I did not keep track of Mr. Janisse's appointments."

"Baloney. You knew all right. What the hell's the matter with you? You got no call to clam up about his goings-on now. He didn't leave you nothing did he? You're out on your can now, ain't you?"

The old man said stiffly: "Mr. Janisse treated me very well. I have no complaint. I hardly expect to live in a house where I'm no longer employed, no. But if I had any reason to wish Mr. Janisse ill, I still couldn't tell you what you ask. I really don't know."

O'Near made a husky, disgusted sound. "Hell, you gimme a pain, you do."

THE MARQUIS ducked back into the shadows of the yard as the Indian-faced detective strode out. There was a fresh stab of worry in his thinking. How had O'Near learned about the pictures? In hasty review, he could not see how the thick-headed homicide officer could have learned about them.

Did it mean…?

He set his jaw. He was in too bad a spot now to spend time worrying what anything meant. All that mattered was finding the rat-faced private detective, Boering and getting the evidence away from him, before it fell into the hands of the rest of the feverishly seeking police force.

And Ronola—he could not shake clear the impression that the shrewd, fast-thinking Latin was the means to that end. If he could get the truth about Ronola—get him thoroughly under his hand—

He reached the silled door, just as the old man was closing it. The Marquis checked it with a foot, looked into the weary eyes and said: "I'm sorry. Could I trouble you just a few minutes more? I'm another police officer."

The old man sighed, "Oh, yes," and let him in.

"I want to get a little information about Ronola, this Latin whom you visited that night."

"Mr. Ronola didn't kill Mr. Janisse. That's all I can tell you. I was with him at the time."

"I understand that. But we need some information that I know you have—for another reason. About Nina Porter."

The old man looked dully questioning. "What about her?"

"Was it true that Mr. Janisse did her an injury—that he offered her twenty thousand dollars to keep it out of court—through her manager, Ronola—and that he failed to pay it?"

The old man looked unhappily at the Marquis, then down at the floor for a long minute. Then he sighed. "I don't suppose there's any harm in telling that now, since you're familiar with it. Mr. Janisse was a great artist. He— his temperament was such—"

"I understand all that too. But about Miss Porter...."

"Miss Porter accompanied him on a trip. There was some accident, for which Mr. Janisse felt responsible and he did make the offer you mentioned. That was a month ago. Since then, Mr. Ronola was constantly attempting to bother him about it. Last week I made bold myself to mention it to Mr. Janisse and he seemed to believe he had already forwarded the money. He was sometimes very careless about money—even large sums. He—he was quite a wealthy man and it seemed to mean nothing to him.

"I informed Mr. Ronola of what he said, and Mr. Ronola denied having received the money. When I urged Mr. Janisse to recall definitely what had happened, he seemed very vague about it. He—he suggested that I visit Mr. Ronola and ask if he would accept half the money and call the matter closed."

The Marquis blinked. "Why? If he thought he had paid it."

The old man looked worried. "I really didn't understand it myself. Mr. Janisse sometimes had violent spells of parsimoniousness. I didn't know but what he had re-pented the offer. At any rate, it was not my place to ask questions. I simply did as he ordered me."

"What did Ronola say to the offer?"

"He refused it."

CHAPTER FIVE

BOERING—OR ELSE

RACING UPTOWN again to try the Druitts once more the redhead asked: "Did you get anything more on Ronola?"

"I don't know. I don't think so. Hey—step on it! It's damned near two."

When they finally pulled up in front of the Fifth Avenue apartment house the hands of the dashboard clock showed exactly ten after. The Marquis ran into the lobby. "Mr. Druitt—fast!"

The switchboard attendant leaned maddeningly back. "Just a moment, sir. The line's busy."

The Marquis groaned, leaned swiftly over and snatched the headphones—and at that very moment a tiny light went on.

"Here—wait!" the terrified attendant yelped. "He's through now."

The Marquis swore, dropped the phones and swung toward the elevators. Of the two in operation, both were closed, humming somewhere in the upper stories. He chafed, sweated, as the little green lights on the panel indicator blinked the sequence of floors. It seemed an age till one opened—and Carleton Druitt and his father strode out.

The Marquis checked them. "Mr. Druitt!"

The youngster was worried-looking. His ruddy, clean-cut, cleft-chinned face was a little pale. The older man's smooth, pointed face was somber, his grape-blue eyes discontented.

The Marquis showed his badge hastily and drew them over to an alcove. "I'm a friend of Miss Hays. I understand you've been getting—uh—threats or something against her.… Wait! You can treat this as confidential—not a police matter."

The youngster looked bewildered, uneasy. He glanced at the older man.

"I'd suggest you tell Lieutenant Marquis exactly what you've received," the elder Druitt said drawlingly. "I'm sure he'll tell you as I have—that they're beneath notice."

"Someone called me earlier and said he had some dangerous information about Syl—Miss Hays. He asked if I would pay money for it. I—I said I guessed so. He was to call later.

"He called just now. The—the person said there would be some pictures to prove the information. I—I'm to wait until morning and he will contact me again."

"Where?"

"I don't know where. He's to call me here." The youngster's troubled face was flushed. "I—I know it can't be anything legitimate, of course."

"Of course not," the Marquis said. "Listen—do me a favor and don't go out. Stay in—and I'll keep in touch with you. We'll fix this crank."

The youngster frowned. "But I—"

"It may be more important than you think," the Marquis urged.

"I'd suggest you do so," the older man said smoothly. "It isn't really necessary for you to go out—and I will be back shortly."

The youngster looked discontented, but said: "Well—all right."

WHEN HE sank down beside McGuire again the Marquis' voice was a little thick. "Missed him, by God! We can't hold out much longer, Ace. With every cop in town burning to get Boering, our chances are fading by the minute. One more bad break like that—" He was silent a moment, then said doggedly: "Drive back down to Horatio Street."

McGuire's chubby face was pinched. "Whatever you say, Marty—but nosing around Ronola's private life isn't going to save your skin or the girl's either."

"How do you know it isn't? Young Druitt just got another call from his blackmailer. The rat talked pictures this time."

"Eh? Good Lord, does that mean that Boering has already reached him?"

"God knows. But there's something damn queer about this Ronola situation. If I could get on top of it I've got a hunch I'd have my answer. The more I think about him, the shrewder he seems to me. I—damn it, Ace—he's got to be the one."

"You're certainly sold on it."

"I've got to be. Stop here—I'm going to phone the agency. There's a chance some of the boys may have stirred up something by now."

The squad member who answered his call nearly knocked his heart into his throat with a false report that precinct police had Boering surrounded in a Harlem tenement. Fortunately, the report was exposed as a fake while he was actually on the phone, but there was sweat on his neck as he ran back to the coupe.

"Get down there, Ace. We're damn near at the end of our string, or I miss my guess. This can't go on much longer."

The minute they drove past Fourteenth Street, both of them leaned sharply forward.

The redhead said quickly: "What the hell? Look at the dolly cars? What are they doing? Using one to a block down here?"

They drove another square. Streaming silently, criss-crossing back and forth, in every direction, were the small police cars.

The Marquis said huskily: "Park—wait a minute. Stop there!" He pointed swiftly to a street corner ahead where a tall man with a wide-brimmed black hat stood chewing a toothpick. They were not sure it was O'Near till they stopped beside him and the detective's thin Indian face swung sharply towards them.

"What goes on, O'Near?" the Marquis made his voice drawl. "Training these drivers for the rodeo?"

The homicide man spat out his toothpick. "We've got a little rat of a cop-killer bottled up somewhere around here. He was seen five minutes ago right where I'm standing. The guy that shot Soldier last night."

"Yeah?" From the corner of his eye, the Marquis looked at the store-lined yellow-brick apartment house, almost diagonally across the street—Ronola's apartment house. "Quick work. Hope you get him."

"Don't think we won't."

Around the corner, McGuire blurted: "My God, what are you going to do?"

"Shoot the last shot in the locker. Park anywhere. I've got to get to Ronola." His face was a little white and stiff. "If this fails we're done for."

They jumped from the car, slid into the side entrance of the apartment house—and then they were before Ronola's door, and he was opening it.

He was dressed exactly as before, save that he no longer wore the red bathrobe. Nina Porter was back in exactly her same position on the couch, one foot under her, as they strode quickly in, slamming the door.

"All right, Ronola—this is your last chance! Look at me!" The Marquis' small eyes were like fire. "I'm going to make you a promise. I never break one. And it's not often that I've had to frame a guy—but when I do, they go away. You got that?"

Ronola's face was a little pasty, his eyes worried. "Look, copper—be reasonable—"

"I'm through being reasonable!" the Marquis' voice was slaty, clipped. "You're going over for that murder—unless—" He shot a quick look around the room. "Where's your phone?"

The Latin ran a finger inside his collar, nodded toward the closed door.

"Come in here."

THE MARQUIS led the way into a fluffy, rose-and-orchid bedroom. He flung a doll off the telephone, snatched up the phone book, got his finger on a number and leaned over it, his eyes driving into Ronola's. "I've got you cold on a dozen motives. I've got your alibi broken down. If necessary, I'll produce an eye-witness to your murdering Janisse—and I mean every word of it. I've found out about your trying to collect twice from him on the twenty grand and although I don't understand it, maybe there's something there to add to my picture. Wait a minute."

He hastily called a number. After a wait, a tired voice answered and said, "Yes," to his, "Mr. Hazelton?"

He identified himself and said: "About that twenty thousand dollars that may or may not have been paid to Mr. Ronola. This is the ninth of the month. You should have your canceled checks back from the bank by now. Maybe it was paid by check and maybe you can find me the check. Please look. I'll call you again in a short while."

He faced Ronola again in the living-room. "I don't know what that'll bring up, if anything," he said. "But you understand where you stand?"

Ronola's face was shining now. He licked dry lips. "I didn't kill Janisse."

"Who said you did? All I said was that you're going to burn for it—so help me—unless you do what I want."

The Latin swallowed. "What—what is it?"

"I want Boering—and I want a gun he has—and I want some pictures he has."

For the first time real terror crossed the dark man's features. He sank on a chair, pulled at his collar. "Listen copper—I swear to God—" he began hoarsely.

"Don't bother," the Marquis clipped. "Boering was seen a half-block from here five minutes ago. You've got to have him—or know where he is—but not as much as I do. Listen to me, greaseball. Boering has my gun. He's a cop-killer and a rat. If the guys out there run him down—and they're bound to before long—I'm liable to face a murder charge. An innocent girl is sure to face one. Besides my gun Boering has pictures and he's cagey enough to make the most of both gun and pictures. Once they get him he'll squeal like a pig—and then there's no out for me. You got that?"

"I—I got it, but I still swear—"

"I'm not interested in your swearing. I've pegged you as my meat. You're going to produce Boering, and that gun, and those pictures—or you're going to burn for murder. Never mind talking—it won't help you now! Just go and do it."

Sweat beads came out on Ronola's forehead. His eyes were hollow. "You—"

"Get him!" the Marquis thundered. "Get him before those bulls do—or else. That's all—or else!"

Ronola licked his lips and his face was haggard. "I—God, copper, I—" Suddenly hope leaped into his eyes. He stood up, his eyes fixed desperately on the second button of the Marquis' chesterfield. "I—" He started and stopped. "I—" His eyes were glazed, almost with wonder, under their stark fear. He swallowed and said huskily: "If he's in the district maybe I—I got one chance of—of—"

"You better take it—and fast," the Marquis assured him grimly. "This is the payoff, brother."

Ronola swayed toward the bedroom, stopped. "You'll let me make a phone call?"

"You've time for just one."

RONOLA PULLED at his throat again, went quickly into the bedroom and closed the door. The Marquis looked over at the China-doll girl. For all the expression on her face, she might not have heard a word. Her eyes stared blankly.

A minute passed. Only the quick, husky rumble of Ronola's muffled voice came through the door.

Then he came out. Sweat was streaming down his face as he said: "Maybe I can get him. But you got to give me a half-hour—and let me alone."

"We'll let you alone. We'll wait right here."

"You got to pull that flatfoot—the old guy that looks like John D. Rockefeller—away from me. The one you got downstairs."

The Marquis snapped: "Go get Tecumseh, Ace." As the redhead ran out, he shot at the dark man: "What are you going to do if you find him?"

"What—what do you want me to do?"

"Kill him—but I'm not sending you to do that. I want the gun and the film primarily. Without them, he isn't half as dangerous. Where is he? What kind of place?"

"I don't know yet—that's on the level." Ronola wiped his palms along his trouser-seams. "Look—if you tail me and these people see it—I'll get a blast and you'll get no guy."

"We're not going to tail you, but it's up to you to get the gun and the pictures. And tell us where we can get the guy. We'll sit right here with your babe—for fifteen minutes."

"God—wait a minute—I said half an—"

"Who cares what you said? In half an hour, those prowl cars'll have him."

Ronola cursed brokenly, swung and jammed into his clothes. McGuire came back in, leading the frail-appearing, wiry old Kavvelfoot. The old man's little brown eyes lighted as they saw the girl in the salmon-pink silk and he hastily lifted his hat. *"Ahhh!"*

"Shut up," the Marquis told him.

Ronola nervously jerked his tie straight, snatched a hat from a table. In the door he stopped and said through lips stiff with bitterness: "This is the lousiest deal any copper ever gave anybody. I won't forget it."

"You won't if you miss," the Marquis assured him.

He swung out the door, and his footsteps padded swiftly away. The Marquis stepped to the door, listened till he heard the elevator stop, the gate open, close again, and the car again begin to hum.

"All right," he snapped at the oldster. "Tecumseh—tie that girl up, or gag her or do anything, but—keep her quiet."

McGuire blinked. "Huh? You're going to tail him?"

"You think I'm crazy? That guy's too damn smart for my liking. Maybe's he's leveling—maybe he isn't. This is our last hope—and I'm not taking chances. Come on and for God's sake don't let him spot us."

They hit the street cautiously, caught sight of the strolling Ronola, heading across toward Seventh Avenue.

"Be careful," McGuire said worriedly. "I think you got him scared enough so he was telling the truth. You don't want to tip his hand, like he said."

In a minute, it became obvious that Ronola was suspicious of a tail and was trying to lose it. He turned corners, doubled back, stopped in store fronts.

The Marquis swore fretfully. The dolly cars passed them and repassed them. Then Ronola straightened out. He stopped strolling, walked swiftly northward, up to Fifteenth Street, then across to Eighth Avenue, over to Hudson and turned left again under the thick shadows of the 'El' along Ninth.

Far ahead, the dolly cars passed occasionally. Ronola walked close to the building fronts, hugging them, obviously hurrying yet just as obviously treading with an excess of caution. By a miracle neither he, nor the two shadows slipping along a block behind him, were actually hailed by the searching cars.

Then suddenly, the Latin turned and ran quickly up the steps of a tenement house, vanished within.

The Marquis whispered, "Come on!" and increased his silent pace.

CHAPTER SIX
THE LAST SHOT

WHEN THEY reached the black, sagging entrance of the brick building into which Ronola had gone they went up three steps noiselessly and touched the door. It was unlocked and they eased into a noisome, evil-smelling hall. There was not a light in the building from cellar to garret—nor was there a sound.

For just a second they stood there listening. Then a board creaked somewhere over their heads and the Marquis glided silently toward the stairway.

They went up one flight, walking on tiptoe, close to the wall to avoid sagging steps. There was no sign no sound of movement on the first floor—nor on the second.

They were just mounting to the third floor when it came—a loud *thunk!* For a second, it was impossible to judge from where it had come—and then a door banged open in the cellar.

The Marquis moaned. They both whirled back.

Far below them, there was the sound of a man sobbing crazily, the clatter of racing feet.

McGuire cried hoarsely, "Boering!" and they both plunged headlong downward and the clanging of the areaway door out front sent the Marquis' heart into his boots.

They plunged out into the dark street—and there was a racing figure almost at the corner ahead. The Marquis roared, "Hey—come here!" and the fugitive ahead sobbed once and fired.

Lead whined off the wall beside the Marquis as they both leaped wildly aside. The Marquis' gun thundered, and the running man cried out as he spun around the corner.

From far down the street into which he had turned, came the roaring shout of two men. The Marquis sprinted madly, rounded the corner just as a dolly car squealed to the curb ahead, and a hoarse voice yelled again: "Hey you—put up your...!"

In the same second that he saw the huddled fugitive, halfway between himself and the dolly car, the Marquis realized where he was. The tenement he had just left was the one directly in the rear of Janisse's studio!

He called out, fairly in a frenzy, "All right—I've got him!" and the huddled figure swung back on him, pumped two fast shots. The Marquis' side was creased by red-hot fire and he whirled round. Gunshots roared from the side of the dolly car. The sobbing fugitive suddenly dived for the studio's gate, flung himself against it as more dolly cars poured into the street as if by magic. The gate fell open under his weight and he was inside, men streaming after him, even as the Marquis tried to throw himself ahead of the streaming bluecoats.

He wrestled through the gate with four others, had one quick flash of the desperate Boering as he tried frantically to beat open the door of the studio, then sobbing, squealing with fear, turned back to empty his gun.

He went down, riddled, under the crashing reports of half a dozen guns. A tall figure in a broad-brimmed black hat plunged through the men that crowded around the fallen killer, smashed men against the Marquis.

O'Near's hoarse, panting voice raved, "Got him! Got the ————!" and the Marquis blood was cold.

O'Near yelled, "Carry him inside!" and hammered the door once before it burst open and the Marquis could see the floodlights in the corners of the room within.

And then—at the last instant of defeat—something exploded in his brain and he caught his breath. If only—

He whirled back, struggled out the gate again, as more dolly cars roared into the street. He was halfway to the corner when he ran full-tilt into the running McGuire. He hardly saw the redhead. McGuire grabbed him, whirled around beside him and whipped in his ear: "Ronola! Boering shot...."

The Marquis ran as though dazed and they plunged down the areaway of the tenement, ran along the hall to an open door in the rear of the cellar. McGuire's torch stabbed the blackness.

IT WAS a large, low cellar room with wooden walls. Big barrels, covered with wet cloths and smelling of clay, a half dozen armatures, pots of paint, tool chests, piles of thin timber, two small blocks of bronze, stood around the walls. Ronola was on the floor, on his knees, his forehead on the floor, half propped against one wall.

"He's dead," McGuire said hoarsely. "Shot square in the heart. Boering must have been waiting for him—out of his mind with fear."

The Marquis' face was like stone. He turned and trotted back up to the street again.

McGuire said: "Wait—hey—for God's sake, Marty—you're licked! Don't go there! Let's get—"

The Marquis' voice was grating. "Come on! This isn't over yet!"

They ran through the gate, snarling lower-ranking police out of the way, pushed through the throng in the yard—and then through the studio door. O'Near was yelling over his shoulder, "All right—get out! We've got him. It's all over. Go back to your cars!" and the bluecoats were silently filtering back. The Marquis wriggled forward. When he burst into the floodlighted living-room, only O'Near, a bald-headed detective named Miles, and the shivering old man, Hazelton, were in the room, with the body of the bleeding, blasted Boering. Even as the Marquis came in O'Near leaped up with a hoarse bellow.

"Got it!" he cried. "Got the film and everything. This breaks Janisse's killing."

The shivering, frantic-eyed, white-haired old Hazelton stammered: "What—what…?"

O'Near roared triumphantly. "This here is a film showing the dame that was with Janisse the night he was killed. She killed him. When I have it developed, I'll have a picture of the killer. By God, it's irony, ain't it? We shoot this rat down here, right on the front door—and he's got the whole case in his pocket." Then he stooped again and came up with a pistol.

"Hey—look at what the rat was toting. It looks like a service— Hey, Miles—phone headquarters to send up a developing outfit fast—and tell them we have a picture of the jane that killed Janisse."

The Marquis said harshly: "I wouldn't do that, O'Near."

"Huh?" The Indian-faced detective spun around. "Oh, you wouldn't, wouldn't you?" His voice was nasty, his face glowing with triumph. He laid the gun down mechanically on the table behind which the old man was standing, came over, hands on hips. "And why not?"

"Because you'll make a laughing-stock of yourself."

"You're the laughing-stock, wise guy."

"No girl killed Janisse."

O'Near made a derisive throat noise, then sucked in a great breath. "You're nuts. If these pictures show what I was told—"

"They show nothing but a girl who was posing for Janisse a little before the murder time. What's that got you?"

"If she was innocent, why didn't she come forward…?"

"Because she knew a lunkhead like you would make trouble for her. Listen, stupid. Janisse was an eccentric in money matters…. Right, Mr. Hazelton?"

The old man's agonized eyes blinked. "Yes. Yes."

"He kicked away twenty thousand on a girl—and then maybe pinched on somebody else. Right again?"

The shaky old man nodded.

"How long did you work for Janisse, Mr. Hazelton?"

"Six—six years."

"How much did he pay you?"

"Well, he—he didn't exactly pay me. He—he looked after me—"

"Did he? Then why did you have to clip that twenty-thousand-dollar check that he gave you for Ronola? Why forge it and then endorse it yourself on the back so that the bank would cash it? You must have gone there in person to get it cashed. The bank will know and you're nailed."

FOR AN instant there was a stunned, awful silence. Then the old man said, gaspingly, uncomprehendingly: "You—you—I don't understand. You—you are accusing me...." His skinny old hand half stretched out in appeal.

"Certainly, you scheming old pack rat. You clipped that money. Ronola wanted it. He started getting nasty. Finally he said he was coming over. You had to keep him from confronting Janisse. You were in a panic—for fear of exposure. Luck sent you this girl and made Janisse pull his rotten marihuana act. While they were wrestling around, you jumped in and killed him. Then you beat it for Ronola's—only he was already coming in the gate.

"That wasn't too fast for you to think out. You hit him with something, knocked him out, went on to his place just the same—because you were smart enough to know that in his position he would have to build an alibi and you gambled that he'd build one for both of you.

"Then when stupid here overlooked the camera with the films in it which you left in plain sight, no doubt, you were afraid suspicion might come your way after all. So you staged a little act to draw attention to them—to make them seem important. You hired this rat Boering to stage a blackmail racket, to make a meet with the girl's representative—and then you tipped the cops off to it! You wanted those films to fall into their hands and you wanted the cops to think them the answer to the murder. You knew you weren't dealing with a very hot brain here, and you— Look out!"

The old man's shaking, outstretched hand had, incredibly, extended over the Marquis' pistol on the table—the one O'Near had taken from the dead Boering. With one flashing leap, he snatched it up, flung himself backwards and elbowed down the master switch, plunging the place in pitch blackness.

"Don't move!" he shrilled. "Don't any of you move!" His panting was audible in the dark. "I'll kill anybody who moves!" His voice became bitter, almost sobbing. "All right, I did take that check. I—I worked for six years and he never gave me a penny! Not a penny! I couldn't leave him because I had nowhere else I could get a job! But he gave me nothing—nothing but a bare living. I had to do all his dirty work. I saw him toss away thousands. I had nothing.

"When I saw that check, I—I thought I had some information. I thought I could make some money—take the check temporarily, gamble with it—make something for myself to keep me when I couldn't work any more. I—I gambled five thousand, and something went wrong. I lost. Then I—I kept trying to stall off Ronola while I made it back. He got more and more insistent. I tried to settle with him for less, but he wouldn't. Then I couldn't stall him any longer. He insisted he was coming to see Janisse himself and I knew Janisse would go crazy. He'd either kill me or put me in prison the rest of my life. I—I was frantic. I had to do what I…."

O'NEAR'S HOARSE curse shook the room. McGuire started to slide away from the Marquis, but the Marquis snatched at his sleeve, yanked him back.

"Hey!" McGuire gulped.

The Marquis started backing towards the door. He put his mouth to the redhead's ear. "Don't be a damn fool! He's—"

There was suddenly a heavy crash—and then a rumbling thump—just as Miles, the baldheaded detective, reached the light switch and the flood blazed up.

For a second O'Near stood gaping, a gun in his hand.

Of the wizened old man there was not the slightest sign. He had disappeared.

The Marquis, still backing toward the door, yelled hoarsely: "Trap door—under the rug there! Didn't you hear him shoot the bolt? He's down in the cellar! I'll get a crowbar!" He turned and ran out, McGuire at his heels.

Outside he yelled, "Get a crowbar—get a couple of crowbars—Mr. O'Near wants a crowbar," and the group of men still in the yard stirred into activity.

The Marquis ran through them, turned back toward the corner. "Come on!" he raved at McGuire. "That room in the tenement was Janisse's store-room. Ten to one he had a passage...."

They ran around and burst down the areaway steps, just as light flashed in the room at the back. The little white-haired man came racing out. McGuire's torch caught him full, impaled him.

For a split second he came up on one toe—then the gun in his wizened hand flashed up.

The Marquis shot him through the shoulder and through the abdomen in the instant that the old man's weapon flamed, smashing plaster in the ceiling. The gun dropped from his hand and he went crashing backwards into the room he had just left, crying out gaspingly, his arms going over his stomach.

The Marquis dived for the gun—his own gun—snatched it up and pocketed it.

They stood over the groaning old man. His bright eyes were filled with pain, but the Marquis' voice was harsh and savage.

"Just a pitiful old guy, eh? You had to do it, eh? And you had to frame an innocent young girl too, I suppose?"

Through pain-worked lips the old man said huskily: "I—I didn't think she'd be convicted. And—and the girls Janisse had were a bunch of hussies. But I didn't think she'd really—"

"No. So you framed her. And like an ass, you let a rat like Boering know who he was working for. You could have stayed anonymous and then, when he got in the grease, he wouldn't have come running to you."

"I—I didn't mean for him to know. But—but he traced my second phone call. He was waiting for it."

"I get it. So you hid him when he came, and then when I prodded Ronola into thinking of you tonight, you jumped at the chance. What with the check coming up, your forgery would be shown—if Ronola were alive. If Boering were alive, you'd be in the soup anyway. So when Ronola called, you were glad enough to throw them both in that room together, figuring the cops would pick off the survivor. Mister, you sure gambled plenty."

Shouting bluecoats, having finally located the shots were pouring down the cellar stairs. It didn't matter to Hazelton. He had toppled over dead.

AS THEY walked away an hour later McGuire jibed: "So you were positive Ronola was your man."

"He was, wasn't he? I made him do all the detective work. I have no kick coming. Wait here a minute. I have to make a call to Big Bella, the queen of the honky-tonks," the Marquis said.

ALBINO ALIBI

BECAUSE THE FIRST MURDER WASN'T EVEN CLASSED AS A CRIME AND THE SECOND WAS OUT OF HIS DISTRICT, THE LITTLE CZAR OF MANHATTAN'S MAIN STEM WAS LEFT TAGGING AT THE HEELS OF ALL THE COPS AND D.A.'S MEN IN TOWN, RIGHT FROM THE START. HOW COULD HE HAVE GUESSED THE TWO DEATHS WERE TIED IN WITH HOLY JOE BANNON, THE ONE KILLER HE'D HAVE GIVEN HIS IMMORTAL SOUL TO TRAP—AND A SEVEN-HUNDRED-GRAND RACKET THAT WAS DUE TO BLAST RIGHT IN HIS OWN FACE AND PUT HIM ON A MURDER SPOT HIMSELF—TO SAY NOTHING OF WRECKING HIS PRECIOUS SQUAD?

CHAPTER ONE
THE CORPSE IN THE
ORANGE PAJAMAS

THE LITTLE monkey-faced man ran down into the San Sylvan's miniature lobby at four minutes past eleven. He was bare-footed, clad in flapping-open, thin, orange-silk pajamas, his scrawny pink chest visible. His silver hair was carefully combed but his wizened face was the color of dull copper, the veins swollen out, his little blue eyes feverish, irrational. He pattered suddenly down the stairs from nowhere, crouched, panting, at the foot of the curving staircase, as though poised for instant flight, while his eyes roved cunningly around the luxurious cream-and-blue-leather lobby. Fortunately, except for attendants, the tiny lobby was deserted.

Merlin, the uniformed youth at the switchboard behind the circular desk, saw him first and stumbled instantly to his feet, flabbergasted. Prior, the other lobby attendant, was screened behind the grilled-in half of the circular desk and did not become aware of the startling apparition till Merlin stammered out: "Mr.—Mr.—Torgenson... What...?"

The old man's fever-ridden eyes sparkled and he tensed to run. His suffused face worked and his little tongue flicked out over his lips. "I'm going," he whispered huskily. "Going."

PRIOR, POKING a curious head around the grill-work, stared in turn. Both attendants—the redheaded Merlin and the blond Prior—were quick and intelligent. Both, utterly uncomprehending, nevertheless used their wits exceptionally quickly and rationally. So far from being at fault for what transpired, they came within an ace of preventing it. But the geography of the San Sylvan's lobby left them almost helpless. The ultra-exclusive apartment hotel towered on the Avenue opposite Central Park. There

Dimples LeSevre went
on with her strip—

—while the crippled man struggled
to withdraw the knife.

were two entrances—the red-canopied one on the Avenue
and the revolving door on the side street. The chromium-
railed staircase down which the old man had run was
across the lobby from the desk and only a few yards from
the propped-open door onto the busy Avenue.

Merlin and Prior realized that he was irrational when he suddenly croaked in a crafty voice: "You may tell my wife I've left."

They both believed that he had no wife. They knew him as a five-year tenant of the building, a reputed multi-millionaire, a quiet little old man who lived with a niece in a sixth-floor suite. And they knew, of course, that he had been dangerously ill for nearly a year.

Prior called hastily: "Mr. Torgenson! Wait—wait a minute!"

"Wait?" his odd, whispering, breathless snarl ripped at them. "For what? For you to torment me for her? No! Not again. No, indeed—you'll never spy on me again, you foul devils. I'm leaving—now!"

The white-faced Merlin gasped under his breath: "Matt—he's gone batty!"

"I know it. You block the revolving door. I'll try and beat him to the oth—"

"And don't deceive yourselves," the old man panted. "Neither of you fooled me for a minute. I was on to you from the start—and I laid my plans carefully. You can't stop me now—not ever!"

Prior tried desperately, as they both eased close to the counter: "I'm sure you did, Mr. Torgenson. It was all a mistake. If you'll let me call Miss Dorinne...."

"Ha! A trick!" He raised a fist to shake it over his head. There was a smooth, pale-blue pasteboard box clutched in his small, red hand. "I know you hate her—that you'd do anything...."

Merlin whispered *"Now!"* and both attendants threw themselves over the counter—but they didn't have a chance.

The old man, fist still on high, was away like a bandy-legged streak, head still over his shoulder, raving at them sobbingly: "No! You'll never catch me again! You—and that hell-cat...!" He tripped on a rug-edge, just a yard ahead of the desperately diving Prior.

"Mr. Torgenson! Hey! For heaven's sake...!"

The old man went stumbling, plunging headlong through the wide door, would have pitched down on his face on the brilliantly lighted, crowded sidewalk, save that he crashed into a knot of pedestrians. The pedestrians were sent spinning one way, the old man bounced crazily off the other, head still peering back over his shoulder, raving shrilly: "Never another penny! Never! It's no use...."

He plowed straight across the sidewalk to slam obliquely into the rear of a parked car, to scramble frantically on around it.

He screeched, "Stop them! Stop them!" as the starch-faced attendants shot from the lobby after him, and clawed himself past the parked car, jumped out into the street.

He was still screeching, "Don't let them get me again.... *Don't...!"* when the speeding taxi hit him.

It caught him with the mudguard and it was going fast. It blasted him, screaming, six feet in the air, a crazy orange jumping-jack, slammed him high up against the rear of the parked car. His head whipcracked on the car's top and the noise was like a bursting paper bag. His mouth was still open squarely in a scream as he pitched off headfore-most into the gutter, blood and brains spattering out around him like a star. He shivered a little while and was still. Then bedlam and hysteria took hold of the street.

Two hours later, a medical examiner's preliminary report revealed that the old man had been dying slowly anyway. He was a diabetic, and the condition was complicated by Bright's disease and a kidney condition. The pasteboard box that he still had clutched in his hand when he was carried into the morgue was—or had been—a freshly opened box of insulin ampules. Since he had been in the habit of administering his own insulin shots, it was fairly obvious that he had miscalculated somewhere and given himself an overdose. Death was recorded as accidental while suffering mental disturbance due to insulin shock, and so entered on police records.

The D.A.'s office received confirmation—insofar as the actual details were concerned—promptly, although the matter was outside its province. One of the D.A.'s investigators, off duty, idly roaming the district, happened to be an onlooker and conceived it wise to write in a report. The investigator was named Rhode. This was on Tuesday.

THE THEATER of Fine Arts had its trouble Thursday. It was a burlesque joint, a pistol-shot from Union Square, currently featuring Dimples LeSevre, premiere stripper of the circuit. There was practically a full house for the eight o'clock show. Nevertheless, it was almost impossible to get witnesses to what happened, partly because of fear of publicity, principally because every eye was on the stage where Dimples was doing her stuff at the time. What the police did get, came almost entirely from a voluble, fat Long Island grocer who sat obliquely behind the crippled man.

The crippled man came in and took his seat before the show started—while the management was still giving away fifty-dollar watches in ten-cent packages of candy. No more could be learned than that he was thin-haired and sandy, wizened, with one pointed ear and that he kept his head down. He was in an aisle seat, halfway back—at the extreme right of the theater—and he had a black topcoat folded in his lap.

He was alone for a while.

The beautifully dressed, thin-hipped man with the black hairline mustache, strolled down the side-aisle halfway through the first act, just at the close of the "Cucumber Factory" blackout. He slid past the cripple and into the vacant seat beside him, did not remove his coat.

Nobody saw them speak to each other.

The show went on for about thirty-five minutes before the third man came in—presumably the third actor in the little drama. He was no more than a dark, muffled figure, even to the garrulous grocer. He came in when the theater was in pitch blackness save for the glow of the spotlight reflected from the powdered, bead-clad, writhing body of Dimples LeSevre, on-stage.

He paused in the aisle, just behind the cripple. The sallow-faced youth in the aisle seat of that row perforce got profanely up, trying to crane hastily around the other, as the topcoat-muffled man edged in sideways.

The muffled man took only one step—and stopped. He looked along the row of seats. They were all full. He bent, peered at his ticket, mumbled something, withdrew and walked up the aisle again and on out of the theater.

Nobody saw the cripple fall, nor saw nor heard anything pertinent, but when the rose-colored lights went up and the orchestra burst forth for the chorus number he was down. He was down on his knees, half in and half out of the aisle, his head almost touching the floor, his coat a pile in front of him, using one hand for a prop while the other clutched frantically and fruitlessly at the black handle of the knife in the middle of his back.

The dapper man beside him saw it first. He glanced down obliquely—and was up on his feet as though galvanized.

After one startled glance, he moved like a flash, clambered swiftly over the prone man, jerking coat lapels up around his throat. He scurried, head bent, up the aisle—and straight into the arms of Rhode, of the D.A.'s office, at the rear of the theater.

Rhode, unknowing what had happened, saw the other's panicky eyes and diving haste and grabbed for him, tried to peer over his shoulder to see what he was running from. "Just a min...."

He saw the cripple just as the stricken man finally got the knife out of his back, dropped it tinkling on the stone flooring and clawed himself madly erect.

His prisoner made a throat sound and dived from under Rhode's clutching hand, scampered for the entrance doors. By the time Rhode had dived after him, recaptured him and whirled the panicky dandy back, the wounded cripple down the aisle had staggered and fallen over against the fire-doors at the side of the house. Before the investigator could make any effective move to stop him, the stabbed man had fallen against the opening-bar of the fire-door and plunged out into the alley. Whirling back against the door from the outside he slammed it closed. His trailing topcoat caught in the latch, and when Rhode's bulk did hit the door, it would not budge. It was jammed tight.

The audience was beginning to stand up. The manager hurried out and Rhode sent the dapper dandy hurtling into his arms, shouted, "Hold him—your office!" and raced round into the alley.

A few drops of fresh, shining blood and the jammed topcoat in the door were all that remained of the cripple. He was gone.

When Rhode shouldered through the cascading audience back into the manager's office, he found he'd drawn a complete blank. The manager was swaying over the desk, blood trickling from his temple, still half-dazed. A small plaster statuette of Gypsy Rose Lee lay in pieces on the floor. The dapper man was gone.

So was Rhode, when the police arrived. He had left for them—in the manager's office—the fat grocer, the knife, the topcoat, and a scribbled reassurance that he, Rhode, had been in position to see that the dapper man had not done the stabbing.

NO ONE suspected any connection up till then, or so much as thought of the one criminal whose name alone, even after eight years, could sting the Marquis to instant murderous rage—Holy Joe Bannon. No one but the amazing opportunist, Rhode.

The theater-stabbing was at nine. At ten he stopped Bleazeby, radio-patrol sergeant, in the Murray Hill district and led him up four flights of stairs in a shabby apartment house, to an open suite.

A thin-lipped, stiff-faced youth with a hairline black mustache and fear-ringed hard little eyes, stood smoking a cigarette in a corner. He had oiled, curly black hair and wore a black coat, knife-edged gray trousers, gleaming black shoes. A raddled, squat-bodied woman of fifty, with wads of brassy blond hair, sat on the edge of an armchair, glazed eyes staring at the carpet. She wore a pink, feather-trimmed wrapper.

The sergeant was a good cop and knew his district. He knew the dapper youth vaguely as a slick article, a "sweet" man—but no charges had ever stood up against him. Once a small lot of jewelry, reported stolen, had been traced to him through a pawnshop, but the charges had been mysteriously withdrawn by the complainant.

"Ha! Blakeney, eh?"

The woman staggered up. "O' coursh, Blakeney," her drunken voice shrilled. "Wanna make someth'n of...."

The sergeant's eyes were sour. "And you're this Queenie Day he's hangin' out with now?"

The woman tried to draw herself up with dignity, tottered and collapsed in the chair. "Sher'n'ly. Queenie Day—queen've shlack wire. Internash—internass—known all over th' worl'."

Rhode said dully: "Sergeant—this is the man who was in the Fine Arts Theater tonight, sitting beside the man who was stabbed."

The sergeant's interest roused. "Yeah? Well, well. Maybe I better take 'em both over to the station-house, huh?"

The white-faced dandy said: "Give me a break, Sergeant. I've told this guy what happened. Somebody sent me a ticket to the burlesque house—nothing else in the envelope. Then he called this afternoon and asked me if I wanted to make a lot of money. Naturally I said yes and he told me to use the ticket. When I sat down beside him in the show, he asked if I was Blakeney and when I said I was he said to follow him out in the alley when he went. Then when I see him keel over—hell, I don't want to get dragged into no—into any station-house, so I dust. I don't know what I'm into. I never saw the guy before—haven't seen him yet, for that matter. I don't know what it's all about."

"Maybe you'll remember over at the precinct."

"I swear I don't know a thing."

"We give a memory-course in ten easy lessons over at the station-house."

The fat woman's muddy face came up blearily, worriedly. "Shta—station-house? I ain't going any station-house! I can't!" Two big tears suddenly muddied her mascara and she tried vainly to get out of the chair, sobbing shrilly: "No, no! Can't go—mourning—m' husband. Died lash Tuesday. Dear devoted husban'—died—can't go...."

"That's a hot one," the sergeant growled.

"Torgenson—dear Charlie—m' husban' th' old skinflint. Dies lash Tuesday."

"Huh?"

"That's right," the dapper youth said quickly. "She used to be married to the old guy that was knocked off by that cab up in front of the San Sylvan day before yesterday—Torgenson, the chemist."

STATION-HOUSE OR no station-house, that was all the precinct police got. Not another ounce of information could they wangle. When it came to doping out a charge for the gigolo, Blakeney, they looked round for Rhode, but he had disappeared. By then howls were going up—the raddled old Queenie Day hadn't been drunk enough to forget a lawyer—and enthusiasm fizzled out to a trickle and evaporated.

No one saw any reason to notify the Marquis.

Except Rhode.

CHAPTER TWO

THE D.A.'S MAN

WITHIN TWO hours, the D.A.'s man was at the door of the Marquis' apartment, looking into the green-and-oak living-room. He was a big man, solid, with a big cheerful face, ruddy and glowing with health, his bright-red lips and twinkling brown eyes lending him an electric appearance. He was nicely tailored in three shades of brown and a diamond twinkled on the plump, nimble hand that held his brown hat.

He said quickly: "My name's Rhode. I have some information which I hear means a lot to you. I'd like to talk it over."

The Marquis' round, red-cheeked face was curious, his deep-set, China-blue eyes quizzical. He put small, broken-knuckled hands in the pockets of his wine-silk dressing-gown and, after a minute, said, "Why not?" and stood aside to let the big man in.

"I won't quibble or beat around the bush with you," Rhode said from an armchair. "In a year and a half in New York, I've done certain people a lot of harm. And I've done certain people a lot of good. I've done myself nothing at all—and I may not get the opportunity to be in New York again."

"And…?"

"I got this information by pure luck. I know it means plenty to you. But it's only an opening to a real, cold-turkey discussion. Mr. Marquis, I can hurt you. Maybe I can ruin you. I don't want to do anything of the sort. I'm not a fool and I think I know an opportunity for both of us when I see it. I want to do business with you."

There was vaguely puzzled light in the Marquis' eyes. "Suppose we start with this information."

The twinkling eye almost closed for a minute. Then Rhode said: "I'm full of information—but the important part will have to keep till we thresh out our business. I'll give you this as a starter, though. You had a murder in your district two days ago. It was passed off as an accident. I can prove it was murder. Maybe I can give you the solution—or point you to it, as well."

Vaguely startled light came in the Marquis' eyes. Hastily he searched his mental file—and inevitably fastened on the death of the chemist at the San Sylvan. "You mean Torgenson?"

"Who else? It was a sketchy, trust-to-God sort of murder, but somebody wanted to hurry up that old man's death. The insulin ampules that he had in his hand—a fresh box supposedly just sent up from the druggist in the building—were not ordinary strength. They were concentrated and they were bound to give him insulin shock when he took them. In his condition, almost anything that happened would be a fair bet to finish him."

"How do you know about the ampules?"

"I got the crushed pasteboard box they were in from the morgue. I had a chemist friend analyze them. That's what he found."

For a minute, the Marquis' eyes were intent and curious. He opened his mouth to speak—and the phone on the refectory table rang sharply. He said, "Excuse me," and walked over and picked it up.

The excited voice of McGuire, the camera-eye of the Broadway Squad said quickly: "Hey—Johnny and I are in the bedroom. We came up right behind that guy but when I saw him we ducked in your back door. Do you know who he is?"

"No," the Marquis said.

"Rhode," the redhead said. "The D.A.'s prize investigator. And he's dynamite. Maney brought him down from Boston a year and a half ago in the magistrates' court investigation. He's supposed to have nosed out all the dope on that, and on the two supreme-court judges—and three district leaders. If Maney's set him to get something on us, it means the D.A.'s after us in dead earnest."

"I don't think so."

"Well, for God's sake look out! I tell you the guy is good. He was a police chief in a jerkwater town in Massachusetts, till he cracked some big ones and got nationally famous. Then he went to Boston and opened a private agency—a crackerjack. He had to be good and have an A-number-one rep for Maney to bring him in. I just got a line on him a couple of days ago. I meant to tell you, but he didn't seem to be after us and I forgot."

"O.K. Keep your ears open."

The Marquis hung up and said: "What made you interested enough in Torgenson's death to dig up that box of ampules, Mr. Rhode?"

The big man had settled himself, stretched heels toward the fireplace, crossed his legs. "I happened to run into a little episode tonight down near the club where I'm staying," he said, "but I'm afraid that will have to come second. You'll let me keep you in suspense for three minutes while I talk about my own affairs?"

After a minute, the Marquis said: "If I have to."

THE BIG man nodded seriously. He suddenly leaned forward in his chair and the twinkle in his eyes was replaced by a cold, direct light. "Mr. Marquis, you don't know who I am—but I know the crime business just about as well as you do. I've put in thirty years at it. I've got a national reputation. And I don't fear any man on earth."

"I know who you are," the Marquis said impatiently. "That you work for Maney and so forth."

The big man blinked rapidly but he refused to be disconcerted. "Then you know what I've done," he went on earnestly. "You know I've pulled down some of the people in this town that were considered untouchable. You know I've made Maney a national figure."

"And?"

"Maybe you don't know that I very nearly have *carte blanche* in that office. He's given me a list of possible things to look into. You're on that list—you and your Broadway Squad."

"I'm always on those damned lists. It doesn't mean anything."

"It does if I choose to go after you. I know all about you, Marquis—and I know I can find something to hang on you—maybe hang you on. I've got all the patience in the world, I promise you—and I have a rough idea of the fortune you and your bunch of thugs take out of your district every year. You've got your system running pretty well—your blackjack-all-but-the-petty-chiselers-out-of-town-and-keep-the-pickings-for-yourselves system. But if I can't find a hole in it somewhere, then I'm not the man Maney thinks I am."

"You're completely off your head—but go on and get it over with," the Marquis said.

"There isn't much more to it. I've worked all my life—hard. I've played for a reputation for being straight, because I thought it was smart. It was. But it hasn't got me much in the bank. I've been waiting for my opportunity—and it's here now. Don't interrupt.

"As I say, I can ruin you, I'm quite sure. Or I can leave you alone—in which case Maney will still have you on the books and you'll at least be pestered constantly as long as he's in office. But there's a third course—one that ought to be worth plenty to you. I can investigate you, whitewash you, give you what will amount to an ace-high standing with Maney—all without interfering for a minute with your affairs."

The Marquis' eyes were incredulous, puzzled. "And…?"

"In return I want your cooperation."

"In what, for God's sake?"

"I've certain friends in Boston. I want to bring them in—with assurance of protection from you for six months. There are certain angles that you haven't allowed to operate in the district the past few years…."

The Marquis exploded. "My God, man, you're utterly mad!"

"Am I? Marquis, listen to me. For the first time in my life I see a chance to clean up for my old age. I'm not going to fool around. If you don't want to let me cash in as I just suggested—then pay me off."

"For this whitewash-investigation?"

"Exactly. But I'll come high. It'll cost you about six months of your take—but you'll get your money's worth. Think it over. Because if you stand me off, by the living Judas, I promise you that there isn't going to be any more take for you—ever! I'll go after you and I'll keep after you till I get you. With Maney behind me, with the political party that backed you hanging on the ropes, with the courts on my side, you're against a tougher rap than you ever were before. On the other hand, at my price, you're aces with the D.A. and you go right on with your present set-up. The price, in cash, is fifty thousand dollars and I mean exactly that."

IT WAS a minute before the Marquis could speak. Then he said weakly: "I've heard some propositions in my time, but that takes the all-time high." He hesitated a long minute. "I don't suppose you'll even begin to understand this, but I'll try and set you straight. We're cops, not crooks. We make a little white money here and there—but this fortune you've got in your mind is madness. You can hear anything—anything at all—about the Broadway Squad if you ask enough people. There are more fairy stories about us than any other squad on the force. But we're just cops like anybody else, except that maybe we have to use our own technique on our own problems.

"We're on the outs with the rest of the force because they can't see that—and maybe because some of them believe this fantastic tale you seem to have swallowed. But you're all wrong, Rhode—all wrong. You're so damned wrong that I'm afraid there isn't a chance of your getting right. So the answer just has to be—no. We've survived other investigations and maybe we can survive yours. But as for your proposition—take it away."

The investigator's face was flushed, his thin eyes flinty. "Yeah? Information and all, eh?"

"I'll pay you for the information on Torg...."

"I don't want small change. But—with the proposition—there's more. It might let you put your hands on a certain party connected with it. A certain party that I hear you want—like you want to breathe."

"Who?"

Rhode's eyes were thin and greedy. "There was once a little redheaded girl newspaper reporter, who had a Broadway cop for a friend. He suggested that she write up a certain tricky racketeer who was operating a hole-in-the-wall mission in Pell Street, with a coast-to-coast broadcast every Sunday that brought him a fortune in the mail. She practically cut the racket out from under him, and her body was found hacked to pieces in the East River—and

the racketeer got off on a phony insanity plea and escaped…
one Joe Bannon….”

The jolt—even after eight years—was like being hit by
a sledge-hammer in the dark. The Marquis was suddenly
on his feet, his face pinched and livid. He was suddenly
standing over the investigator, deep-set eyes blazing
bluely—so suddenly that a gun jumped into the startled
Rhode’s hand.

“If you’ve news of Bannon, mister—out with it—fast!”
he said chalkily. “And don’t pull guns on me. Your proposition’s cold. But I’ll pay anything in reason—for Joe
Bannon.”

The investigator’s jaw was set, his face dark. “I said the
information goes with the deal. And don’t think I haven’t
got it. I learned plenty tonight. Your friend Bannon is here
to kill—he’s got some mysterious racket—some big
racket….” He jumped up, kicking the chair away from
him. “Keep away from me, Marquis! If you want what I
know….” He backed a step further—right between the
rigid forms of McGuire and big Johnny Berthold.

He gasped, his big head whipping back and forth. Big
Johnny’s huge hand smacked down on the gun, wrenched
cruelly—and almost brought the investigator to his knees
before the gun came free.

“We don’t pull guns on the Marquis,” the redheaded
McGuire said.

Big Johnny flung the gun in a corner, snatched the
purple-faced investigator’s tie, whirled him round, chest
to chest. He yelled: “Who the hell do you think you
are—coming in here and waving guns at the chief?”

“Yeah—you big hick!” McGuire took up the chorus.

“I oughta sock you one!” Big Johnny roared.

"Or maybe make a charge against you!" McGuire hammered.

Snarling, yelling in his face, they shouted him, step by step, across the room, their chests tight to his, never letting his apoplectic gasps form words, blasting a steady stream of invective at the top of their lungs—till the big man backed into the wall with a thud that shook the room.

Twice, the Marquis opened his mouth—and twice closed it, his eyes hollow.

"You ———— ————— thugs!" Rhode finally gasped out—and his hair almost lifted from his scalp at big Johnny's: *"What!"*

Casually, McGuire wandered away, while the shaggy giant renewed his yelling, still holding the struggling, gulping investigator by the tie.

"Of all the damned nerve! Calmly walk in here and shoot your ———— ————— face off about...."

McGuire hooked a hip on the table just inside the door, fingered his take. There were a number of papers, a black leather wallet, even the investigator's small, shiny badge. Carefully, one by one, he examined them, while the roaring Johnny wrestled the investigator, now clawing at the tightening tie to swing him around so that his back was to the redhead.

McGUIRE EMPTIED the wallet, went through half the folded papers—and was suddenly on his feet. Across the room, he met the Marquis' eyes as he slipped swiftly to the bedroom door and through it.

Somehow, big Johnny sustained the uproar for the minutes the redhead was inside. Then McGuire came out, a sheet of white paper in his hand, tucking a pencil in his pocket. He went over and tossed the slip he had taken in with him on top of the investigator's other belongings.

The Marquis said: "All right, Johnny. I think Mr. Rhode understands."

McGuire walked over and stood by the fireplace, his hands behind him. "I hope he does."

The purple-faced Rhode straightened his tie. "Damn you, Marquis! You don't think this is going to get you anywhere? I'll build a fire under you that will smoke you right out of town! And as for the information—you can whistle for it." He clenched his teeth but he could not resist a tormented, bitter: "I'll give you one more chance. Play with me...."

"It's cold," the Marquis said.

"You know what you're asking for?" Rhode almost sobbed.

"Go back to Kokomo," big Johnny snarled at him.

Rhode's teeth snapped and there was the rage of disappointment in his eyes. "All right." He went over and snatched up his gun from the corner, jammed it in his pocket, walked to the door. He yanked the door viciously open and through tight jaws said, "If I never pull another—" and his eye fell on the table-top.

He almost strangled. His Adam's apple did wild contortions and his face turned maroon. His diamond-twinkling hand finally snatched out, crushed the lot from his pockets together. He swallowed a last furious "———— ————————— you!" and slammed the door.

McGuire's excited voice said: "He had it, Marty. He had it."

"Smart or not," big Johnny drawled, "his hair's still full of haysee...."

"Shut up. He had a description of Holy Joe Bannon in his pocket. It was in Pop Lee's handwriting, so I just called Pop at the "I" Bureau. Pop had identified a thumbprint on a note Rhode brought him as Holy Joe's. He read me the note from the photostat he took. Then I called Campbell and between shuttling back and forth between the two of them—Rhode seems to have popped off plenty to Campbell—I got the whole story. Listen—

"Last Thursday Rhode saw old Torgenson die. The old man was raving about his wife. Nobody thought he had a wife. Out of curiosity Rhode nosed around and found he'd had one he divorced ten years ago—a Queenie Day, a circus performer. About the time Rhode locates her, she's passing dough to a slick-looking guy named Blakeney. He's her gig, but Rhode doesn't know that. He has a hunch he's onto something and he trails along trying to get a line on this gig.

"Tonight, the gig goes to a burlesque show. He sits down beside a cripple and he's trying to talk to him. Presently somebody comes along and stabs the cripple—only the cripple makes a getaway—doesn't die on the premises. So does the killer and so does this gig—Blakeney. Only the cripple loses his coat. Rhode gets it and finds a note in the lining—this note, written by Joe Bannon, some time back, evidently to the cripple. Here it is. Listen—

"Dear Al:

"Be patient. The big killing has to wait till this Torgenson dies. He's damn near dead right now and it's madness to try to hurry it up. There's no sense in your coming on here now. Once the old man dies, I'll make the ten-strike, never worry. But get it into your head that this is a big play and a delicate play. We have to hit it exactly right, attend to these certain parties—and get clear, fast. For God's sake, keep patient! (Signed) Joe."

THE MARQUIS' face was like lead. McGuire hurried on excitedly: "See? Bannon is here to pull some big killing—or killings. He can't start until old Torgenson dies. Now he's away. Maybe the cripple at the burlesque show was supposed to be the first—"

"Come to think of it," big Johnny said, "maybe he changed his mind and did hurry up that Torgenson killing. Rhode said it was mur—"

"Call up the M.E.," the Marquis said. "Tell him to hold Torgenson's body. Unless he's been wised up, just say it's a favor to me. We'll get what start we can on the homicide squad."

McGuire jumped to the phone.

"Call the boys," the Marquis said when that call was finished. "Get the word around that Bannon is in town— and that I want him. I'll pay anything. Did the M.E. have any suspicion that the old man's death wasn't accidental?"

"No. Rhode must have held out on him."

"Well—get those calls out."

CHAPTER THREE

DRAGNET

BY MORNING the net was spread and the most urgent alarm the Marquis had ever sent out was having its effect. With no charge whatever against the gaunt-faced ex-evangelist, stoolpigeons and informers in every section of the city were being threatened, beaten, bribed, hammered at. Even those police officers not normally addicted to doing anything for the Marquis were not deaf to the announcement that he "would pay anything" and the web tightened over the city.

Evidently Rhode did not think it expedient to report tardily the things he had discovered. There was no whisper through the morning that Holy Joe Bannon was in any way connected with the "accidental" death of the millionaire Torgenson.

The Marquis, his head in unfamiliar turmoil, sat in his apartment trying to get eight-year-old pictures out of his mind. Pictures of the pert, boyish little redhead, Nan Ames, with her quick charming smile, and a trick of twiddling her fingers good-bye. There'd been no love affair—just a deep, exhilarating friendship that had grown for two years up to the fatal night when he had suggested she write up Holy Joe Bannon and his odorous Pell Street mission.

Pictures of the gaunt, starch-faced, hoarse-voiced pseudo-evangelist—of his cramped, dismal little hole-in-the-wall on Pell Street, with its meager kitchen and dormitory, its racks of dog-eared magazines and games—and its all-important microphone. Pictures of the merciless printed estimates that the little redhead had made of the golden stream that flowed from that microphone into the greedy hands of the racketeer, and out again to the gambling-joints, the dream-sellers, the Harlem hotspots.

Nightmare pictures of that last Sunday night—the gaunt, fanatical looking Bannon thundering hoarsely from the pulpit, his long, skinny arms upraised above his husky black hair, his wild little eyes gleaming blackly in his long, doughy face—and his eyes jerking down to little Nan Ames sitting with her pretty legs crossed in an otherwise empty rear pew—the last picture the Marquis had of her alive.

Her body—white, trim, lovely—stretched on a slab in the morgue, almost cut to pieces, seaweed in her glorious hair. The frantic ill-luck that had put two inspectors in the Harlem tenement to pull the Marquis away from the half-throttled murderer and, hence, the trial.

Bannon in the dock—the terrible shrewdness that gradually became apparent behind every one of his wildly blurted outbursts about divine voices and visions. His never-ceasing, wary scrutiny of the Marquis from the corner of one eye. The high-priced mouthpiece with his sonorous, infuriating pleas and, finally, the stunning verdict of temporary insanity and the subsequent disappearance from the Tombs, around which the entire Broadway Squad was grimly stationed, of Holy Joe Bannon.

The Marquis paced the apartment in a fever, forced his mind to race over the mystery behind which Bannon was now hiding.

McGUIRE BROUGHT in the whole dossier of the dead Torgenson early in the afternoon, summarized it for the Marquis.

"Nobody knows where he came from before he was clerking in that Times Square drug store. That was twenty years ago. Then he figured out this coal-tar dye and sold it on a royalty basis to a big company and started getting rich. He was married to this Queenie Day then, and stayed that way for ten years more. He made a settlement on her and she has no legal claim to any part of his estate, because he made a will—four years ago—giving his niece every-thing. The niece is his dead brother's daughter and a little sweetheart, if you ask me. She came to live with him about six years ago.

"Torgenson was a chess player till he got so sick and had to go to bed. Apparently he never left New York, except once—four years ago—when he went away for six months and didn't tell the niece where he was going. He was in touch with his lawyer, Howard Dusk, all the time, however—according to Dusk, was just on a pleasure trip through the West. I tried to make something of it but it doesn't seem to jell. And apart from that, there isn't a damn thing to fasten to."

"Howard Dusk is his lawyer?"

"Yeah. And the niece's too—guardian, trustee, executor of the will—everything. He handled most of the old man's financial affairs the last couple years. But you've got Dusk wrong, Marty. He's tough, but he isn't a thief."

"I wouldn't trust him any farther than I could throw him. He was born in the same block on Avenue A that I was."

McGuire looked helpless.

"What about the ex-wife?"

"Nothing about her. She's just traveled around, spending the dough he gave her in keeping stewed and getting young gigolos. This Blakeney is just that—a gigolo." He hesitated, his forehead wrinkled. "What do you make of it, Marty? You see anything?"

"Not yet. I've got more hope of finding Bannon through a stoolpigeon than in trying to figure out what he's doing."

Amazingly enough, they did just that, within twenty-four hours.

There were two false alarms. Two detectives in a waterfront precinct cornered and slugged down a dock rat who bore a fair resemblance to the gaunt-faced Bannon. A fast car raced the Marquis through the city in nothing flat—to the bitter disappointment of mistaken identity.

Just after nightfall, a city fireman fancied he recognized a body in a Chelsea fire as that of the former evangelist. When the Marquis reached the scene it was discovered that the charred corpse had a glass eye.

Then, at midnight, a detective in an uptown precinct rang in excitedly and fate took another sardonic jab at the Marquis.

"In Sevens Richardson's gambling joint," the detective told him hastily. "I saw him through a crack in the office door. I'm sure, Marty. I didn't tip my hand. I couldn't jug him and my skipper wouldn't give me any medals for helping you. I thought I'd better leave it up to—"

"Where is Sevens' joint now?"

"Same old place. The Tolliver Hotel, down on lower Madison. He's got half the third floor. What used to be a private ballroom and a few rooms off it."

THE MARQUIS saw the lookout in the shadows when he sailed into the sagging, broken-tiled lobby of the old hotel, saw him slip furtively around behind the elevator bank, but he didn't care about that.

He did not even bother with the elevators. There was an ancient, lazy-tong type of gate stretched across the stairs just above ground-floor level. The Marquis swung around it, over the banister, and ran on up. In the third-floor hall a broken-nosed pug with a cauliflower ear, wearing a dinner jacket, popped out of a doorway. "Hey buddy—just a min—" he gulped. "Oh—uh—hello, Marty."

"Open up, Pants—it's no raid, but you'll think the building's falling down if you stall me."

The suddenly sweating pug ran a finger inside his collar and his mournful eyes were tortured. "Uh—yeah, Marty. Sure."

He swayed from one leg to the other, finally waddled unhappily to a door down the hall, tapped in cadence and the Marquis stepped through into the lush, gray-satin-walled former ballroom.

His eyes went across the humming, dim little layout, beyond the three busy crap tables to the closed door of Richardson's office. He paid no attention to the uneasy eyes of the employees who saw him, but strode quickly around the crowds that packed the tables and grabbed the doorknob in one small, black-gloved hand, rattled it.

When the tall, languid albino opened the door, the Marquis marched almost into him, forced him to fall back and swung the door closed behind him. He put his hands in his tight Chesterfield pockets and said: "All right, Sevens. I won't kill you as long as you tell me where he is."

For all the gambler's amazing poker face—he looked no more than eighteen, with silky, honey-colored hair, a pinkish complexion and pink eyes with white lashes, fluttery white hands—some of his color went. "Make it clearer, Marty."

"Holy Joe Bannon. And I'll give you one minute to produce him." He looked swiftly around the office at the maroon rug, walnut furniture, filing-cabinets, flat-topped desk—at the small, green-metal lock-box on the desk.

"Marty, I give you my word, I haven't seen Bannon in years."

A little white corner of paper hung out of the closed, but not locked, green-metal box. The Marquis' eye was caught, only vaguely, by the white corner, but the gambler was evidently too jittery to realize that. He started to edge silkily toward the box, and that *did* rivet the Marquis' attention.

"I heard he was in Europe—" the gambler began.

The Marquis caught the panicky move, grunted and stepped forward, drove a shoulder into the languid gambler's chest and sent him stumbling. He snatched at the white paper curiously. Then was when the gods gave him his break.

It was a small slip, bearing a handwritten—*I.O.U. $500—J. Bannon.*

There was a flush on the Marquis' forehead as he faced the sweating gambler. He said softly: "Now, Sevens—you were saying?"

The gambler took a handkerchief from his sleeve, drew it across his forehead. His pink, moist-looking face had no expression nor his pink rabbit-eyes. He said hoarsely: "All right, Marty. He's been in a—a couple of times lately. Yesterday—and today. I swear to God that's all I know."

The Marquis' China-blue eyes were flint. "Yet you extend him credit when you know I want him."

The other swallowed desperately. "Marty—give me a break. I'm running in the red here. There's some motor guys from Detroit that have been taking me for two weeks. Bannon came in with a roll that would choke a horse and I—well, I needed the money and I took a chance. When— when he went broke, I would of turned him in—"

"Where is he, Sevens?"

"On the level, I don't know."

"When will he be back—assuming you don't cross me?"

"He—he said tomorrow night."

THE MARQUIS stared at the effete-looking gambler, recalling that he had once moved him out of the Broadway district as too deadly.

"It doesn't go," he said grimly. "Where do I get him now?"

The albino licked his lips. "I swear to God, Marty—I don't know. But he'll come tomorrow. I'm into him for thousands. I'll guarantee—"

"Get your hat, louse."

"Marty—for God's sake—then he *will* hear about your being here and *won't* come back. I know how you want him. I admit I was dumb to cover him—but I'm leveling now. I swear you'll get him tomorrow night—here. I'll turn him in to you—I swear it!"

The Marquis' teeth showed between his vermilion lips. He started to speak, stopped, clamped his jaw.

"You can take me," the albino pleaded, "but you'll miss him—for sure. Use your head, Marty. I'm the only guy in New York he trusts. If you scare him away now, we both lose."

The Marquis' teeth set. "All right," he decided finally. "I'll give you till then—then big Johnny takes you into a room."

The sweating gambler gulped. "Marty—listen—if he finds out about you being here, of course, he won't—"

"Never mind welshing. That's up to you. I'll go out your icebox door, wherever it is. Nobody but your employees noticed me come in and you can handle them. This is your one chance of being able to walk the rest of your life, so don't flub it."

"So help me," the gambler blurted earnestly, "I'll do what I can. Put—put one of your guys near here and give me the phone number. Not too near, because Joe's no fool. If he comes in before, I'll flash you the office fast. I swear it."

"I ought to kill you just on principle."

The gambler plucked at his collar. "Give me a chance, Marty." He stepped over shakily to the filing-cases, swung them aside and opened a panel-door onto a flight of fire-stairs. "I'm not mad, Marty. I know how my bread's buttered. I'm not likely to cross you."

In the doorway the Marquis still stood, tormented by indecision. "Not unless you thought you could get away with it. Don't think so, that's all."

He went down the stairs, still wondering if he'd done the right thing, brain-stormed by the tearing urge to buy anything to get Joe Bannon in his hands.

And within a block of the shabby hotel he saw the murderous ex-evangelist!

THE FIRE-STAIRS from Sevens' office led down to a landing, dividing into two final flights. The Marquis chose the left-hand service stairway, which led him down through the kitchens and out into the alley. He had walked to the street, walked half a block to the nearest cigar store, intending to phone McGuire to tell the redhead to post himself nearby—or in the hotel—in the rare event of a hurry call from Sevens Richardson. He had one foot in the entrance of the store when a man hurried out of a watchmaker's cubicle on the opposite side of the street, strode quickly across—and vanished into the row of store-fronts. Just as he vanished light fell across his gaunt face under its wide hat brim—and the Marquis went on fire.

Instantly, he was running, blood pounding in his ears, hand diving for the gun on his hip.

He raced past wondering eyes, slid to a stumbling stop at the place where the gaunt man had disappeared—and found himself staring down one of New York's rare street-to-street alleys through into the next block.

The alley was fully lighted from blazing store-fronts along the street at the opposite end and for a feverish second the Marquis thought he had made a mistake. There was not a soul in the alley or any moving thing. He started in, pulled back, hot eyes flashing around him for some other avenue down which Bannon might have escaped.

In one long rush, headlights blazed alight, a car roared forward somewhere midway the alley, rolled out and pounded away from him, heading the other way, evidently from an invisible parking-space somewhere along the little artery.

SOME GLIMMERING of sanity caught the raving Marquis just as he jerked the gun up to fire. The agonizing realization struck him that he could *not* fire at a man not wanted for anything—even Bannon—here in the heart of the city, in reach of a score of witnesses. Not without giving the reform prosecutor, Maney, undreamed of ammunition for ruining him and his squad.

He held his fire just in time and his eyes tried for the license number. He couldn't catch it, but in the instant the vanishing car turned and bumped down the curb into the next street, he identified it as a three- or four-year-old Buick.

He whirled back, groaning, flying back toward his own parked convertible near the hotel, white-hot prayer in his heart that he would get a break. The Buick was turning over toward Fifth Avenue... Maybe....

He dove into his own car, kicked it to life and sent it spinning down the street, paralleling the Buick's course. He raced it through the gears to the first corner, took the corner on two wheels, driving for the street below and, before he could even attempt to tread on the brakes, the Buick shot directly past him, going uptown on Fifth Avenue, the gaunt-faced evangelist crouched over the wheel of the speeding car.

The Marquis jammed down on the brakes, squealing the tires, spun the wheel as soon as he dared, got tangled maddeningly in traffic, finally was pounding up Fifth far in the wake of the vanishing Buick.

Only prayer kept him from losing his quarry on the chase up Fifth. The old Buick still had plenty of power and the devil himself contrived the traffic snarls. Four times, between Twenty-third and a Hundred and Tenth, the Marquis was held up while the other car scooted away from within a block of him—and then the Buick ducked into the Park. It was sheer luck that the Marquis saw that, for Bannon was two full blocks ahead.

As he spun, in turn, into the curving dark roadway, the Marquis had a sudden scare that someone was chasing *him,* and for the time that it took to get through the Park, up Central Park West to a Hundred and Twenty-fifth Street, his attention was divided between trying to make certain of that, and keeping the Buick in sight ahead. If he drove the gaunt-faced evangelist to the curb, there could be only one possible upshot. The murderous Bannon would never surrender to the Marquis—not alive. And the Marquis did not want him dead. He had to hold back, agonizing and sweating, while he tried vainly and desperately to determine whether or not he actually did have a tail. Naturally, he had a fleeting thought of Maney, and the prosecutor's new imported bloodhound Rhode, but when the Buick plunged into Harlem he found himself finally with no one behind him and cursed himself for his worries.

The Buick nearly ran away from him up Lenox, was far enough ahead when it turned off so that he did not know into which cross-street it *had* gone, and he coasted right by.

Not till he had circled an entire block did he finally relocate the Buick, parked almost directly before a tall, dingy tenement, but of the gaunt man there was no sign. A service alley led to the rear of the dingy building and, after a swift moment's survey as he coasted by, the Marquis parked his own car, got out and hurried around. No lights save a perpendicular string of hall-lamps were visible from the little court behind the building—the court that also served the building facing on the street above, and he hurried back to the front.

He looked up. Only one window in the whole building-front glowed—a shaded casement on the fifth floor.

He wasted three minutes in tight, sweating indecision before he tried the front door. It was locked and no light burned inside, but there was a dim glow, presumably from the hall-lights higher up.

He was shaky with eagerness, and jittery with fear that something might, even yet, snatch Bannon from him. He vacillated between the front and the rear of the building, unable to decide either to go in, or to wait outside.

Once he heard something bang faintly, far up in the building, but it was too modest a sound to whet his curiosity.

CHAPTER FOUR
HOLY JOE

IT WAS nearly ten minutes before pounding impatience drove the Marquis into the building, via a picklock on the front door, and he stood in the dank, filthy odors of the darkened ground-floor hall. He heard no sound.

He went soundlessly up the worn wooden stairs. Nothing stirred on any floor. Then, at last, he was in front of the door under which the crack of light shone. Service gun in one small, black-gloved hand, he turned the knob slowly, with infinite care.

The first of the cruel payoff came when the door opened easily under his hand. It was so unexpected that he almost stumbled into the apartment. He caught himself, hastily cocked the gun, stepped on in and threw himself aside, low, let the door close itself.

Fever grew in his eyes.

There was death in the shabby, scantily furnished living-room. A single fly-specked bulb hung from the ceiling, gave sick yellow light. On a couch in the corner lay a wizened little man, on his face, hands and feet roped behind him, naked to the waist. An ugly-looking, swollen, black knife-wound was halfway between his shoulders. A dirty, blood-soaked bandage with tips of adhesive lay on the floor by the couch. His clothes were in a heap. There were thin blue bruise-lines around the lips of the wound as though someone had laid on with a whip. The man's wizened little face was contorted in agony.

The Marquis jumped quickly to the couch, ripped off a glove to feel for pulse. There was no pulse. But the body was still warm. Bending over, he saw the curtain-rod that had been used to beat the dead man's back—and he saw the mechanical brace on the dead man's leg.

He caught his breath, jabbed a hand hastily into the inside pocket of the crumpled coat on the floor—and had a handful of papers. Quickly, he jerked them out, glanced at them—and knew that at least he had something. This was the "Al" of Bannon's long-ago letter—the cripple of the Fine Arts stabbing.

A sound from the rear jerked his head up. He crammed the papers in his pocket for future examination.

A door at the rear of the room whined open and Holy Joe Bannon, gaunt in a black shirt, his wild bushy hair awry, stood spraddled in the doorway, swaying. One hand held a square black pistol pointed at the floor. His mouth was working soundlessly, his face a mask of cuts and welts and one arm hung limp at his side. His black eyes were pin-points of daze—and then of terrified recognition. He tried vainly to raise the gun. His breath whistled as he croaked, almost in a whisper, "You!" and fell back into the bedroom as the Marquis sprang.

There was no control, no rationality in his pounding head, other than mechanical realization that the gaunt-faced evangelist was powerless to shoot and that he had him trapped at last. Eight years of fury sent fire surging through his blood. He was a diving streak as he plunged after the moaning, terrified man.

The bedroom was dark and he lost a split second before he saw Bannon fumbling at the hall door. Even as he leaped for him, the door became a square of light and Bannon fell out—just as the Marquis' furious blow caught him at the back of the head.

He was flung, stumbling, across into the banister and for a second is seemed he would topple over. The Marquis dived, yanked him back by the coat-collar, spun him around upright and let his cocked right explode in his face.

"Try and remember Nan Ames, you scum...."

It nearly tore Bannon's head from his shoulders, sailed him backwards to crash into the fire-door—and the Marquis, his teeth bared, leaped after, lifting an upper-cut from the floor.

Only it didn't work that way.

Something was wrong with the fire-door's latch. Bannon slammed against it—and it whipped open like paper. It did not even check the gaunt man's frantic heel-stagger. He went through it as though it were not there, a terrified scream on his lips, tried crazily to twist himself as he was flung, arched backwards, over the fire-escape railing, clawing frantically.

FOR AN instant the murderous haze in the Marquis' brain gave way to a flash of alarm. Wildly he leaped, grabbing—and the evangelist's feet flew up in his face. He could not clutch them. The murderer screamed, went hurtling over, slamming down on the fire-escape railing below, bouncing off, one whimpering sob bursting from him as he hit the second railing, making it whang like a guitar string. He bounced off, crashed on still a third, finally slammed down with a terrific metallic *bong*—and there was silence.

The red haze evaporated from the Marquis' brain and he was instantly crouched, frozen.

It was then he saw Rhode.

Not for a fraction of an instant did he have the slightest doubt as to the identity of the man in the courtyard—despite the five stories that separated them. The shaft of light from the open fire-door behind the Marquis fell aslant on the big, crouched, brown-clad body and upturned pink face and, in the instant that the man below drew in breath sharply and whipped out blue metal, the flash of the diamond on his hand twinkled—and realization of the terrible pitfall in which he was trapped crawled in the Marquis' heart. He leaped backwards into the hall, yanking the door with him.

Murder!

He was facing a charge of murder without the faintest shadow of a doubt, if the sharp-eyed D.A.'s investigator below had recognized him. And burning recollection of the car he had fancied seeing following him on the way up here jumped back into his mind.

Recognized him? Rhode had followed him here, prowled around waiting for him! There was not a bit of doubt of that. Even in the fraction of a second that all this whipped through the Marquis' mind, the tenement below him started to stir to life.

A fresh stab of fear sent him scuttling for the stairs. At best, he had fallen into danger of a kind that made his head swim, but if so much as one person in the tenement were to recognize him, he was done for. As he stood, he was poised on the edge of disaster. With one confirming witness to add evidence to that of the big investigator below, he was *over* the edge!

In something approaching panic the Marquis raced downward through the building, plunged for the front door—and almost broke his neck stopping short as he heard the glass being kicked in. He turned and raced down the long corridor toward a door at the rear of the hall.

By a miracle it was unlocked and he plunged through, was halfway across the court, when he remembered his car parked in front. It was almost as dangerous as confirming witnesses—or was it?

His burning brain suddenly saw one gasp of hope and he ran on.

Getting around the building in the rear was no problem. There was a delivery alley debouching into the court and he raced silently along it, out into a deserted street.

He had to force himself to a walk, with ice tapping at his spine, till he reached Lenox, and the sleeping driver of a parked taxi. Deliberately, he knocked his imported hard hat into a shapeless blob as he ran up, turned the collar of his Chesterfield up around his face and growled, at the abruptly awakened driver: "Over to Broadway, in a hurry."

HE STARTED to breathe easily again as the cab whirled him out of the district—just as the first police siren cut through the night, blocks distant. But the knife of fear in his chest was not withdrawn till he had dropped from the cab in the shadow of trees near Columbia University, huddled there till the dismissed cab bowled away over the hill, then found a phone in a dingy, apparently untenanted all-night drugstore where he called McGuire.

His round face was stiff and lined as he made another call to report his car stolen. Then there was a ten-minute wait for the chubby redheaded detective to arrive and pick him up, race him downtown to another phone—one in a night club which he could reach through the alley door where it was a certainty that no one would see him.

He clipped in flat, bitten phrases to the redhead, exactly what had happened as they darted through traffic.

McGuire's voice was husky as he finally blurted: "Good God—what are you going to do?"

"There's only one thing I *can* do," the Marquis said. "Get me to that phone."

The redhead's bright blue eyes went wide as he stood beside the Marquis in the little room where the phone was and recognized the number the Marquis was calling.

"Sevens Richard— Judas! What...?"

The Marquis' lips jerked to the phone and he said: "Sevens? Are you alone?... Be damn sure you are. How many people have been in your office since I left there?"

Little beads of relief stood out on his forehead as the albino gambler's puzzled voice told him: "Why, as it happens, no one. I've been doing some book-keeping and— Listen, Marty, he hasn't shown. I swear...."

"Never mind that. Listen to me—and listen carefully, if you want to live. I need an alibi. I went into your office an hour ago—and I left by the icebox door. Nobody saw me come out. Now I'm coming down there and come back in again the back way. Never mind Joe Bannon or his hearing about it. I've been in your office the last hour and a half—never been out of it. Understand? If you stick to that—no matter what else happens—you're in the clear with me. If you don't—God help you! Got it?"

The gambler's gulp was audible over the phone. He said huskily, but almost eagerly, at that: "I—I got it, Marty. O.K."

McGuire said in a strained voice as they raced downtown again: "Will it hold up?"

"Why not? Sevens is a rat, but he's never had a conviction against him. He's legally as good in court as your friend Rhode—if that was Rhode."

They made the last lap of the mad race in seconds and the Marquis was back in front of the shabby hotel on lower Madison. The street was utterly silent, deserted as he piled out, ran down the delivery alley and picked the lock into the kitchens. No one saw him on the fire-stairs and the panel-door that let him into the albino's office opened instantly at his first tap.

The gambler's pink eyes were curious, startled, as he backed away from the Marquis after letting him in, but he licked his lips and said nothing.

"Everything still clear?" the Marquis wanted to know.

"Absolutely," the other said huskily. "Listen, Marty—am I likely to get into trouble…?"

"Plenty," the Marquis assured him grimly. "But you can survive. If you let me down for one second, there's twenty-two tough guys on my squad that will give you trouble you *won't* survive. Is that perfectly clear?"

The other gulped and sweat shone on his face. He wiped his palms with his handkerchief. "Yeah, yeah. It's clear, Marty. I'll—I'll do what you say."

ANY DOUBT that it was Rhode who had seen him from the Harlem courtyard ended forty minutes later. Following the only sane course—stepping at once into the routine he would have followed had he not seen the murderous evangelist at all—the Marquis was strolling unhurriedly from one of the squad's telephone stations—a cigar on Broadway near Fiftieth—when the black coupe whipped into the curb beside him and the red-lipped, ruddy-faced investigator jumped out.

"Lieutenant Marquis!"

The Marquis looked politely curious, stopped, strolled over, his round face somber and unexcited.

"Yes?"

"I think the district attorney wants to see you." It was no twinkle in the brown eyes. A cold, blazing fire of triumph burned deep within. "I phoned him and he asked me to bring you right down."

The Marquis cocked his head. "Are you crazy? I'm working right now. I don't leave the district at this hour, except on business."

"This is business."

"I mean *my* business."

The ruddy face darkened a little and fury trembled the big man's voice. "Cut it out, Marquis. This is for keeps."

"What is?"

"Can it! Harlem—and Holy Joe Bannon—and that cripple you killed about an hour ago."

The Marquis gasped. "*I*—killed? You must be mad. When am I supposed to have…?"

"Cut this crap!" Rhode snarled. "An hour ago—and I was on your tail and saw you at it. Come on—get in the car—give me your gun and I'll take a chance on driving you down."

The Marquis grunted. "Behave yourself. An hour ago I was downtown—not uptown. I'll give you a break, because I don't want to leave the section right now. I'll save your boss a nice suit for false arrest—oh, yes, you'd have to make a formal arrest to take me down—by telling you where I was. You can check up for yourself—and then maybe think up something to phone your boss so that he can go back to bed. Do you know where the Tolliver Hotel is? About twenty people saw me in one of the rooms there. Go in here and call this number…."

When the ruddy-faced man emerged four minutes later from the cigar store, his face was purple. He said through set teeth: "You think I believe that crook? If ever an alibi was phony as hell, that one is."

"You frighten me," the Marquis said sarcastically.

The other's lips were like paper. He was silent for a full minute, before he blurted uncontrollably: "I'm going to make you pay for this, Marquis, if it's the last thing I do."

The Marquis shrugged, turned away. "Have a field day," he invited—and breathed again as the big, brown-clad man flung himself into the coupe.

CHAPTER FIVE

DUSK

THE REAL, nightmare twist to the fantastic horror did not dawn till the morning papers reached the street. McGuire, white-faced, caught the Marquis, waving the fresh sheet, in a Forty-second Street shooting-gallery. The gulping redhead made no comment, simply jammed the paper under his skipper's face.

Even then, it was a second before the Marquis could read through the not-too-prominent item, find the stunning news.

> … one Joseph Bannon, who was visiting the murdered cripple at the time, was unable to give any clue to the murderer. He was slugged over the head as he entered the apartment and, apparently in an effort to kill him as well, dropped over the edge of the fire-escape in the rear. By a miracle, he escaped with only serious bruises and contusions, and with two broken ribs. Before leaving the hospital, where he was treated for his injuries, Bannon gave a vague description of the two masked men whom he says he believes he saw.…

The Marquis' eyes raced to the bottom of the page, but nowhere was there anything to deny that the seemingly unkillable evangelist had been allowed to walk calmly out of the hospital without a detaining hand being laid on him.

The Marquis jumped to the phone, hastily dialed the hospital, where the special officer on duty moaned miserably: "My God, I know it now, Marquis. I didn't then! The coppers who brought him in should have recognized him—not me: His face was all swole up and, anyhow, he told a straight story and who cares about the punk that was killed anyway?"

"You madman! Every cop in town knows I wanted Bannon!"

"Don't take it out on me. Nobody recognized him. He gave his address—the place where this cripple was killed. Rhode was off chasing downtown somewhere and he didn't tell none of the prowl cops who the guy was. When the docs seen he was all right, the cops questioned him but he didn't see nothing and he was no good as a witness anyway—even if they was going to try and make something of the killing. Why should...?"

The Marquis slammed down the receiver. Through tight teeth, he said, "The lamebrain ————s!"

"Why didn't Rhode identify Bannon? Didn't he know...?"

"That fool didn't even go to the hospital—he was too busy chasing downtown after me. And the dope didn't even bother to tell the cops before he ran off."

He stood there, while the whole tormenting situation burned in his mind. The murderous—and unbelievably tough—Bannon, was free again. The whole mess was rushing forward once more.

Not till then did he fully realize his own folly. The evangelist was working to drive through his murderous scheme and to depend on informers to turn him up—now, at any rate—was madness. It was absolutely necessary to discover what he was doing. Discover it—and crack down on it. He realized his own wildness of purpose up till now with agonizing fury.

For the first time the frightening possibility chilled him that, while he groped and stumbled around blindly, the deadly Bannon might drive his evil schemes to completion and vanish again. That would wreck not only the Marquis but his squad. By his broadcast he had declared himself. If Bannon succeeded now—brought off whatever his murderous plans called for—it would be a devastating slap in the face to the squad's precious prestige. It suddenly dawned on the Marquis that he had succeeded in getting himself on highly dangerous ground. As long as the murder of the cripple was a mystery he stood in danger of facing the charge himself. Only the tenuous wall of Sevens Richardson's alibi stood between him and the savage determination of Rhode and the D.A., Maney, to trip him up.

He spurred his brain almost in panic to try and divine what he was up against—what Bannon was contriving.

Torgenson—the death of the chemist had let the racket loose. Was the stabbing of the cripple—the "Al" who was apparently Bannon's accomplice—part of it?

That the chemist's millions was the bait seemed almost inevitable. But how would Holy Joe Bannon, hiding in some other town, even be aware that such people as the Torgensons existed? How—unless he had some accomplice on the ground?

ONCE STARTED, questions raced through his mind. He tried to see the picture. Someone on the ground, sending for Joe Bannon to drive the racket through? The "Al" of the note, waiting somewhere out of town impatiently? His finally coming here—and the final killing of the almost-dead Torgenson—did they tie up? And why was the cripple himself stabbed?

He rejoined McGuire and strode grimly back toward the theater-ticket agency on Times Square that was the squad's unofficial headquarters.

McGuire blurted: "The guy's unnatural! You can't kill him! He has the gall of a goat—to come back into the one town in the world where even the pavements are too hot for him—and coolly hammer away at some racket! It must be tremendous, Marty."

The Marquis scarcely heard him. He said: "Go back inside when we get to the agency and build a fire under everybody. It's a forlorn hope, but somebody might spot the rat somewhere else."

This time he knew they wouldn't—knew that it was up to him—and that only by using his head could he hope to dig him out. The racket! What was the racket? Who had originated it? Bannon? The crippled "Al"?

And for the first time his mind really turned to Howard Dusk. Dusk, the up-from-the-gutter, shrewd, ruthless Broadway lawyer—and the financial agent, apparently of long-standing, as well as the attorney, of the Torgensons.

Certainly, if there were any angle connected with the chemist that could be exploited by murder, Dusk would know of it. How, for argument's sake, could Dusk tie in with Bannon, with the crippled "Al"?

McGuire went on ahead of him into the agency. When the Marquis was abreast he merely slowed, took in the crowded little mob of telephoning detectives inside, would have walked on past, save that McGuire came bouncing out and called after him.

"Marty—a call for you. Torgenson's lawyer—Howard Dusk." It was as though fate had been watching his swarming thoughts.

When he answered, the harsh voice in his ear was quick and anxious. "Have you seen Dorinne Torgenson?" Dusk snapped.

From the plain question, the Marquis' hot mind jumped. Dorinne Torgenson! The heir to the chemist's fortune! If this ominous scheme had any logical development, and if the old man's money were at the root of it, the girl would seem to be the storm center now.

Was she the "big killing?" Was she next in line?

"Well, have you?" the lawyer's voice cried fretfully.

"No. Why?"

The receiver was slammed down in his ear.

He sat, hot-eyed, while Kavvelfoot, the mummy-faced oldster of the squad, on whose phone the call had come, teetered from one foot to the other, a small address-book in one wrinkled hand.

He suddenly thought of the papers he had taken from the crippled dead man in Harlem, pulled them hastily from his pocket. His quick eyes sifted through them and he reached for a phone, saw Kavvelfoot, got up and went to the front of the agency. Lean, stringy, washed-out-looking Harry Derosier was standing to one side. The Marquis stopped beside him long enough to tell him: "Go over and get on Howard Dusk's tail. Stick with him from now on and phone reports here. No, I don't know what I expect him to do. You'll probably find him at his office."

He went on up to Lindy's, got a handful of change and took the cripple's papers into a phone booth with him. He made long-distance calls for twenty-five minutes, and wound up with the dead cripple's dossier.

Al Tromper was his name. He was a hospital attendant by trade who had worked, satisfactorily, in various hospitals around California, mostly in his home town, San Jose. He found nothing against him and nobody seemed to know whether he had a family or not. He had hurt his leg in a fall suffered while employed at the State Mental Hospital, some eight years before.

A REALLY disorganizing thought struck the Marquis then. What if Bannon were only a henchman, a hired hand, a specialist of some kind. For—suddenly—he realized that both the killing of Torgenson and of the cripple, Al Tromper, were out of line for Bannon. In his note to Tromper, Bannon had inveighed against hastening the dying Torgenson's death. And Tromper, the little cripple, was undoubtedly his accomplice in whatever racket was going forward. But if Bannon were not the head man— then who? Who had murdered Torgenson—and Al Tromper?

He groped hastily. Who could profit from the old man's death? Who would have reason to pursue the ex-hospital attendant and finally do away with him?

He sat there in the phone booth, his head hot, and his mind returned inevitably to the shrewd, ruthless Howard Dusk, the dead millionaire's lawyer. Then he thought of the blowsy, run-down ex-wife of Torgenson—and her gigolo boy friend. Instantly, he knew that in neither of the brains of that pair was there the subtlety to engineer the insulin-shocked death of the chemist.

The girl? Was it conceivable that, instead of being the next victim on Bannon's list, she was actually behind all this? Had he been too quick to accept the usually reliable redheaded McGuire's stamp of approval on her?

He jumped back to the phone call of the lawyer. Was Dorinne Torgenson missing? Could it be that Bannon was already striking?

He felt a little chill in his spine, slid to the edge of the booth with his face worried—and a black silk dress stopped in front of him.

A girl's husky voice blurted, "Are you Lieutenant Marquis of the Broadway Squad?" and he looked up at tormented, shining, long-lashed brown eyes. She was not more than twenty, with dark-brown curls low on the back of her neck, her velvety white face touched with fever spots. Her desperate eyes searched his somber ones and he got quickly to his feet.

She said breathlessly: "I'm Dorinne Torgenson. Oh, please—please—why won't you let me bury my father?"

The Marquis looked down at her rounded little figure under the black dress, the short black Persian jacket. In his mind he raved at the M.E. who had exposed his request to hold the body—but he could not really blame him. The girl was exquisitely lovely. "It's just a formality, Miss Torgenson." He groped hastily. "I'm sorry if it worried you. It'll be only a day or so now."

"Then you don't—you—I'm the only—oh, Mr. Marquis— what is it? My—my lawyer wants me to let him go into court and force them to give him up, but if—if you want me to—I know you're an experienced police officer—oh, please, what is it that made you ask Doctor Hernandez to—to hold him?"

He looked at her tormented brown eyes. There were tears under her lashes.

He said uncomfortably: "I'm quite sure it's all a mistake, but—"

A gray-faced, bald-headed man with shoulders so wide that they made his really sturdy body seem wasp-like burst up the aisle and took her arm. "Dorinne!"

The bald-headed man's eyes were gray ice, his long lined face like granite. He said through stiff lips: "Dorinne— please go out and let me talk to the Marquis."

Her frightened eyes went from one to the other. The Marquis said dully: "Hello, Howard."

"Please, Dorinne—I'll ask him for you. I know what you want. But please—go home and stay there."

"Oh, Mr. Dusk—if there's any reason—"

"Dorinne—please!"

WHEN SHE backed miserably away the lawyer turned feverish eyes on the Marquis. "Marty—for God's sake, that girl's had enough grief. Can't you get her father's body released?"

The Marquis' eyes were blank. "I'll try." He hesitated. "She inherits Torgenson's money?"

"Yes, yes of course."

"There's a will?"

"Certainly. I was his lawyer for twenty years—ever since I was defending gangsters and he was clerking in the drug store. He made a will four years ago." There was a queer frightened light deep in his gray eyes, "Marty, you're not going to make any trouble for her?"

The Marquis eyed him carefully. "Howard, if you're in love with her, take my advice. You're twenty years too old."

"Oh, my God, I know that. It isn't that. But she's—she's so damn sweet, Marty." There was still that vaguely frightened, questioning look in his eyes. He said huskily: "I want to talk to you, Marty."

He slid into the booth. The Marquis' eyes squinted as he suddenly realized that the lawyer's attitude of an hour ago was completely, utterly deflated. He was frightened. He licked his gray lips, mopped the lining of his fedora. "Marty—" He started twice and could get no further. Then he choked it out. "Marty—I'll pay ten thousand dollars for fifteen minutes alone with the person who killed that cripple—that Al Tromper—in Harlem last night."

The Marquis' mouth opened. "You *what?*"

The lawyer repeated.

"My God, you don't think I have him, do you?"

The lawyer's eyes held the Marquis'. "Holy Joe Bannon didn't kill him, Marty."

"Who did then?"

The lawyer winced. "If I knew that, I wouldn't come to you. But I've got to see him—got to get to him, Marty. I'll pay—"

"Why?"

For another long second, the lawyer's eyes searched the Marquis' desperately. Then he seemed to sag. "If you don't know why, then I can't tell you, Marty. But for God's sake catch him—I'll pay anything you ask—only let me see him. I swear to God, I won't make trouble for you. I'll do exactly as you say—"

"Wait a minute," the Marquis said bewilderedly. "Do you think I killed him?"

The lawyer swallowed, ran his eyes away from the Marquis', a finger inside his collar. "Well, no, Marty, but I heard something from the district attorney's office. I—look, Marty! Something was taken from the cripple, I think. The killer took it. Maybe he doesn't know its importance. Hell, it isn't important, except—except to me. No—I'm not going to explain. I can't. Only, please, Marty—get him—and it—for me. I'll do anything you say."

The Marquis' eyes were thin. He hesitated a long minute. "Howard—in case you don't know it, your client, Torgenson, was murdered."

"What! Why, you're—you're crazy, Marty—crazy...."

"No. The same rat killed him that killed the cripple."

The lawyer's eyes were stunned and hollow. "But—but it—oh, my God, it's insane!"

"What's the answer, Howard?"

"I swear I don't know, Marty—any more than you do. And believe it or not—I don't even know what it was that was stolen. I only know I've got to have it. I can't tell you any more than that if you jug me, or third-degree me. Marty, I guess I made a mistake coming here. I don't know why I listened to— Oh, hell, Marty, all I can say is that the offer still stands."

THE BEWILDERED Marquis searched his eyes. "One of us is crazy. Will you answer me one thing. Did anybody have reason to kill Torgenson, your client?"

The lawyer hesitated, his eyes racked. "Marty—I don't know. Maybe—but I can't believe it. He died a natural death—in a way. He took his own insulin shots and maybe—maybe the box he took the ampules from was fresher or stronger than what he was used to—I don't know."

The Marquis got up quickly. He said: "Howard—for God's sake, if you know anything, come clean. Maybe this will help you. I know for a fact that Joe Bannon is still planning his big play—that up till now everything is only preliminary. If you can tell me what it is—for God's sake do it!"

There was no mistaking the sudden, amazed fear that leaped into the lawyer's eyes. He blurted hoarsely: "Marty— are you positive? You know that—you *know* he's planning...."

"Yeah. You tell me who."

The lawyer's shaking hand ground over his bald head. "I—I haven't any idea, Marty. I swear it. I—Marty—I've got to go. I've nothing more to tell you. I've got to get up and see that Dorinne's all right."

The Marquis grabbed his arm. "Howard—when you called me an hour ago, you were tough as nails. Now you're scuttled. What happened in the meantime?"

The lawyer's face was stiff and white. "I—I was in my office. I—well, when I got up to go out, I found a note under the door. Oh, hell, Marty, it's nothing I can tell you about. I swear that. It—it wouldn't help you."

The Marquis searched his eyes, said, "All right, Howard. Call me if anything happens," and watched him hurry out of the restaurant.

He strolled in his wake a minute later, stepped onto the sparsely populated, brilliant street, his somber blue eyes darting along the lawyer's back-trail, hunting for Harry Derosier. He was blessing himself for having put the droopy sergeant on the lawyer's trail just, apparently, at the right time. If Derosier had been watching the lawyer, there was an outside chance that he had seen who had slipped the note under the lawyer's door—if indeed there actually were such a note.

Sharp lines came on his forehead as he failed to spot the English-looking Derosier.

The sharp lines became a scowl, as it began to be apparent that Derosier was not tailing Dusk. Had the sergeant missed him at his office? Had he arrived there after the lawyer had left?

It did not seem possible. He had dispatched him an hour ago. The office was within two blocks of the ticket agency. He must have arrived within minutes of the lawyer's phone call to the Marquis.

He strode down Broadway, over the one block—and was in front of the narrow, rickety anachronism of a wooden building that housed the lawyer's office. There was no sign whatever of Derosier.

CHAPTER SIX
ALBINO ALIBI

AS FAR as the Marquis could tell, there were no lights on in the building except the hall lights. The lobby was open, its yellow marble dinginess empty save for a dog-eared register propped open on a small table. The single elevator was closed, humming, the attendant presumably in it.

The directory told him that Howard Dusk's office was on the fourth floor and he went quietly up the wide marble stairs, then two flights of shabby wooden ones. He saw no one, heard nothing, till he turned into the corridor along which the lawyer's office fronted.

The office was dark. The boards under his feet were worn, sagging, and they creaked shakily as he walked.

Maybe the catch on the broom-closet was feeble, or maybe the weight inside had slowly forced it almost open. At any rate, when the Marquis' weight sagged the boards in front of the scaly yellow door, it burst open and a man jumped out at him.

In instant reflex, the Marquis' elbow jerked up and back, caught the man under the chin, sent him flopping back against the wall, while the Marquis jumped back, snatching at his hip.

He did not need a gun. The man's big body hit the wall and folded up like a concertina, flopping, sprawled out on his back, his arms flung wide, his eyes staring sightlessly up at the ceiling. The front of his brown coat was a sopping mass of blood and his big face was starch-white.

He was Rhode, the D.A.'s investigator, and he had been knifed to death by someone who knew how to use a knife.

The Marquis' hair stood on end.

In one clear, devastating flash of light, he saw the perilous position that this might place him in. Dusk had said that he had heard something—obviously the suspicion that the Marquis had killed the cripple uptown—from a leak in the D.A.'s office. Obviously, Rhode had voiced his suspicion—and probably the whole story—in the ear of the brilliant reform prosecutor, Maney. It needed no imagination to divine that the big investigator would have sworn as to the Marquis' guilt—and as to his own intention of nailing him.

And now he was dead—and his pockets stripped.

The Marquis knelt, made a flashing search, straightened, wiped his gloved fingers on a handkerchief.

The sound of the elevator stopping at the ground floor, its door clanking open, and a man's sharp steps across the tile below, jerked his head round to the stairwell.

Somebody below said, "Hello, Ben," and there was answering mumble, then the elevator shook as someone boarded it and the door clanked slowly closed.

Agony of indecision racked the Marquis for the space of two heartbeats. He was not panicky enough to think that he could be convicted on this—not unless they convicted him first on the murder of the crippled Al Tromper—but he knew Maney would believe him guilty. Believing that, he would throw the full force of his office at the Marquis—and just how much danger there was in that, the Marquis sweated to consider. If he were found here, with the body still warm....

He sweated afresh at the prospect of running out, of leaving the murder unreported. If only he had some inkling of Holy Joe Bannon's scheme—but he didn't. He was still straining, desperate for the truth, without a valid hint of any part of it. And if he were found here, he would, beyond any possibility or shadow of doubt, be held by the vindictive D.A. for at least forty-eight hours.

The urge was too much. He turned and ran on whispering feet to the stairs, waited till the elevator had passed him, then crept as fast as he could down the staircase. If he allowed himself to be held, conceivably the one slim reed that supported him now—the alibi given him by Sevens Richardson—would collapse and he would find himself deep in the mire. As long as he could stay in action, there was a chance that he might somehow crack the riddle—and save his own skin.

HE DID not think he was noticed as he hurried out. There were pedestrians in the street, but he recognized no one. He hurried back up Broadway, heart pounding, till he was far enough away to make a chance meeting meaningless, then swung for the ticket agency.

Thought of the English-looking Derosier burned in his mind. In spite of the painfully obvious fact that Dusk had managed to get rid of his shadow somewhere, there was an outside hope that Derosier might have seen something—seen someone enter the office building after the lawyer.

There was a touch of desperation in the Marquis' mind as he burst into the agency. He did not fool himself that he had escaped much by running from the corpse. The minute it was found, he would be in almost as bad a spot with the infuriated district attorney—though the question of whether he could be held was a delicate one.

Kavvelfoot, the squad's oldster, was just hanging up his phone as the Marquis strode in. He called instantly: "Oh, ah, Marty—Harry Derosier was just on the phone. He said to tell you that the party gave him the slip in the Sheldrake Hotel lobby. He's coming down here to commit suicide, he says."

The Marquis could not restrain a bitter, "Tell him he'd better," as a fresh stab of desperation tore him. Could Dusk, after all, be behind this reign of terror? Could he have killed the old man to cover up some defalcation—and maybe Tromper—and now the investigator Rhode to cover up the first crime? Was his tender solicitude for the girl Dorinne no more than a fraud and could he conceivably be going to strike his final blow at her?

The Marquis decided he had to see the lawyer at once.

Even that was denied him.

After twenty-five minutes of sweating on the telephone, after a futile chase uptown to the lawyer's Beekman Place apartment, he was back in the agency again, lacing his brain, groping, juggling, reaching desperately for an opening.

He had already called the radio-room at headquarters and put out a private alarm for the lawyer, Dusk. Now, with no slightest whisper of him, his suspicion began to mount—and with it the realization that the girl Dorinne was entirely in the lawyer's hands.

He called the San Sylvan hastily, got the girl's suite—and was answered by a harsh masculine voice that gave him a qualm, till he identified himself.

The voice said: "Oh, yeah, Lootenant. This is Cummings, Eighteenth. Wait a minute, I'll get her."

"Never mind. I just want to make sure she's protected—all around. And I mean *all* around."

"Why? What's up, Lootenant? You think she's in dang—"

"Somebody is—something's going to happen, any time now. It may be to her. God help you if it is. And don't let that lawyer of hers near her."

"Huh? Hey, he was the one—"

"I know it."

He hung up, hesitated just a minute, then once more dialed the lawyer's office number, his curiosity beyond bounds. Little beads of sweat came out on his neck when a man's voice answered.

He said: "Mr. Dusk, please."

"This is Mr. Dusk," the voice said and there was the click of a tracer going in on the wire. The Marquis hung up hastily.

He called the homicide bureau, got in touch with the one inspector he could trust and asked: "Is there any report about an investigator for the D.A.'s office, or anybody else, dead up around Times Square recently?"

If anything could have alarmed him more, it was the inspector's "No."

He squeezed his brain when he hung up. Why? He was perfectly certain that the dead Rhode had been discovered—that the news was being kept quiet for some reason—that the D.A.'s men must be in the office building now. That tracer was not the mark of anyone else except the police—and the police were still in ignorance. Why— why were they keeping it quiet?

Half feverish with suspense, he started out the door— and the next frightening blow fell.

Asa McGuire, white-faced, leaped up from behind a phone and yelled hoarsely, "Marty! Marty!" and ran for the back room. The Marquis hurried at his heels.

Behind the closed door, the redhead blurted: "They raided Sevens Richardson's joint ten minutes ago—the D.A.'s crew. They claim they found some dope as well as the gambling equipment. They've got him on the way to jail on both a federal charge and a gambling charge! You get it? They're trying to spike your alibi—discredit…."

"Get Solly!" the Marquis clipped. "Get him down there quick before that damned D.A. makes a deal with Sevens."

"You think Sevens would fold up?"

"If the D.A. can convince him there's a real rap hanging over him, and that he'll protect him from me if he breaks I wouldn't doubt it for a minute. —————— ————— that Rhode! This is trouble, Ace. Move, for God's sake! This may block us off completely from the payoff."

THEY RACED downtown desperately with the little mouthpiece to the house of a friendly judge for writs, called bondsmen by the score, as the grim-faced, mustached little D.A., Maney himself, hurried from his office to fight the release of the albino gambler.

For an hour they fought and argued—but they could not hold him in the face of the legal situation.

The red-faced, glittering-eyed little Maney faced the Marquis outside the Tombs and there was fury in his stare. He said softly: "This won't help you, Marquis. You're done for. I'm going to get you—any way I can."

"I'll survive," the Marquis said.

They climbed into McGuire's car—Sevens, dirty, disheveled, his hair matted and lumps on his jaw.

The gambler blurted bitterly: "They're going to get me, Marty. He swore he would—if I protected you. God, what a spot you've put me in."

"I'll make it up to you," the Marquis promised. "Whatever they do, they won't kill you, mister. And if you think I won't—you're crazy. You've got trouble coming—but there's less of it playing with me. And I'll go to bat for you when it's all over."

"All over? How can it ever be all over? I'm giving you a phony alib—"

"Take my word for it—it's going to break any minute," the Marquis assured him—without the slightest notion of how explosively right he was.

THE DESERTED gambling-room was a shambles. Axes and crowbars had done their work. The Marquis cocked a sour eye at the albino as the arrangement of wires and magnets beneath two of the three tables was exposed to light, but he said nothing. Even the gambler's office had not escaped. Desk drawers, filing-cabinets, papers, ornaments, clothing, were a mess on the floor.

The albino sat on a chair in his littered office, held his head in his hands. He looked ready to collapse—and the fear of it was a sting that anchored the Marquis. He was afraid to go away. Now, with Maney out for his blood, he realized how dangerously everything was pyramided on his alibi—and how close that was to dropping from under him.

Desperately, he tried to guess Maney's next move.

The gambler looked wearily at the Marquis' feet, said nothing.

The Marquis said through tight lips, "Just a minute, Sevens," and led Asa McGuire outside, out into the hotel corridor.

His forehead was flushed as he told the redhead: "You stay with him. I think he's wilting. I don't have to tell you what it means if he reneges on me."

McGuire said, "No,"—and the murderous tangle exploded.

The sound of the shot beyond the double thickness of walls was a dull boom! The sound of the slamming door was a thud.

The Marquis whirled.

McGuire cried out, "My God!" as they both raced back into the suite, dived over the debris of the gambling-room.

White-faced, the Marquis ripped, "Get down into the alley—the icebox door lets out there," and the redhead flew down the hall.

The Marquis dived for Sevens Richardson's office.

The albino was on his knees on the floor, crumpled, his face twisted in pain, one hand clutching his shoulder.

The Marquis yelled hoarsely, "Sevens! Are you all..." and at the gambler's pain-racked nod, he leaped for the icebox door behind the file-cabinets.

He ripped it open, gun in hand, plunged out onto a dark landing. Feet were racing far down ahead of him. There was light at the third landing down. The Marquis leaped to the banister, caught a glimpse of a body—and fired. He pumped three shots as fast as he could, whirled round and down. Below he heard a gasped curse. He flung himself down another flight—and racking tongues of orange fire jabbered up at him thunderingly.

He yelled, "Come back here—you're done—you can't get..." and heard a door slam far below.

He fairly dived the rest of the way to the landing, yanked open the door of the service stairs and plunged down and into the kitchens. He raced ten feet, threw his shoulder against the service-alley door and plunged out.

McGuire yelled: "Don't move! I'll let you—oh, God, *you*, chief!"

The Marquis groaned, flung back without a word and plowed up to the landing again, took the other stairs down as fast as he could—the fire-stairs—but when he emerged on the side street the pavement was bare for rods.

He bit at the tumbling McGuire at his heels: "Get an ambulance—fast.... What's that?"

McGuire handed him a blue square of cardboard six by four inches. It had a trailing wet blood spot at one edge. It was a card of admission for a California State Hospital, dated August 14, 1935, for one William Black. Evidently William Black had filled in some of the entries as well as his own signature.

"It was on the landing," McGuire said. "Maybe the guy dropped...."

"All right. Get that ambulance."

He tried to convince himself that the blue card meant something as he raced back up, but he couldn't figure it. He burst back into the office, slipping the card in his pocket.

Richardson had one hand on a chair, was trying to hoist himself up. Blood ran down through the fingers of the other hand, clamped to his shoulder. The Marquis jumped to give him a hand. The gambler's pink face was waxy, sweat-stained, his pale hair matted.

"Who was it?" the Marquis flung at him.

"God knows," the albino gasped. "I was sitting there— he busted in—put a gun on me and blasted. He—he called me something. I dunno what. I tried to fall when I guessed he was going to shoot, otherwise he'd have got me for keeps."

"The voice? My God, didn't you recognize…?"

The gambler shook his head. "No…. Get… get a doc, will you, Marquis?"

"An ambulance is on the way. But you've got to remember…."

"I didn't have a chance, I tell you? I didn't see him—and he just growled."

The Marquis showed him the blue card. "Have you ever seen this? Do you know what it is?"

The gambler said, "No," hazily, and slid in a dead faint.

CHAPTER SEVEN
THE BLUE CARD

NOT TILL they were in the rushing ambulance did the white-faced McGuire whisper: "You don't think Maney would go this far to nail you, do you?"

"God knows." The Marquis' pinched eyes were on the now-moaning gambler in the stretcher. "How is he, Doc?" he asked the bored-looking interne.

"Didn't even hit a bone. All he needs is a dressing. Just a big sissy, is all."

Not till they had bandaged the wound and Sevens was on a bed, half-dressed, in the private room the Marquis ordered, did the gambler fully come out of his daze.

Instantly, the Marquis hammered at him: "Was it Bannon? Surely you'd know if it was Bannon!"

"I think—I think I would. I don't think it was."

"And he didn't say anything—just opened the door and let you have it? He didn't want anything? Ask for anything?"

"No. He growled. That's all."

McGuire said: "Hey, Marty—what if some of these other bulls come around? Or even somebody from Maney's office?"

"Go down and find some doc that has the authority and bribe him or something to say no one can see Sevens."

While the redhead was gone, he paced the room. "You can't explain it at all? You don't know why you were shot?"

Sevens' waxy face was drawn. "No. No, I don't, Marty. Listen, Marty." He swallowed. "Listen—I got an idea. Let me see Maney for a minute...."

The Marquis was suddenly over him, his forehead flushed. "You damn rat—so you do want to belch!"

The gambler's eyes crawled sickly. "No, no, Marty. It's not that. I—it's not...."

McGuire came back in. The Marquis' eyes were hot on the gambler's bloodshot pink ones. "This baby wants to crawl, Ace. Maybe you better tell him what happens to him—*after* Maney gets me behind b...."

A worried-looking nurse came in. "Is Lieutenant Marquis—are one of you...?"

"I am, yes ma'am."

"There—there's a phone call for you."

"Can you bring a phone here?"

The minute the instrument was plugged in, the Marquis recognized the voice of the mysteriously vanished Howard Dusk. Even as the lawyer asked, "Marty—is that you?" the Marquis had his hand over the mouthpiece, clipping at McGuire. "Dusk—trace it fast—send a radio car to pick.... Yeah, Howard. What is it?"

The lawyer's voice was angry. "Did you give orders that I wasn't to be admitted to Miss Torgenson's apartment?"

"Yeah. I said no one was to be, Howard. If it's something important come down here and I'll go up with you."

"I'll do no such thing. You've got your damned nerve...."

Hastily, the Marquis groped. "Well, I'll tell you Howard..." but the receiver was hung up in his ear.

The Marquis swung toward the door. McGuire hurried in after a minute. "A drug store—in the building where the Torgenson's apartment is—the San Sylvan...."

The Marquis started for the door, hesitated, went over and looked out down the fire-escape, finally said: "The hell with it, if they think they can stop me, let them try it." At the door, he told McGuire: "It's up to you, Ace. See that this rat doesn't get a chance to talk to anyone. Lock the door from the *out*side."

He hurried downstairs, avoiding the crowd of bluecoats and detectives by taking the stretcher elevator, ran out the ambulance entrance. He had no trouble finding a cab to race him uptown to the San Sylvan.

HE FLUNG off in front of the hotel, saw the green-and-white prowl car angled in at the curb, ran in—and almost collided with the two radio cops coming out. One of them said glumly: "He seems to have pulled out just before we got here, Marty. Some guy came from across the street and spoke to him and they got in a cab and drove off. The cab was a regular here though and maybe—" He glanced at a number on a slip of paper in his hand and then sharply up at a cab wheeling to come in line before the hotel.

"There he is now! Hey—you...!"

To the Marquis' quick question, the driver of the cab said: "Yeah. I know who you mean—a big guy like a football player only with a bald head. Him and this guy looked like a wild man."

"Wild man?" The Marquis' eyes jumped and he flung a furtive look to be sure the radio cops were out of hearing. "What do you mean?"

"Well, a tall, gaunt-faced guy—sort of crazy eyes...."

The Marquis' heart leaped. "Where'd you take them?"

"To the Normandy Garage."

The Marquis was already inside, slamming the cab door. "Take me there."

A white-jumpered attendant at the mammoth garage told him: "Sure, Mr. Dusk came in and got his car, made sure it was tanked up and drove off."

The Marquis almost piled back into the cab, then, instead ran into a phone booth in the garage and demanded to be connected with Sevens Richardson's room.

"Just ring it," he raved when the operator began the customary sing-song. "There's an instrument already plugged in there. I just had it...."

The phone rang. It rang again—and again—and again.

Not till the fifth ring did the Marquis' heart actually stop, while sweat drenched him and his scalp crawled.

Not till the seventh did the hoarse voice of the red-headed McGuire burst onto the wire.

"Ace—do you know where Howard Dusk lives? Somewhere out of the city...."

"Yes. Croton-on-Hudson," the redhead almost sobbed, "But Marty—he's gone! Sevens is gone! The fire-escape—I never thought—I was outside, keeping the bulls away—you said—oh God, Marty, what'll I do? Do you think he'll go to Maney?"

The Marquis' teeth were clenched. He did not answer. He could not answer. He jammed down the receiver, hastily called his own apartment on Central Park West, clipped instructions at his Jap, ran out and piled back into the cab.

By the time the cab dumped him off in front of his own address and he had piled into the long convertible that the Jap had ready at the curb, his face was a white, set mask.

He kneed the siren, sent the powerful car leaping cross-town, raced up Broadway—and then over to the Riverside Drive Parkway. He jammed the accelerator to the floor, kept the siren going till he was well outside the city limits, trying to squeeze the last notch of speed from the car.

He could not dare even consider that he was wrong. He couldn't be wrong—now. Everything was pyramided on the one wild gamble he was making.

He almost went crazy when the toll bridge made him check his thundering pace, and again when he took the wrong road at the Hawthorn traffic-circle. He shook off half a dozen speed cops with a flash of his badge—and then the stoplight at Harmon twinkled and he jerked his foot from the accelerator, let the car sag, pounded forward at a moderate forty.

HE SAW no one from whom to ask directions till he rounded the silent policeman in the heart of Croton's upper-village business district. At this hour of the morning the streets were bare and deserted, only the lights of a gas station and one or two taverns burning redly.

A gas-station attendant said: "Sure. It's right at the top of the hill—what they call Mount Breeze. It's a fair-sized place—has a fieldstone wall round it. Don't go in the first gate—that leads you round to the garage, sort of under the back of the house. Go on past it to the next one—that's the driveway. The house is set back maybe fifty yards—sort of a rock garden for a front yard and quite a few trees. You can't miss it...."

Then he was plunging up the side of the steep slope of the hill, his heart in his mouth, his eyes hot and straining through the darkness.

He saw the house as he crept past the garage drive-way—saw the light in the front room, and saw the shape of the house. It was built on the side of a hill. The garage was at basement level, and there was a sun-deck atop the garage, a railed veranda running along almost all of three sides of the house, at the level of the ground-floor rooms.

For just a minute, after he had flung the car to a halt on the tree-lined road forty yards beyond the second entrance, he sat with a hand on the door, lacing his brain. He jumped out, started down the road, ran back and took a small black cylinder from the glove compartment of the car, held it for a moment in the glow of the dashlight, palmed it.

He ran right back past the first break in the fieldstone wall that circled the place, swung through the second, and followed the curving driveway till he was at the side of the veranda. He went up like a cat, was across the narrow veranda in two strides, crouched, peering through the casement window, blessing the absence of beclouding curtains.

His heart gave a leap.

The bald-headed, gray-eyed Howard Dusk was at a wall-safe in the far wall of the vast aquamarine-and-cream living-room. Even as the Marquis looked, he worked the opening lever, swung the door back, reached inside, flung an inquiring look over his shoulder.

Holy Joe Bannon, his black clothes rumpled and baggy, the black cap on his forehead dabbed with mud, stood ten feet behind the lawyer. His bruised face had its same wild, fanatical look, his bushy black hair straggling from under the cap. His long, bony hand held a square black gun centered on the lawyer's back.

His words came through the casement window, bitten, harsh. "There'd better be no tricks, mister. One hand will do. Bring the dough out between your fingers—slowly."

For a minute wild rage began to swell up inside the Marquis—the eight-year-old rage at the murderous evangelist—but he set his teeth, stifled it. This little drama had to be played to its end carefully, delicately. It was not time for blowing up. He still lacked one or two answers.

Half his gaze was on the fastenings of the small-paned folding window before him, as Dusk's hand slowly came out of the safe, bearing a thick wad of currency. The fastening—if it were the usual kind—would be a small lever inside. It would not be too strong to snap with a heavy blow—and once the windows were folded aside, the opening was large enough to admit him.

Dusk was facing Bannon now, the money still between his fingers.

Bannon snarled: "All right, throw it over."

Dusk complied. The wad fell at Bannon's feet, bounced up onto his shoe. He stooped, without taking his eyes from the lawyer, picked it up and stowed it in his coat-front.

"There's ten thousand here?"

"Yeah, maybe a little more. It's every cent I can get my hands on tonight. Now for God's sake, give me that thing and clear out. You ought to make the Canadian border by morning but if you're going to take my car, I've got to report it stolen almost as soon as you leave—or the police will think I'm mixed up with you."

The evangelist's teeth showed. "Well, aren't you? Paying blackmail is some sort of a crime isn't it?"

"Stop wasting time," the lawyer bit. "Hand it over and go—now."

THERE WAS a second when silence held the room inside. The Marquis crouched, his deep-set eyes pin-points of light, settled himself to absorb every word. This was the finale.

It came too abruptly.

The lawyer repeated: "Come on—put it on that table and get out, will you? That Broadway copper has an alarm out for me. How do you know somebody didn't spot me. Give me the damned thing!"

The evangelist's teeth showed in a grin. "Don't be a fool. You think I'd give it up for this much dough? The original proposition still stands, mister—*seven hundred and fifty thousand dollars!* This is just a token payment."

Even the Marquis' imagination had not visualized the extent of the racket. Mention of such a sum startled him— startled him so that he almost let the whole mess slip out of his fingers.

He saw the red surge sweep up Howard Dusk's face and bald head, saw the wild fury leap into the lawyer's gray eyes, saw him sway. "Why you double-crossing—"

The evangelist yelled sharply: "Stay back! I don't need you—I can go direct to her...." Even through the window the whitening of his finger on the trigger was visible.

The Marquis' hair stood on end. He whipped up his own gun, dived with the heel of his hand out to smash open the window and shoot the gun out of Bannon's hand.

It didn't work. He had underestimated by a fraction the strength of the latch. He dived, hit the window—and it burst halfway open, held, bounced back. Inside, Bannon instantly whirled—and red thunder jumped from his gun. Glass stung and sprayed in the Marquis' face. He had to fire. His own gun bucked and jumped, even as he hit the window again—and Bannon dropped to his knees, his face contorted. His gun blazed again from the floor and white fire nicked the Marquis' ear as he plunged half over the sill. Panic made his shooting an instant too quick. To save his own life, he had to pound two more shots into the huddle that was Bannon, as fast as he could. The first caught the evangelist in the chest, slumping him—and the second tore away part of his nose.

Then the Marquis was in the room, wild fury making his head thunder. He sobbed, "——— ——— you! I wanted you alive…" as he dived over beside the now-still, blood-spurting gaunt man.

He cursed wildly, feverishly, as he squatted there. Bannon was either dead or seconds from it. He flung him, almost viciously, over flat on his back. The evangelist slumped, clapped down spread-eagled, like a sack of meal. The Marquis scrabbled nearer, one gloved hand whipping back his blood-soaked coat, probing into his inside pocket quickly.

Howard Dusk's voice was suddenly harsh and grim. He said: "Drop your gun, Marty—and get away from that. I'll do all the searching that's necessary."

Red-faced, the Marquis dropped his gun. "Howard—you damned fool…."

"Stand up! Step away—over there!"

"Are you mad? You'll get what you want—what you paid him for…."

"I know I will. Marty—don't cross me—" the lawyer's face was harsh and pale, shaky. "I'll kill you if I have to, so help me. Keep clear...."

Wild, the Marquis backed away. "Howard—I'm not a fool. I know what you're after—I know all about it."

CHAPTER EIGHT
ENTER—THE D.A.

IN MID-STRIDE, the lawyer stopped. He seemed to crouch a little lower and his eyes were white-ringed, frantic. He licked his lips. "You"—his voice was so husky that he had to clear his throat—"Think—think damned carefully, Marty. *Do* you know?"

The Marquis' eyes were hot. "Of course I know. If I hadn't been blind chasing after that rat, I would have spotted it before. God knows I was told. Torgenson's trip to California four years ago—out of sight for six months— Al Tromper, a male nurse in mental institutions. What exact date was Torgenson's will written, Howard? You want me to tell you?"

The lawyer's croak probably meant yes.

"August fourth, nineteen-thirty five. Right?"

The lawyer's eyes were pin-points.

"And he wrote it out himself, mailed it to you from California. Right?"

"Yes."

"Still hoping I don't know, Howard? Or figuring you'll have to kill me after all? Go on, search him."

The crazy fire did not leave the lawyer's hollow eyes as he knelt by the dead man, groped hastily through his pockets. Red touched his temples.

He got up slowly, empty-handed.

The Marquis drove on: "Bannon hasn't got what you want. He came here to New York with it—and waited for the old man to die. But, you see, it was taken away from him."

The lawyer's voice croaked again: "Marty—for the last time—don't fool me. If you know...."

"Know? Sure, I know. I know that Torgenson, when he took that six months' trip four years ago, went to California. I know—as well as though I'd been there myself—just about what he did. He must have been uneasy about the state of his mind—the way he died proved that it was none too stable. He went out there and had himself examined under the name of William Black. Either that or he was cutting up in a hotel or something and somebody else had him examined. I think probably he submitted himself—because, when he found out he was crazy, he evidently wrote out his will and mailed it to you.

"Maybe he wasn't crazy. No two alienists get together very well now. Four years ago it was even more a matter of opinion. At any rate, some alienist found him insane and committed him to the State Hospital. No matter how or why—he was declared legally insane. He was legally insane when he entered that hospital. Right?"

The lawyer licked his lips.

"As a matter of fact, he must have been a little hazy to make his will the same day. What's the first line in a will, Howard? *I, So-and-so, being of sound mind and body....*

"At any rate, the will is dated the same day that he was legally declared insane and committed—and that makes the will not worth a drop of water in court. Or am *I* crazy?"

"Go on."

"Go on? With what. Anybody can see the rest. He was there six months and then declared cured. Only—there was a male nurse named Tromper in the hospital who found out who 'William Black' really was—maybe through rifling his effects or his papers or something. Evidently it didn't mean anything to him at the time, but sometime later he must have had it brought to his notice—some time after Torgenson had been restored to circulation. He fell in with Holy Joe Bannon, and I don't doubt for a minute that they started off with the simple idea of shaking Torgenson down to conceal the fact that he had been in a nut-house.

"Then they found what they really had—a million-dollar racket. They must have pinched or bribed his admission card out of the state hospital—his own handwriting's on it so there would be no trouble proving it was Torgenson.

"They had to wait for him to die, of course. If he had gotten the slightest wind of the situation, he would have made a new will when he was legally sane. Or, I don't doubt, if he had told *you* the truth about that six-months' disappearance you would have made him do it. But it didn't happen. A certain party killed Torgenson before it happened—and the racket was on."

Dusk nodded at the prone Bannon and croaked: "He killed Torgenson."

THE MARQUIS shook his head. "No. A certain accomplice killed Torgenson—or hastened his dying. Not Al Tromper. Because Al Tromper died at the hands of this same accomplice—or maybe I shouldn't call him an accomplice. He started out that way—and wound up by taking over the whole racket. He killed Torgenson because he needed money soon, and he killed Al Tromper because

Tromper was an obstinate dummy—because Tromper insisted on trying to contact Torgenson's separated wife and getting a bit out of her—a bid to expose the truth, thus making the whole estate revert to her, instead of the niece. Tromper was too dumb to understand that the whole value of the secret would be destroyed if more than one person knew about it."

The gun was steady in the lawyer's hand. He licked his lips. "I hope you realize what you just said, Marty."

The Marquis shook his head. "You're not going to kill me, Howard."

"No? This is a lonely spot. Those shots a minute ago haven't drawn any attention, have they? I—"

"You forget the blue card, Howard. If you kill me, you'll never find it."

Dusk's Adam's apple bobbed. "Where—who...?"

"It's been around, Howard—that slip. Tromper had it—Bannon had it—and the accomplice that Bannon went to saw it. This accomplice was in a bad spot. He had been losing money heavily in his business. When Bannon came to him for financing while waiting for the deal to go through, he jumped at it.

"He jumped at it—and he watched Bannon like a hawk. It wasn't too hard a job to find where Bannon was holed up—along with this Al Tromper. As soon as he knew, he calmly walked up there and beat the evidence—the blue slip—out of the two of them, killing Tromper finally in the process. Then he walked off with it.

"He knew Bannon had already gone to you, as the girl's protector—just as he knew every move of the whole game. He got a superb break because the D.A.'s office were so busy trying to hang it on me, and I was so busy trying to run down Bannon, that he was overlooked.

"That is, he was overlooked till tonight, when he went to contact you at your office—when he slipped that note under your door. The note, I suppose, was to inform you that the blue slip had changed hands and that you would have to make your deal with him?"

"Ye—yes," gasped Dusk. "But I didn't believe him. I—he didn't say who he was—just that he would get in touch with me later—that I was to raise all the cash—seven hundred and fif—"

"Sure. But while he was slipping it under, Rhode came along and caught him. He had no out but to kill Rhode. Rhode seeing him, put him on the spot in the first place. And if Rhode got the note out, which he undoubtedly would, the racket was blown to pieces. So he knifed him and left him in your office building.

"He thought he was safe because he knew I was hot on Bannon's trail—that even if I did catch him, Bannon's talk wouldn't interest me—that I'd kill him out of hand.

"Maybe that was close to the truth—only Bannon was too tough. He wasn't willing to call himself washed up—so he came back and took the blue slip away again tonight, shot down his accomplice—and in turn got the blue slip shot out of his hand by me."

"Then you've got it!" Dusk blurted hoarsely. "I—"

The gun at the window crashed, without the slightest warning. Dusk's gun flew up out of his hand and he staggered backwards cursing, clutching his blood-spurting wrist.

Sevens Richardson's pink face came through the window, tight, hard and pretty, his pink eyes shining. "Yeah. He has it—but not for long. You must think I give up a million bucks awfully easy, Marty."

THE MARQUIS' face was like rock. The albino climbed into the room and his little white teeth showed between his lips. "All right, Marquis—hand it over."

"What for?" the Marquis said. "You're going to have to kill me anyway—if you hope to cash in on the blue slip. And you don't think I'd be fool enough to carry it around with me, anyway, do you?"

"Yeah. I think just that. In fact I know it. Since the minute you showed it to me in my place, I been awfully close to you, Marty—and I know you haven't had a chance to ditch it."

"You're crazy," the Marquis said. He started forward, lifting his hands—and letting the little black cylinder roll down his pant leg, his own movements concealing the move. "Take a look if you don't believe me. I mailed it to myself—at a certain address." He swiveled sideways, stood invitingly.

The albino's pink eyes were hard and searching. "You—" he started forward, his teeth tight. "I'll shoot you down in a minute. Don't think I won't."

The Marquis shrugged. "I'm not arguing."

The albino stepped forward, jammed the gun into his midriff. His pink fingers flew to the Marquis' inside pocket. Sweat stood out on the Marquis' neck. Inch by inch, with desperate care, he maneuvered the albino around so that his back was to the dead man on the floor—and the little black cylinder.

By a miracle, the albino's fingers dipped into every pocket but the right one first. The Marquis, every nerve strained on the black gun a foot from his heel—the gun that Dusk had had shot out of his hand—held his breath. If anything had gone wrong—if that cylinder had gotten damp in the car....

There was a minute when it seemed hopeless—a wash-out—a pitiful fizzle....

Then the albino's hand dipped into the Marquis' pocket, closed on the blue card. His breath went out in a sharp exhalation. "So you didn't have it on...."

The cylinder jumped an inch in the air and its hiss was like a burst steam valve. White smoke spewed from the end like a plume. The albino tried to jump back as he whirled, but the Marquis, already on his toes, clamped his gun like lightning, wrenched.

He had no illusions about the desperate chances he was taking, but there was no alternative. The albino swore wildly—and pulled the trigger.

The gun was like searing bucking flame in the Marquis' hand. A line of white cut the inside of his calf as the bullet ploughed into the floor. The albino yelled, "Drop it—I'll..." and fired again. The shot smashed out a window as the Marquis flung himself aside, threw all his weight on the gun arm—but ill luck intervened.

The gun flew out of the albino's hand, but it flew out of the Marquis' half-numbed fingers as well, went sailing—straight out the window.

There was a split second when both men flung wild glances behind them—and dived together. The albino, the fallen Bannon's gun in his hand, fired in exactly the same instant that the Marquis got a hand on Dusk's. The two shots interlaced. Numbing pain burnt the Marquis' left shoulder and the albino, squatting, was knocked over backwards. He fired again as he fell. The Marquis flung himself wildly aside—as the frantic, moaning Dusk clawed with his good hand into the open mouth of the wall-safe.

He whirled back, a second gun in his hand. The albino had started to crawl toward the door, his head down, one hand on the floor, the gun-hand clutching his stomach, gasping, sobbing. He blurted out, "I—all right, I'm done—" and as the Marquis and Dusk relaxed, he suddenly spun, was on his feet like a cat, the gun in his hand spitting flame and roar, backing toward the door.

The Marquis was hit the second time in exactly the same spot and the pain maddened him. He fired blindly, his teeth clenched—as the lawyer Dusk crashed down— and then the albino was somehow at the door. Miraculously, he stayed erect. The Marquis saw his shots kicking dust from the albino's clothes—but the gambler somehow fell out the door.

The Marquis stumbled after—and there was a sudden shout, a smash of bone on flesh—and the albino sailed back into the room, crashed bloodily on his back and lay still.

OVER THE sights of a police positive, Ace McGuire's white, bewildered redhead appeared in the doorway, "What— What—?" he stammered, then, as he caught the scene, "You mean Richardson was…?"

"Of course he was," the Marquis gritted through tight teeth. "Get an ambulance or something. Howard—where did he get you…?"

"In—the chest—" the other gasped out. "And in the arm. I—"

"Wait!" McGuire burst in. "I came here to tell you—" He broke off, as the strident wail of a siren sounded outside.

"About time these local laws…" the Marquis started.

"That's not the local laws. It's Maney. He had your call to me tapped—the one when you mentioned this house. I found it out just a few minutes later.…"

The Marquis groaned, and his wild eyes searched the floor. He dived, splattering blood across the carpet, over to the still faintly moaning albino, snatched at his hand. He had to pry the fingers open to claw out the bloody, crumpled blue card. He flung it toward Dusk.

"Get it out of sight," he snapped, as the white-faced lawyer snatched it with his frantic free hand. "Listen—the story is this.

"I was after Bannon. Bannon came to you and tried to blackmail you on some unmentioned deal. Being a lawyer you can get away with that—even say it was pure extortion. Wait—say he threatened to kidnap Dorinne Torgenson— that'll explain the guard. He and Sevens Richardson were in it together—that's why Sevens didn't want to back my alibi. You were picked up at the point of a gun by Bannon. You managed to get a message to me that they'd snatched you and were bringing you here. I got out to save you, but Sevens was tailing me. We got here in time to have a rare gun battle.

"Sevens confessed in front of the pair of us—both of them did. Sevens hired a gunman—we don't know who— to kill Tromper and beat up Bannon, when they quarreled about the size of the loot. God knows that ought to drive them into a madhouse—all of them. Will you stick to it?"

"You—you're not going to expose the—the blue card?"

"And let that old harridan of an ex-wife and her gig take the dough from Dorinne Torgenson? Hardly. Is it a deal?"

Sirens were screaming to a halt, the sound of running, shouting men surrounding the house as the lawyer said hastily: "A deal."

Blows pounded on the door. Outside, Maney's crisp, angry little voice yelled: "Open up—you're surrounded."

"You'd better open up, Ace," the Marquis told McGuire. "We're surrounded."

THE COMPLETE CASES
OF BILL BRENT, VOLUME 1

Frederick C. Davis

FREDERICK C. DAVIS

THE COMPLETE CASES OF

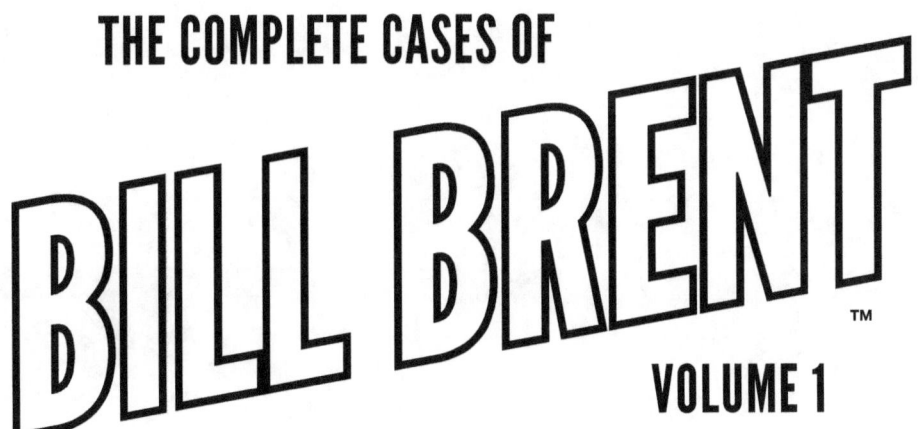

BILL BRENT™

VOLUME 1

FREDERICK C. DAVIS

ILLUSTRATIONS BY
JOHN FLEMING GOULD

ALTUS PRESS

BOSTON • 2016

EDITED AND DESIGNED BY
Matthew Moring

PUBLISHING HISTORY
"Please Pass the Poison" originally appeared in the February, 1941 issue of *Dime Detective* magazine. Copyright 1941 by Popular Publications, Inc. Copyright renewed 1968 and assigned to Steeger Properties, LLC. All rights reserved.

"Let the Skeletons Rattle" originally appeared in the May, 1941 issue of *Dime Detective* magazine. Copyright 1941 by Popular Publications, Inc. Copyright renewed 1968 and assigned to Steeger Properties, LLC. All rights reserved.

"Killer, Stay Away From My Door!" originally appeared in the September, 1941 issue of *Dime Detective* magazine. Copyright 1941 by Popular Publications, Inc. Copyright renewed 1968 and assigned to Steeger Properties, LLC. All rights reserved.

"You Slay Me, Baby" originally appeared in the July, 1942 issue of *Dime Detective* magazine. Copyright 1941 by Popular Publications, Inc. Copyright renewed 1969 and assigned to Steeger Properties, LLC. All rights reserved.

THANKS TO
Joel Frieman & Rick Ollerman

TABLE OF CONTENTS

PLEASE PASS THE POISON 1

LET THE SKELETONS RATTLE . . 71

KILLER, STAY AWAY

FROM MY DOOR! 161

YOU SLAY ME, BABY 227

PLEASE PASS THE POISON

TAKE A BRIEFCASE CRAMMED
WITH UNDERDONE PORKCHOPS,
COLD BUTTERED ASPARAGUS
AND HALF A DOZEN BUCKWHEAT
CAKES—A BOTTLE OF LUXURIO
SCALP ELIXIR—THREE HUNKS OF
SALTWATER TAFFY CLUTCHED
IN A DEAD MAN'S HAND WHILE
A HORDE OF GUINEA PIGS
FROLICKED OVER THE CORPSE—
AND STIR THOROUGHLY. GIVE
SAME TO A VETERINARY SURGEON
AND AN ADVICE-TO-THE-
LOVELORN COLUMNIST TO HAGGLE
OVER—AND WATCH THE MURDER
WHEELS BEGIN TO SPIN AS THEY
SALT THE UNSAVORY STEW
WITH CYANIDE AND ATTEMPT TO
DIGEST IT BETWEEN KILLS.

CHAPTER ONE
GRANDMA WAS A QUACK

THE GIRL was breathless from having run up six flights of stairs and as her high heels tick-ticked to a standstill just inside the city-room, Brent squinted at her from the amber shadow of his eye-shade.

He peered at her warily over a scented lavender letter, got up and closed the door because he sensed that she was one hundred pounds of trouble looking for him.

In this stuffy cubicle which served as his office he hid himself as best he could. Partitioned off the remotest corner of the big littered room, it was not much more commodious than a telephone booth. The rest of the *Reporter's* staff worked in the open, moving about like reasonably free citizens with reasonably clear consciences—but not William Coleridge Brent. They exchanged gossip, wise-cracked, grinned and even laughed occasionally while Brent labored in his crowded cell and sweated in solitude. Like a haunted man he shrank behind his typewriter, watching, through the glass panel, the girl who had just hurried in, and hoping, with all his heart, that she would go away.

She didn't, but gazed about, confused by the clatter and hustle, her eyes coffee-colored and big. She was well worth noticing—her hair had the tint of fine sherry, she was over twenty-one and still cute as a kitten—but nobody except

Brent paid her the slightest attention. Garrett, the city
editor, ensconced behind a rolltop desk in the corner, kept
scowling and slashing his blue pencil across a sheaf of copy.
Valerie Randall, whom Brent considered the most lusciously vine-ripened brunette ever to grace a newspaper

staff, was pounding the keys as rapidly as the eight other reporters who were steaming into the day's assignments. Unlike them, Brent had never convinced himself that a deadline was more important than a live woman, and this one's bewilderment was so painful to see that he simply couldn't ignore her.

He trudged to her, shaggy head lowered, blunt chin down, and her intelligent eyes flashed him her gratitude.

"Lora Lorne," she said quickly. "I want to see Miss Lorne."

In her hands she had one of Lora Lorne's columns, clipped from a recent *Reporter*. Lora Lorne was the paper's love oracle, its own Dorothy Dix or Beatrice Fairfax, who sagely advised her harassed readers concerning their philandering husbands, their faithless wives, their nagging mothers-in-law, their broken troths, their unrequited passions, their illegitimate children. Above Lora Lorne's intimately sympathetic letters her portrait was printed— a picture of a sweet old soul, combs in her white hair, wise eyes in a kindly crinkled face, eyeglasses dangling from a reel pinned to her grandmotherly shoulder. Obviously, however, no one resembling Lora Lorne was present in the city-room.

"Afraid you can't," Brent said. "She never comes in here."

"But—but there's no one else I can turn to, no one else who would really understand." The girl's appeal was earnest, heartfelt. "I must see Miss Lorne, really I must!"

"Sorry, too busy," Brent insisted. "Wrapped up in hundreds of problems, you know—can't see anyone personally. Her advice is given out exclusively in her column." He screwed up his face as he said it. "Just write her a letter, and she'll print her answer in a few days—"

The girl murmured in a sick voice: "A few days!" as if he'd said several decades. "But I can't wait, can't possibly. This is so terribly serious, and horrible things might happen before then." Her tearful eyes pleaded with Brent. "Please ask her to make an exception just this once. She's so wonderfully sympathetic, I'm sure—she'll— I'm so desperate for her help— If I can't see her, I—I'll just give up."

The girl choked off a sob and Brent wagged his head, wondering how he could make her realize that she'd never see Miss Lorne. Not today or tomorrow or ever, no matter how plaintively she might implore it. He couldn't tell her the real reason for that. He'd sooner shoot himself than reveal that it was he—a husky, rugged guy whose fullback's shoulders sagged under the weight of his own woes—he who daily wrote the agony column. He, God help him, was Lora Lorne.

BRENT GENTLY took the girl's arm and led her to a chair near his door. She perched on the edge of it, all tense, her chin puckered and quivering, still pathetically believing that only Lora Lorne's homely counsel could rescue her from misfortune.

"I've already written her so many letters. Dozens! I began when I was just a little girl and she's been like an aunt to me. But lately—things haven't turned out the way she thought they would. In fact they're worse—so much worse—that's why I know she'll want to talk to me. If you'll remind her that it's about my mother, and another man, and my step-father, and the awful things my grandfather whispers to me— You *will* ask her, won't you?"

"Can't, damn it," Brent muttered. "Don't know where she lives. Don't even know what her phone number is. Neither does anybody else on the paper, except Mr. Palmer, the publisher. He lives in California, and won't tell. It's been tried hundreds of times. No go. The only way of reaching her is by letter. That's all. No other. Absolutely. An old Negro manservant with a game leg comes in here every day—name's Mose—picks up her mail and that's the closest any of us ever get to her. Sorry. Now please pull yourself together, and if you'd like to borrow somebody's typewriter—"

"No." The girl distraitly shook her head. "Tomorrow it will be too late. Even a few hours—" She stared out the window, stared widely across a checkerboard of roofs, and there was fear in her eyes. "I've always depended on Lora Lorne. Everything's gone wrong now, everything, and it's so terribly hopeless without Lora Lorne's advice." She lowered her head, bit her lips and silently cried.

"Suppose you tell me about it," Brent said miserably. "Maybe I can help somehow."

"You?" And her tone was scornful. "A man! Why, you couldn't understand. But Miss Lorne is so sweet—and wonderful—"

She blinked at the engagement solitaire she wore and again she burst into silent, anguished sobs.

"Now look, I'm far from being hard-hearted," Brent assured her, "but there's only one suggestion I can make. Go home, and figure it out your own way. Whatever the difficulty may be, and whether you can get anywhere with it or not, go home!"

She blubbered again: "Hopeless, hopeless," and a tear fell on her clipping, on the picture of the lady which topped it, on the saccharine face supposed to be that of Lora Lorne.

Brent didn't know who the hell the old dame really was. Nobody did. Probably it wasn't a photograph, but a drawing, and she'd never actually existed. The picture had been run every day, month after month, never changing since the column was begun twenty-two years ago. A long succession of female busybodies had hidden behind the copyrighted nom-de-hooey. The last of them was Mrs. Smithers, the art editor's wife, who had abandoned her amatory

expostulations to run away with a mortician named Quack-
enbush, who was married to Hannah Heckhimer, the
editor of the Saturday children's page, who had no children
and thereafter, likewise, no husband. So much for the
damned column's moral value.

Bill Brent was the first man ever to suffer the indig-
nity of being Lora Lorne, and remembering this didn't
help to get his mind off the girl who was still sitting outside
his door, utterly bewildered by her tribulations.

He wished to God she'd go away, and Garrett was
waiting for today's love feast, so he re-read the last item
he'd written: "You must realize, dear Worried Wife, that
the romance of courtship cannot last forever, and that it
is only when love settles down into glorified friendship
after marriage that there is any peace or comfort in it."
That was no help, either. He poked into the mound of
varicolored correspondence on his desk, and grimaced. "It
happened when Phil and I were deeply in love, and it
didn't seem so wrong. Now Herbert wants to marry me.
Shall I tell him about the sin in my past?" "Would it be
terribly bad if I went to Atlantic City for the weekend
with my boy-friend?" In various forms those two questions
cropped up in practically every mail, but here was something special. A man signing himself B.D. wrote: "I suspect
my wife is trying to kill me. I don't want to tell the police.
She's too clever for them. I want to catch her at it and
show her I'm not so dumb. I know all about her and the
man she wants to take my place. She's watching her chance,
planning to murder me—"

It was something to get jittery about, all right, but B.D.
had nothing to fear half so deadly as this stuff that de-
scended on Brent by the ton, day after day—this stuff that
was polluting his mind and sickening his soul.

ABRUPTLY BRENT marched past the girl who was still sitting morosely near his door, marched across the city-room to the desk in the opposite corner, stared down at his city editor.

"If you've got the time, Garrett," he said, "I'd like to murder you and separate you into small, bloody parts, you jackal."

Without glancing up, Barrett said: "Go back to work, Lora."

Brent set his teeth. "Isn't there a drop of mercy in you? Isn't there a spark of kindness? For God's sake, man, you know it's months now since I've been blotto. Months since I've been stinko, or sozzled, or even mildly squiffed. Months since I've so much as smelled a cork or pinched a lady's hinie. I've done my penance. You've punished me more than enough. I'm licked. I'm crying uncle."

"Lora, go back to work, now," Garrett said, going on with his own work, "like a good girl."

Brent closed both fists. "On my word of honor, I'll never get drunk again, I'll never make a pass at another woman, I'll never miss another day's work, not another hour's. Suffering cats, Garrett, put me back on the police shift where I belong!"

Garrett sat back and looked bored. A muscular, ruddy, dynamic man, with granite-gray eyes and a jaw which a bulldog would envy, he'd come out of the first World War a major at twenty-three. He was still a military martinet, an inflexible disciplinarian.

"Do I have to go into that again?" he complained. "There's a contract, remember? You agreed to accept assignments and execute orders as required. Remember? A smart New York reporter should know better than to sign legal documents without first carefully reading same, don't you think? Yes. Well, your orders are to keep the love column going, and it's damn near press time right now, Lora."

Brent said levelly: "Garrett, that column's driving me crazy. I can't stand it any longer. I tell you, Garrett, it's driving me nuts and *I can't stand it!*"

"Any contract can be broken, including yours." Garrett shrugged. "Is that the way you want it?"

That was the way Brent didn't dare have it. He'd get the pants sued off him, and besides he'd be blacklisted. Another reason well worth considering was that Garrett had lured him out of New York with an upholstered salary, payable regularly and unfailingly until the contract expired or was fractured. And furthermore— Brent sent a yearning glance at Valerie Randall, the most delectable brunette he had ever seen inside a city-room. In any department other than Miss Lorne's he would be most happy to remain. But he was stuck with the love column, until such time as Garrett might relent, and his only hope of escape was to persist in appealing to the reason of a thoroughly unreasonable sadist.

"Look, Garrett," he said, controlling his tone. "Our column of medical advice is written by a doctor, not by a blacksmith. Our financial stuff is written by an economist, not a grocer. But me! I'm a fake, even down to my pen-name and my sex. Well, a quack cure for rheumatism may be bad, but a quack cure for an unfaithful husband is plenty worse."

"You're doing fine," Garrett said, his blue pencil streaking across a page of copy. "The column has improved since you took it over, Grandma."

"But it's too damned dangerous! I'm not qualified to play God. Look at that girl sitting over there, for example. She just told me that the advice I gave her has made her troubles tougher than they were in the first place. Look at her! Isn't she a pathetic picture?"

"What girl? Oh, that girl. *That—that girl—*"

Garrett was staring across the city-room, straining up, his face blanched. Brent spun about and swallowed his breath. He'd left the girl sitting in the chair, head bent, sobbing silently because she had failed to see Miss Lorne. Because she hadn't seen Miss Lorne she was now hopelessly leaving. But she wasn't going out the way she'd come in.

She was going out the window.

"Hey!" Brent yelled.

He startled everyone in the city-room except the girl. Every head swiveled toward him except the girl's. She was intent on her purpose and her knees were on the sill and she was crawling out. She was gripping the awning brace, bringing herself to her trim little feet, poising to jump. Brent scrambled to the window as she tottered forward. He dove for her, wrapped his arm around her legs, dragged back.

"Let me go, let me go!"

She pulled at the awning, struggling to free herself, to fling herself into the chasm of the street.

"Stop that!" Brent howled.

She didn't stop.

He tried to brace himself and couldn't. He had nothing to hang onto except the girl. She was dragging him across the sill, slapping his face, and he couldn't see, didn't dare loosen a finger. He was off balance, his head and shoulders out, and the floor was slippery. She was going down in another second and very possibly Bill Brent, alias Lora Lorne, would take the trip with her.

"Don't!" he gasped. "Lora Lorne would advise against it!"

Maybe it was those crazy words that got to her and changed her mind about dying. Maybe it was just a lucky fluke that she fainted then. Brent didn't know which and didn't care. He was too deliriously glad to find himself backing away from the window, clutching the girl's limp body against his, her sherry hair spraying over his shoulder, her dreamy face peacefully upturned, her lips close. She was dead to the world, but not nearly so dead as she might have been when picked off the pavement six stories down.

CHAPTER TWO

THE PRICELESS
PORK CHOP

SINCE THE city-room provided no accommodations for unconscious girls, Brent headed for the women's lavatory, where there was a wicker chaise-longue. He had to plow his way through the entire staff and he put her down in reverse, feet on the tilted head. He was splashing water in her wan face when Valerie Randall tugged him aside.

"You're Lora Lorne professionally," she reminded him, smiling in her sweetly taunting way, "but not anatomically. Let me take care of her."

"You'll take care of her like a tigress takes care of a rabbit," Brent answered grimly. "Even if she were your own sister, you'd take care of her so well she'd find herself splashed all over the front page."

With a nod, Val calmly agreed this was true. "After all, *I'm* a reporter," she said, "so go away and let me get to work on her."

"I feel sorry for the kid—feel responsible. Besides—well, this is a hell of a place and a hell of a time for it—but I'm working myself up to the point of asking you to marry me in the good old-fashioned way."

Val's smile became a bit superior and disdainful. "This isn't at all sudden," she remarked.

"I know. I've got troubles. My job's turning me into a walking mass of inhibitions. I have nightmares. Not just now and then, but every time I try to sleep. Double-feature nightmares. In the worst one, you and I get married and then everything horrible happens to us. I wake up screaming."

"Perhaps," Val said, turning back to the girl, "you'd better ask Lora Lorne's advice."

He moaned and was still chilled by the nearness of death, and when he sidled out Val was shaking the limp girl and asking: "What's your name? What's your address? Why did you try to kill, yourself?"

Again he elbowed through the curious staff, while Garrett snarled everybody back to work. On the floor beneath that yawning window he saw the girl's purse. He retreated into his office and found, among the usual feminine impedimenta, a driver's license. The would-be suicide's name was Jean Chester and she lived at 1180 Willow Street, in the suburb of Greengrove.

The clipping was also there, wadded up, still tear-stained. Yesterday's, Brent saw. Which one of the printed letters was hers? She'd mentioned her mother, another man, a step-father, a whispering grandfather and she'd burst into sobs over her engagement ring.

Dear Miss Lorne:

My employer is a charming, wonderful man and even though he's married and has two grown children he keeps asking me—

That wasn't it, but the last letter in the column fit part of the set-up.

Dear Lora Lorne:

I'm to be married in less than a week, but lately my happiness has turned to misery. I love my fiancé with all my heart and I'm sure he loves me too, but recently he has been saying that I must give up my work. Dear Miss Lorne, I love my work too, but he insists I can't go on with it, just because he is jealous of the fine, older man who has guided me so unselfishly for years. He's so wrong about that, but last night we had a terrible quarrel and he told me I'd have to choose once and for all between them. I don't want to lose my fiancé, because I love him, really I do, but I know I'll be unhappy all my life if I have to give up my other dreams too. Oh, Miss Lorne, how can I decide?

It was signed "So Bewildered," and Brent had answered to the effect that she should make her sweetheart understand that with his unreasonable, selfish attitude he was smothering the beautiful flame of their love for each other. "If he really loves you, and realizes this, you will reach a new understanding with him. He will see that he must take you as the modern and very intelligent young woman you are, dear."

OBVIOUSLY THE thing wasn't as simple as that. The pat make-him-understand prescription not only hadn't worked but had aggravated the predicament. Grimly Brent dug into his file and came up with another of Lora Lorne's attempts to set the world right for "So Bewildered." The second letter, dated ten days earlier, presented a knottier problem:

> Dear Lora Lorne:
>
> It is a shocking, disillusioning thing to discover that your own mother is not playing fair with your father. He's really my step-father, and I don't want to think that Mother has actually done anything terribly wrong, but I know she has met another man many times, secretly, and I think she's in love with this man.
>
> My step-father doesn't dream what's going on behind his back and I'm so terribly afraid he'll find out that Mother is cheating on him and he'll do something awful. Last night when Mother came home, very late, I couldn't keep quiet any longer. I told her I knew, and she denied it—lied to me—and told me to mind my own business. Oh, Miss Lorne, if it goes on I'm sure it will turn into a ghastly tragedy. What can I do?

Publicly commiserating with "So Bewildered," Miss Lorne had urged her to go forthrightly to the other man and call upon his better nature. Lora Lorne had faith that he would be so shamed and remorseful, that Mother too would mend her ways and thereafter devote herself to the sanctity of "So Bewildered's" home.

Effective advice, that. Brilliantly successful. It had improved the situation so wonderfully that so-bewildered Jean Chester had tried to leap outward over sagacious Miss Lorne's own windowsill!

"God save the *Reporter's* subscribers from my well-intended bungling!" said Bill Brent to himself, very sourly.

He stuffed the purse into a drawer, marched again out of his office, marched again across the city-room, and arrived at the desk in the opposite corner, a second behind Valerie Randall.

"She won't talk," Val reported to Garrett. "Not who she is or where she lives. It would disgrace the family name and all that. But Bill knows about her."

Brent shook his head. "Don't know from nothing. She didn't tell me a thing. Anyway, I'm not a news man any more. My specialty is *l'amour*—remember? I am exclusively devoted to guiding our readers' mad passions."

They eyed him suspiciously and Val said: "I'm giving her the absent treatment and don't worry, boss, once she's had a chance to calm down I'll coax a whizbang of a story out of her."

"Let her alone!" Brent protested. "Haven't we hurt her enough already?"

Garrett signaled Val to her desk to write the story. "Don't bother me," he answered. "I've got a paper to get out today and where the hell, Lora, is your part of it?"

White-lipped, Brent leaned over him. "Lay off the poor kid! Suppose she'd gone down into the street. It wouldn't have been suicide. That, Garrett, would have been murder. With my little column I almost killed that girl."

"You grabbed her in time, so what're you worrying about?" Garrett stuffed copy into the pneumatic tube. "When somebody tries to dive out of one of my own windows, I consider it's news, but the story's not yours. It's Val's. She'll make the most of it. What I want from you is a column. Fast. And no arguments—except in court."

"You—" Brent leveled his finger and his face was slightly green. "You'll get your goddam column!"

He strode back to his desk, plucked a new letter off the heap, read with a nauseated expression: "Will a gentleman make an improper proposal to a girl he really loves?" And, Heaven help him, he had to answer in the negative, making himself, he felt, a traitor to his sex.

He pounded out the last line, which mentioned "the bleached remnants of painful past mistakes," and was disgustedly carrying the stuff to Garrett when Val Randall popped out of the ladies' room with a breathless bulletin.

"She's gone!"

"That's swell!" Brent blurted, grinning.

With a scowl, Garrett snarled: "Go after her!"

"Must've slipped down the stairs when nobody was looking," Val gasped.

"That's swell!" Brent repeated, smiling happily.

"Grab her!" Garrett snapped.

Val tossed copy to his desk. "There it is, unknown girl angle. Add later, I hope. She can't be far."

"Bring her back here!" Garrett ordered.

VAL FLEW out the door. Brent delivered his column to Garrett, and Garrett glowered at him, and Brent kept grinning. He went back, put his head out the same window and shuddered. There was a girl on the pavement who looked exactly like Jean Chester. It *was* Jean Chester, and she was on her feet, which were in rapid motion. She ran across the street and, just as Val appeared on the steps directly below Brent, disappeared into Smitty's Dairy Bar.

Brent saw Val scanning the busy sidewalk, and as she guessed herself off in the wrong direction his grin became even broader.

He sauntered to the swinging doors, gave Garrett a lackadaisical salute, leaned through them—and sped. He made the six flights in fifteen jumps, slowed on the sidewalk, made sure Val was well started on her goose chase, dodged across the street, and found Jean Chester in Smitty's—with a man.

The man was shorter than the girl, round-bellied, jerky-eyed. His clothes might have come out of a Sears Roebuck catalogue, issue of 1920, and he wore a dusty derby. He was drinking a glass of milk. His puckered expression testified that he hated milk, but there were three empty glasses lined up on the bar in front of him, beside his briefcase, and this was his fourth. While he applied himself to it, the girl spoke to him rapidly, in a whisper of pleading. He shook his head and turned away, reaching for his briefcase and looking terrified. The girl's hand reached for it first. The result was a tug-of-war. The man and Jean Chester struggled over the case.

"… Kill me!" Brent heard him blurt, hoarsely. "Trying to kill me. This proves it! Wants to kill me!"

The girl won the tussle, and abruptly she spun about, slapped the swinging doors apart and was gone with the case. The man, still appearing to be scared out of his wits, scampered after her. Brent had seen her slip into a coupe parked at the curb, but the man hadn't. In pursuit of her, he disappeared around the corner at a run.

The car spurted away. Brent broke into a lope, chasing it. At the corner, it encountered a red light. He caught up with it, opened the door and crawled in while the frightened girl shrank from him. The briefcase was on the seat beside her. He grabbed it and she gasped.

"The light's green now," he pointed out. "Better get going—and I think I know how to reach Lora Lorne, after all."

Again the name had a magical effect on Jean Chester. Still frightened she sent the car forward. He opened the case, and noticed that two initials were stamped on the flap: *B.D.*

In one compartment it contained four bottles of a scarlet, excessively fragrant liquid which the labels identified as Luxurio Scalp Elixir.

In the other was a piece of oil-silk, wadded up. Brent discovered as he unwound it that it contained a fried pork chop, two boiled potatoes and approximately a dozen stalks of buttered asparagus—all cold and most unappetizing.

THE GIRL, still shaky, kept the car rolling and turned a distressed glance on Brent.

"Will you really take me to Lora Lorne?" she asked plaintively. "Really?"

Sooner than confess that she was already in proximity to the *Reporter's* love oracle, Brent would lay himself down under a ten-ton truck. Let the truth leak out and he would be a laughingstock, but his fear, strangely enough, wasn't his real reason for guarding the secret.

Being deeply sympathetic by nature, he shrank from the thought of destroying the girl's blind trust. He couldn't bring himself to tell her that Lora Lorne actually smoked a pipe, wore size eleven brogans, had once shattered a nose against a Princeton goalpost, and vastly enjoyed the art of Gypsy Rose Lee.

Evading her question, he asked while she drove: "Who was that man? The one who belongs to this case?"

"My step-father. Bernard Dunbar. Can you really take me—"

"Does he carry this cargo of hair-tonic for drinking purposes?"

"He sells it. He's a barber's supply salesman and," she added irrelevantly, "he works very hard—always on the road, scarcely home at all. He's really a nice man, but his stomach bothers him and he's a little queer. Can you really—"

"Does he usually go about equipped with a cold blue-plate dinner, lacking only a cold cup of coffee?"

She grew a little paler and said: "It will be so wonderful to see Miss Lorne! If you'll—"

"Why were you so anxious to take this tasty little snack away from him?"

"He's wrong about it, I know he's wrong!" Being too distracted to explain further, she added: "If you'll only take me to Miss Lorne right now—"

"Just a minute," he countered. "Sooner or later I'd like to find out what the hell you're talking about. But I didn't say I could bring you and Miss Lorne together. I think I know how she can be reached, but I'll have to feel her out first. I found those letters of yours she printed. Suppose you tell me what's gone wrong and I'll do my best to get her to straighten everything out for you."

"Oh, please!" Hope fired Jean Chester and made her radiant. "You see, about my mother— Well, a few nights ago my mother was out, and my step-father was away too, and I was terrified, thinking he might come back unexpectedly and discover what—what Mother was doing behind his back. At last, long after midnight, a car drew up and stopped and its lights went out, and Mother was in it—with that man."

Brent clucked.

"I didn't know who he was. Mother's been so—so secretive, and this was the first time I'd ever seen him. I—I ran out to the car. I made him listen to me, begged him not to see Mother again. He just laughed and Mother got out and told me not to be a little fool and she wouldn't have me snooping. The man drove away and I still don't know who he is or what he really looks like, and I'm so afraid that something—something horrible will happen."

"For instance," Brent inquired, "a quiet little murder, perhaps?"

"Oh!" The girl's eyes were like frightened saucers of coffee, and she rushed off on another tangent. "My step-father is a sort of hypochondriac, and he thinks he has all sorts of pains inside him, but he only imagines them— Mother was furious with me and ordered me out of the house. Now I'm staying at the Wilburn Hotel and my bill is overdue and I can't pay it because I'm not getting any more of my money. Mother's keeping it and won't give me a cent."

"Let's get this straight," Brent suggested. "About the money."

"It was left me by my real father, who died years ago— just suddenly died, and four months later Mother married Mr. Dunbar. Insurance money, it was twenty thousand dollars at the beginning—supposed to be held in trust for me by Mother. I've come of age, and I've used some of it for my researches, and now I need the rest of it, but Mother won't give me a penny of it."

"Sue her," Brent recommended.

"But I couldn't! Don't you see? If I go to court, the whole awful story will come out, about why Mother turned against me, and all about that other man, and it would be a horrible scandal. I couldn't do such a thing, I just couldn't! It's what I'm trying to prevent. And yet I've got to get my money, I need it so desperately. I'm sure Miss Lorne can tell me just how I can bring Mother back to her senses— aren't you?"

BRENT SWALLOWED a protest. Following the main highway eastward, they had reached Greengrove. The girl braked, watching an approaching car that swung into the driveway of a rambling house surrounded by gardened grounds. "It's Doctor Veach," she murmured. She turned the coupe after Dr. Veach's and both veered into a parking space opposite the porch, where two sedans were sitting. Gazing uneasily at them, Jean Chester said: "This is—was my home, and that's my step-father's Chevvy. He must be inside with Mother, he must've come for a late lunch."

"After four glasses of milk?" Brent wondered. "Since you were ordered to clear out, why have you come back?"

"Because I've got to get some of my money from Mother and I've got to explain to Doctor Veach too, because I'm so anxious to go on with our parasitology, and now I'll have to give it up unless— He's probably come looking for me."

Jean Chester hurried to him. Following her with the briefcase, Brent found that Dr. Veach was a man of impressive presence, brisk, ruggedly handsome, gray-templed, with poise and self-possession that came of long professional experience.

"Jean!" he said in a firm, strong tone. "I've been trying everywhere to find you. I need you at the lab, and your cultures are about to spoil. What's wrong, Jean?"

"I'll—I'll come, Doctor," she said obediently. "This is Mr.—Brent?" Her chin lifted with pride. "I'm Doctor Veach's research assistant, and he's the director of the Veach College of—"

Brent was clasping the strong hand of Dr. Veach when the scream rang out. It came, shrilly, from behind the house. A woman cried: "Father, father, *father!*" The sharp note of terror in her voice startled the girl, turned Brent and Dr. Veach. Suddenly the girl was running. Brent and the doctor followed and saw a man sprawled on the ground.

A lean, snowy-headed man was lying on his back inside an enclosure, one of a series of four large cages formed by steel mesh stretched between steel uprights. The ground around him was alive with small, brown-and-white, nose-wriggling animals—guinea-pigs, Brent guessed. He lay just inside the gate, and Jean Chester was the first to reach him.

"Granddad!" she cried.

She dropped to her knees beside Granddad, caught up one of his blue-veined, inert hands and frantically rubbed it. The guinea-pigs scampered up their runways and into their hutches as Dr. Veach quickly tested the old man's pulse. Veach stiffened up at once, looking startled, taking a wary step backward. He grasped Jean's arm, pulled her to her feet, peered at Brent.

"Take her away!" he said.

He hurried to his car and returned with a black medical case and bent over the old man.

Brent steered the girl through the gate and saw the woman standing at the rear of the house. Jean's mother was smartly dressed and looked almost as young as her daughter. She was wearing an apron and in one hand she was gripping a large wooden spoon from which batter dripped.

"I saw him fall!" she said hoarsely. "I saw him go inside and fall!"

In the door behind her, a napkin tucked into his collar, was Bernard Dunbar, Jean's step-father, the hair-tonic salesman with the jerky, scared eyes.